MW01098641

Flip

Christopher J. Fox

First published by Christopher J. Fox 2019

Copyright © 2019 by Christopher J. Fox

All rights reserved. No part of this publication may be reproduced, stored, or transmitted in any form or by any means, electronic, mechanical, photocopying, recording, scanning, or otherwise without written permission from the publisher. It is illegal to copy this book, post it to a website, or distribute it by any other means without permission.

This novel is entirely a work of fiction. The names, characters, and incidents portrayed in it are the work of the author's imagination. Any resemblance to actual persons, living or dead, events or localities is entirely coincidental.

Christopher J. Fox asserts the moral right to be identified as the author of this work.

Designations used by companies to distinguish their products are often claimed as trademarks. All brand names and product names used in this book and on its cover are trade names, service marks, trademarks, and registered trademarks of their respective owners. The publishers and the book are not associated with any product or vendor mentioned in this book. None of the companies referenced within the book have endorsed the book.

First edition

ISBN: 978-1-7332712-1-9

Editing by Angela Brown
Proofreading by Kate Schomaker
Cover art by Lance Buckley

This book is dedicated with love to the memory of my father, Brian Christopher Fox.

Acknowledgments

First and foremost, my wife, Dora. She and I developed the plot, the characters, and their voices together. This book, like everything else good in my life, is a product of our hard work and God's blessings. Huge thanks to our daughters Anastasia, Gabrielle, and Catalina, who have thought about, read, and provided frank feedback on this book since our long road trip back to Omaha for our eldest daughter Mariana's wedding.

I am deeply grateful to my editor, Angela Brown, and my proofreader, Kate Schomaker for excellent work. Thanks to Lance Buckley who conceptualized and produced the cover art.

Table of Contents

"The more closely you look at one thing, the less closely can you see something else."
~ Werner Heisenberg

***

Once there was an old frog who had lived all his life in a dank well. One day a frog from the sea paid him a visit.

"Where do you come from?" asked the frog in the well.

"From the great ocean," he replied.

"How big is your ocean?"

"It's gigantic."

"You mean about a quarter of the size of my well here?"

"Bigger."

"Bigger? You mean half as big?"

"No, even bigger."

"Is it…as big as this well?"

"There's no comparison."

"That's impossible! I've got to see this for myself."

They set off together. When the frog from the well saw the ocean, it was such a shock that his head just exploded into pieces.

~ Patrul Rinpoche from *The Tibetan Book of Living and Dying*

Prologue

Ahigbe watched his little sister, Ikazuabe, as she played with her pigtails and pulled at her seat belt. She didn't want the restraint to wrinkle her new white cotton dress.

"*Ika, regarde à l'extérieur et dis-moi ce que tu vois.* (Ika, look outside and tell me what you see)," he said.

The six-year-old gazed out the airplane window at the dense tropical jungle sliding away below.

"*Des arbres et des plantes* (Trees and plants)," she answered.

This was her first trip from her home in Cotonou, Benin, to Paris, and though the family had left the central African nation not quite an hour ago, she was starting to squirm, and Ahigbe realized the novelty of flying had already worn off for her.

"*Combien de temps pour qu'on arrive là-bas, maman?* (How long until we get there, Mama?)" Ikazuabe asked.

"Keep looking for the Mediterranean Sea, dear. When you see that, it won't be long."

Ahigbe was in the middle seat, his mother on the aisle. In a bid for temporary peace, he reached under the seat in front of him for his bag.

"Ika, let's read a book. Do you like *Green Eggs and Ham?*"

"Yes, I do, Sam I Am!" The little girl giggled, her hands on her hips, pleased with the word game she had played with her brother. He opened the book and read the first page aloud.

1

Suddenly a ferocious quake jolted them. A loud bang followed it, accompanied by painful pressure in Ahigbe's ears. Screams erupted as the plane lurched to one side, and he could only see the ground below through the window and only bright sky above. Ika was shrieking, her hands on her ears. He grabbed for her before she was thrown from her seat.

The man in the seat in front of him flew up, his head colliding with the overhead compartment with a sickening, wet crunch. Blood sprayed around the cabin and into Ahigbe's face, soaking him.

Everything was chaos. A screaming, howling wind deafened the boy and tore at his exposed flesh. Something hard hit him in the head. Wincing in pain, he wiped the blood from his eyes. Bags and laptops flew through the cabin. The yellow oxygen masks had dropped, but they were waving wildly about, eluding his frantic grasp. Gasping for a full breath, for any air that would come, Ahigbe clawed desperately for the yellow mask. His world constricted to the excruciating burning in his chest and the yellow blob bouncing around in front of him, and black spots filled his eyes. Another savage twist of the plane, and he was crushed into his seat, the remaining breath squeezed from his burning lungs. A moment as long as a lifetime later, mercifully, dark night came down like a curtain before his eyes.

***

Ahigbe woke up and saw...*trees? But where is the side of the plane?* he asked himself. Dazed, he sat for a moment, trying to make sense of his now-stationary world. Slowly reality started to form around him again as he returned to his senses. The trees were still there, and Ika was lying like a limp doll in her seat.

"Ika! Ika!" he cried, shaking his unresponsive sister. Panic clutched the twelve-year-old boy, but then he saw her little chest rise and fall. She coughed and opened her eyes.

"Ahi!" she cried, and reached for her brother.

"It's okay, Ika. I'm here."

Ahigbe winced as he turned his head to the left at the sound of a cough and saw his mother covering her mouth with a bleeding hand. In the rows in front of him and behind, children cried and coughed as

2

smoke roiled through what remained of the cabin. To his right, a woman was yelling. He jerked his head around, which made him wince again.

"You've got to get out of there! Now!" she screamed in French. "Come here, toward me," she said, motioning with her hands.

His mother heard and saw the woman too, and she undid her seat belt. Ahigbe did the same and reached over to help Ika.

"C'mon. Hurry!" the woman yelled again.

Now that he was able to move, he got a better view of her. She was standing on the wing of the plane just a few feet from them, visible through the gaping hole. The woman wore a long white coat over a skirt and a white top. A golden light glinted off something that hung around her neck. She was gesturing frantically, a look of panic on her face.

Clutching Ika to his chest, Ahigbe set one foot on the edge of the broken fuselage and swung his other foot as far as he could to reach the wing, which was about a foot away and two feet above. He thrust hard with his back leg and pushed up onto the wing, freeing the two of them from the wreckage. Ika breathed deeply and coughed once more when she was in the cleaner air.

When he set Ika down on the wing, the woman said, "I'll watch her. Go help your mother and the other children."

Ahigbe turned to grasp his mother's hand and pulled with all the strength in his young arms. In an instant, the three of them were on the wing, sucking in deep breaths. After a few moments, he turned his attention back to the cries of other children carried on the acrid smoke that spewed from the cabin. He took a deep breath and stepped back inside the plane. He bent low and tried to search for anyone alive. The interior of the plane, blurred by the water running from his eyes and a blanket of smoke, was a wreckage of humanity. Ahigbe turned his eyes away from it and focused on the floor as he crawled down the aisle toward the shrieks. His arms and legs wobbled, and a disturbing shiver pulsed through his torso. He wanted to stop, to run back to his mother and sister, but the cries sounded too much like Ika's. He found one little boy pinned underneath a pair of twisted legs and freed the child. The two boys stumbled to the opening, and Ahigbe handed him to his mother.

3

"There's no more time to go back in and search. Call for them," the woman in white said.

Ahigbe nodded, then called to the other children. "Undo your seat belts. Come here. We have to get off the plane!"

Miraculously, a number of small children worked their way toward him, and he handed them out to his mother. Soon half a dozen children were gathered there. They were shaking, crying, and coughing, but otherwise uninjured, standing on the wing of the plane.

Ahigbe paused, sweeping his eyes once more around what remained of the cabin and its occupants. He never had seen death like this before, and he knew the image of it never would leave him. His mother called to him, begging him to get out of the plane, so he did. Once he was on the wing, he looked around for the woman in white.

"C'mon! C'mon!" the woman called, now at the end of the wing, about ten meters from him. "Hurry!"

"Come here," Ahigbe's mother said, bending over to pick up Ika, who reached up, eager for the safety of her mother's arms.

"This way," the woman called again. She was now off the wing, standing on the floor of the smoldering jungle. Ahigbe, seeing flames rise from the rear of the plane, rushed down the length of the wing as fast as he could, making sure his mother, sister, and the other children were close behind. The wing had shorn off the tops of the surrounding trees as the plane had crashed, and its tip had gouged out a trench in the dirt. It was a small step off the wing to the ground.

"Follow me!" came the voice, now more commanding than before.

Everyone moved toward it, into the overgrowth and away from the plane. The vegetation was too dense for running, as much as Ahigbe wanted to. Leaves slapped his face, and branches pulled at his clothes as he pushed them away to allow others to follow. Up ahead, he saw the woman standing in a clearing, just above them on a small hill. He lost sight of her as a leaf swatted him in the face, but the hill with the clearing was just straight ahead.

In a moment, Ahigbe climbed the hill, panting. His mother was breathing hard behind him, and Ika sobbed softly. The woman was gone, but he saw a path running down the other side, the thick jungle undergrowth chopped back away from it.

"This way!" came the voice from down the path.

The group quickly followed, almost at a run now. A deafening explosion thundered at the scurrying survivors for the second time that day, this time accompanied by a rush of wind and heat on their backs. Ahigbe glanced over his shoulder and saw the fireball turn to oily black smoke as the last of the plane's fuel was consumed. As frightening as the massive explosion was, he knew they were safe now. He started down the path again, this time following his mother.

The woman led them down the path for about ten minutes. Ahigbe would catch glimpses of her white coat, or hear her call, then lose sight of her as she slipped around another bend. As he struggled to keep up, he tried to place her. He knew he hadn't seen her on the plane, so where had she come from?

"Over here there's a road," she called to them.

Ahigbe burst ahead at a dead run. He knew a road was their best chance at finding help and getting away from here.

"Please, lady, wait!" he shouted, and then his feet hit the gravel road. "Lady!" he called again, searching around for the woman in white.

"Ahigbe!" his mother yelled from behind as she stepped out of the forest, waving him back with one hand as she carried Ika in the other.

"Mama, the lady's not here," Ahigbe said as he caught his breath and looked around.

"Where did she go?" she asked, her eyes sweeping the area.

"I don't know." The boy shrugged. Ika wriggled, wanting to be put down now, but her mother wasn't about to let her out of her protective arms.

"Who was she?" Ahigbe asked his mother.

With wide eyes, the woman blessed herself. *"Au nom du Père, du Fils et du Saint-Esprit. Un ange,"* she said. An angel.

1 Medic 82

"When sufficiently examined through this extraordinary view of reality, the causes for almost every event can be related to other preceding events or circumstances."

"Master, I noticed that you said almost every event. So some things are random and unpredictable?"

"Perhaps, but remember our ability to comprehend all possible causes is limited."

"So, then, are you saying that nothing is truly unpredictable?"

"Well, there are miracles."

—Lama Rinpoche Matthew Estabrook to newly ordained monks on the subject of transperceptual meditation

From the passenger seat of Medic 82, John Holden gazed out at the maple leaves. Although their centers were still vibrant, the edges were curled and desiccated by the most stagnant, oppressive, sweltering Nebraska summer he'd experienced in his twenty-five years. *This morning is a godsend, though*, he thought. A gentle breeze stirred the leaves as fresh morning air swept over his face. *It's 8:25, and my uniform isn't sticking to me yet.*

As he popped the last bite of his breakfast burrito into his mouth, the radio squawked, interrupting his reverie.

"KEA571 to Medic 82. You have a call. Fifty-year-old woman, unresponsive at University Labs, building 87, room 2361. Campus security is on-site."

"That's a straight shot," John told his partner, Megan. He grabbed the mike while she started the engine and flipped on the sirens and lights. A moment later, Medic 82 rolled on the call.

After keying the mike, John replied, "Medic 82 responding. ETA…" He glanced at Megan, who held up five fingers. "Five minutes."

"Acknowledged, Medic 82."

The unusual thing about driving an emergency vehicle during an actual emergency is that you have to be calm and careful and deliberate, which is incongruent with the sirens, lights, and churning engine. Megan, however, was a natural. She reminded John of the navy helicopter pilots he'd flown with when he was a rescue diver. As she smoothly moved the ambulance into the oncoming lane, weaving sedately to bypass a minor traffic snarl on their side of the road, he thought he heard her hum the Beach Boys' "409" while acting like this was just another 7-Eleven run.

As good as Megan was, the ride to the scene always took too long for John, and he unconsciously leaned into his seat belt. Three minutes later, the ambulance turned onto University Drive South— the heavy traffic obediently parting before it—then headed for building 87. The impeccably groomed campus grounds were in full summer bloom and packed with students and staff arriving for classes. John counted a dozen or so bicyclists just on the visible stretch of road before them, which slowed them down even more. About two miles from the building, he unbuckled and gripped the bulkhead on either side, then stepped into the back to gather their gear. Unresponsiveness in a fifty-year-old woman could be caused any of a million things, but in his experience it was best to prepare for a cardiac, respiratory, neurological, or illness-related emergency. The dispatcher didn't mention trauma, but he would prepare for that as well; maybe she had fallen down a set of stairs.

"Hard left coming up!" Megan shouted.

Suddenly the ambulance heaved, barely giving John time to brace himself. "What the hell!" he shouted back.

"Sorry. Don't whine. A pedestrian redirected us. We're taking University Drive North."

With their gear outlined in his head and a jaw-grinding breath of exasperation, he made his way to the passenger seat and threw himself onto it. The winding University Drive North would add two miles to the drive as it looped around and then deposited them at their destination.

Forty-five seconds ticked by, then forty-five more. Megan expertly moved Medic 82 along University Drive North. She was so much better than John at driving under pressure. She had her game face on and was doing her job to a T. Megan knew remaining unruffled was the best way to help the patient, and John knew he had to do the same. An annoyed, exasperated medic wasn't nearly as effective as a calm, focused one.

In his years as a rescue diver and a medic, he'd learned not to embrace anxiety but to focus on the job. In the medical field, this was called clinical detachment; in the military, it was called keeping your shit together. Setting himself straight in his seat, John took long, deliberate, deep breaths and counted them up to twenty-one, doing the best he could to think about nothing—usually an impossible task. He let his torso muscles relax and his attention focus on the job ahead. He would get to the victim, ensure the scene was safe, and start an initial evaluation. Megan would take the woman's vitals, gather history from bystanders, and make sure the path out of the room was clear for transport. They wouldn't be too far from University Hospital; the ER was just across campus, maybe two miles away and a straight shot, as long as the roads were clear. Calmer now, John watched the campus pass by.

"KEA571 to Medic 82. Campus security advises you to use University Drive North, due to construction on University Drive South," the dispatcher relayed.

"Medic 82 to KEA571. We're already on University Drive North. ETA one minute," John replied. He turned to Megan. "Did you know about the construction?"

"No. A woman in a lab coat was standing at the intersection and directed me this way."

"Nice of her to help, but she could have been wrong."

Megan shrugged. "Dunno. Doesn't matter, really. We went the right way."

Medic 82 pulled into the driveway of building 87 and onto the blacktop emergency apron, then stopped at the front door. John called in their arrival to dispatch. Building 87, built in the 1950s, was a solid brick structure bound by sandstone. Yellow-and-black emergency fallout shelter signs hung by the entryways. A moment later, a blue-and-white University City police car pulled up behind them. The vehicle stopped far enough behind the ambulance to ensure it wouldn't block the ambulance's rear doors.

A campus security guard held the building's front door open with one hand and his radio with the other. He spoke into it; though John couldn't hear him, he probably was telling the other units and the dispatcher that Medic 82 and the University City police had arrived.

John and Megan easily rolled through this part of the call. They were so practiced that it was like a dance. They pulled out the gurney, dropped its legs, placed their equipment on it, and hurried toward the entryway with him pushing and her steering. When they reached the elevator, another guard held the door for them. All three boarded, and the guard hit the button labeled "1" for the second floor. The elevator was old, probably original to the building, and was cramped with the gurney and three of them in it

"Where's the patient, and what's her condition?" Megan asked the guard.

"Dr. Aida Doxiphus. She's is in the neuroimaging lab. My partner is with her. He said she's lying there unresponsive. We'll turn left out of the elevator and head down the hall to room 2361 on the left."

"Any hazards? Chemical? Physical?"

"No. She has some kind of brain scanning machines in there, but those are in separate rooms. No leaks or chemical spills."

A moment later the door slid open. Megan was out first, and the guard held the elevator door until John and the gurney were clear, then followed the EMTs, his rubber-soled shoes squeaking on the floor.

John and Megan made their way down the hallway at a trot, guiding the gurney between them, their equipment safely cradled on it. The lab door, also original to the building, was wooden with security glass in the top half. The letters stenciled on it read

NEUROIMAGING/TRANSCRANIAL MAGNETIC
STIMULATION/TRANSCRANIAL DIRECT CURRENT STIMULATION.

John entered the lab first. Squinting his eyes against the sunlight, which poured in through the eastern wall of windows, he saw a woman, lying flat on the floor. Her legs were straight and her arms at her side, as if she'd just been standing but then decided to lie down on the cool linoleum floor to close her eyes for a few minutes. She lay in an aisle between two long lab benches that held rows of Sigma chemical bottles, a water bath, and an old stirring plate. She had long dark hair and a dark complexion. Under her white lab coat, she was dressed in an expensive-looking white silk blouse, a khaki skirt, and flats. She had the toned look of an athlete; *perhaps she's a runner*, John thought.

He looked around to get a better sense of the room. A man in jeans, a faded Red Hot Chili Peppers T-shirt, and a lab coat leaned on the lab bench for support.

John approached the man. "Hi, I'm John, and this is my partner, Megan. We're here to treat this woman. Do you know her? Did you call this in?"

"Yeah, she's my boss, Aida Doxiphus. I called this in."

John stepped over to the woman. "Dr. Doxiphus, can you hear me?" John called out loudly, but the doctor gave no response.

Megan tossed a pair of exam gloves to John; body substance isolation was mandatory on every call.

Megan continued as John gloved up. "What's your name?"

The man nervously paused; he looked a pale and diaphoretic.

"Megan...," John started, but she was already moving.

"I got him. Sir, let's get you to sit down here," she said. She and one of the security guards helped him to the floor. It wasn't uncommon to respond to a call for one person and end up with multiple patients. They never knew how the situation would go on-site.

"Bill. My name is Bill," he finally choked out.

"What happened here, Bill? What time did she collapse?"

10

As she asked this, John's focus split in two, one part examining the patient while the other listened to Bill for clues. He paid more attention to the first; Megan would handle Bill.

John began his assessment, logging mental observations for later use. The patient was lying there, eyes closed; he didn't see any obvious signs of trauma from a fall, no blood or contusions, no deformed joints or limbs. He knelt next to her and checked the left carotid for a pulse. It was there; he counted them for thirty seconds. "Sixty-five bpm, normal. Color looks good. Skin is warm and dry," he called out to Megan. *Okay, so this isn't a cardiac call.*

"I came in right at eight a.m.," Bill said, "and Dr. D was already here, in her office on her computer. She looked okay to me."

John tilted the doctor's head back as far as possible in order to open her mouth and an airway. The visual exam of the airway looked good; he swept his index finger across the inside of her mouth and throat. Dr. Doxiphus gagged a little, but he found nothing; her airway was clear. He watched her chest rise and fall in slow, regular waves and counted the breaths as he timed out sixty seconds on his watch.

"Respiration fourteen breaths per minute, regular and normal, clear airway, and she's breathing on her own." John relaxed a bit; no resuscitation was necessary.

"I said hi," Bill said, "and put my stuff on my desk. Then I went to go to the bathroom and grab a cup of coffee, right at ten after…"

Megan left the now seated Bill. She had a clipboard in hand and a blood pressure cuff under her arm. "Ready for vitals, John," she said, putting down the clipboard.

"When I came back, at quarter after, I found her right there, just like that," Bill said, his voice cracking.

John opened the patient's blouse and placed the head of his stethoscope on her chest, listening to her breathing.

Megan, looking at the woman closely for the first time, gave a slight start. "John!" she whispered with a note of mild alarm. "This is the woman I saw, the one who redirected us to University Drive North."

"What?"

"Seriously, this is her or her twin. She's wearing the same clothes!"

"Can't be. It probably was just someone who looks like her," he offered.

"No, this is her. I'm sure of it," Megan said as she examined the woman's face and hesitated in bewilderment.

"What are you talking about? I've been here the whole time. She hasn't moved," exclaimed Bill.

"Okay, we'll sort that out later. Right now we need her vitals," John said, trying to get the call back on track.

"Right," said Megan, fitting the blood pressure cuff on Dr. Doxiphus's left arm. "One ten over seventy-five," she called out, then noted it on her clipboard.

"Lungs are clear," John said. "What's her pO_2?"

"Ninety-nine percent on room air. Her vitals are all good."

"I went to the phone right away to call 911," Bill continued. Although his voice was steadier now, he was blinking as though he were trying to send a Morse code message.

John gently lifted the patient's eyelids and flicked his penlight twice into each eye. "Pupils are equal and reactive. Pupillary response normal."

He moved to kneel by her head and quickly ran his hands down the back of her head and neck. No trauma; neck was supple. He continued his exam, feeling her torso, arms, hips, and legs, looking for any subtle injuries that his initial visual exam might have missed. Everything was normal, and the woman had no medical tags.

"The exam is good. The only sign is an AMS–altered mental status–so I'm thinking neurological or pharmaceutical," he told Megan.

Megan nodded. A pharmaceutical check meant looking for obvious signs of drug use. She moved to visually examine the insides of the woman's arms, by her elbows and her fingernail beds—which she pinched to push the blood out and timed how long they took to refill—and behind her knees. "Negative exam. Capillary refill is normal," said Megan.

"Bill, is she on any regular medications? Does she have diabetes or a history of seizures or allergies?" Megan asked.

"Dr. D?" he squeaked. "No, she's really healthy, never misses a day. I don't know about any medications, though."

"When you saw her, did she make any remarks about unusual smells, lights, or sensations?"

"Uh…I don't know. I mean, she was in the other room and looked okay."

John looked up to one of the guards. "I need you to check her purse for any prescription bottles. Look for Keppra or Dilantin or an insulin syringe—she might be diabetic."

The guard moved quickly to the office.

"Bill, are there any drugs or chemicals in here that she might have accidentally been exposed to?" John asked.

"Yeah, we have plenty of chemicals, but I handle them mostly, and nothin' happens to me."

The guard returned. "There aren't any medications in her bag or computer case."

Nothing more to do here, John thought. The patient was in neurological emergency, but the assessment was inconclusive. He had to treat this like a stroke or long-duration seizure, maybe status epilepticus. They had to transport her quickly.

"How old is she?" John asked Bill.

"Fifty, I think."

John stopped and keyed his radio to call in the assessment results and ask for orders from University Hospital ER. He was good at his job and wasn't surprised when there weren't any.

"Let's wrap her up and move her," he said.

He got the gurney and dropped it to its lowest level while Megan finished taking notes. They moved the patient to the gurney, laying her on her side so she wouldn't inhale anything in case she vomited. After he placed a folded blanket under her head for support, they strapped her in and rolled her to Medic 82.

On the way to the ER, John again took her vitals, which were steady. She was a three on the Glasgow Coma Scale, the lowest possible score, which indicated severe neurological dysfunction, and she had no response to a hard pinch of her earlobe. She was possibly in a postictal state from a seizure, though there were no signs of a grand mal, petit, or absence, and she wasn't showing any of the expected signs of recovery. She also showed no signs of a stroke, though nothing could be ruled out with the equipment and time they had. John called this information in to the University Hospital ER.

13

Despite the woman's stability and generally sound presentation, she was in a serious situation and time was against her. If she had suffered a stroke, time was key. John checked his watch; it was 8:38. The tech had last seen her at 8:10 and called in at 8:15. So she'd been down between twenty-three and twenty-eight minutes. He checked her vitals again—no change. As he did, a thought struck him. The call from the dispatcher came at 8:25, and the lab tech said he called it in at quarter after, and he was so sure of the times too.

John stopped himself with an audible, "Huh?" 911 never took ten minutes to tone out—verbal shorthand for dispatching—a medic. He paused, mulling this over. The timeline didn't fit.

2 Equilibrium and Potentials

S itting in the third row of the lecture hall, Natalia Doxiphus yawned once, then again. Any more and she knew the professor would get irritated. Seven thirty a.m. was too damn early for the start of a summer class, and she was on her second cup of iced coffee. It frustrated her that her parents, Doctors Gregorio and Aida Doxiphus, were making her take this class at all, but they insisted that she follow the established series of coursework.

"Talking about neurobiology at home isn't the same as doing the lecture and lab work. You have to take these classes for the experience, besides, they're required for your major," was the response she had received from her parents every time she broached the subject of skipping over the introductory material.

Thankfully the seventy-five-minute introductory biological psychology class was nearly over. Professor LaVista was rushing through the last of the material in his slide deck. They were covering resting potential—the state that neurons always return to after they've fired.

"The sodium-potassium pump, here at point one of the diagram, moves three sodium ions out of the neuron for every two potassium ions it moves into the neuron." As the professor droned on, Natalia's eyes glazed over as she stared at the projected slide. *I know this stuff. This is so boring. No wonder I can't stay awake.*

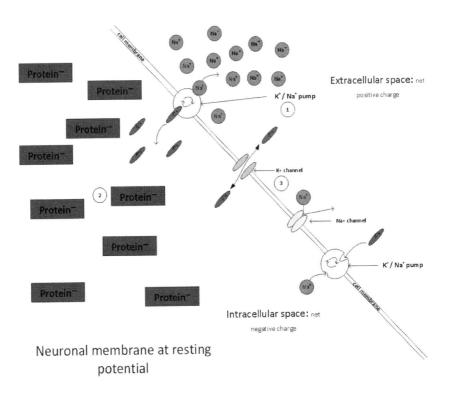

Extracellular space: net positive charge

K⁺ / Na⁺ pump ①

K+ channel ③

Na+ channel

K⁺ / Na⁺ pump

Intracellular space: net negative charge

Neuronal membrane at resting potential

She drew zentangles on the border of her notebook page, and her mind drifted while the professor spent the next few minutes discussing the sodium-potassium pump. Despite her best intentions, Natalia's eyelids started to slide down. They snapped open when the professor said, "The sodium-potassium pump runs all the time, even in a sleeping brain"—he looked right at her— "and is responsible for a large amount of the brain's energy consumption."

He was just too damn awake for Natalia's liking, but then Uncle Tony always had been a morning person.

"Any questions?"

"I'm unclear about one thing, Professor," blurted out a biology major from the front row, for the ninth time this morning.

"Steve," acknowledged Professor LaVista, trying not to let his irritation show, and modestly succeeding.

"Since the pump is always moving sodium ions out of the neuron, and the cell membrane is selectively permeable to potassium only,

16

how did the sodium get into the neuron in the first place, and why doesn't it get depleted?"

"That's a reasonable question but a little ahead of where we are. Anyone have any thoughts?"

No one immediately volunteered, not that the professor would have noticed, as he was ignoring Steve and focusing on his slide notes. After a few beats, and still without looking up, he called out, "Natalia, would you care to help Steve out?"

Natalia groaned inwardly. *Not again, not today. I hate talking in class. I'm a junior. Let the kiss-ass senior figure it out for himself.* But Uncle Tony had asked, so she put on a good face and turned toward Steve. After stifling a third yawn, she explained in an authoritative tone.

"The sodium ions enter when the neuron is propagating an action potential," she told Steve, who looked puzzled. She decided to take pity on him. "When the neuron is exposed to enough depolarizing stimuli, its resting potential—that's the electrical charge difference between the interior of the cell and the extracellular space—starts to move in the positive direction, toward the threshold. When it reaches the threshold, which is about minus thirty to minus forty mV, the polarity of the cell changes briefly and the voltage-gated sodium channels open for about a millisecond, allowing a rapid influx of sodium ions into the cell's interior down the sodium concentration gradient. The potassium channels close during this time. This activity is the generation of an action potential in the neuron. Then the charge-gated sodium channels close, and a combination of the work of the sodium-potassium pump and the reopened potassium channels restore the neuron to its resting state, or resting potential, so it's ready to fire again. That's where the sodium comes from."

Natalia finished and hoped the professor wouldn't ask her to use the Nernst equation to predict the balancing point between the electrostatic pressure and the concentration gradient for potassium.

"That's exactly right, Ms. Doxiphus. Thank you," Professor LaVista said, beaming. Steve looked sheepish; Nat gave him a weak smile and turned back to the front of the room.

"That's it for today. Your last tests have been graded, and the scores are available on the website. Be prepared for next time. We'll be covering action-potential propagation."

There was a general thumping of books and closing of laptops as the class rose as one from their seats.

"Natalia, do you have a second, please?" Professor LaVista asked.

"Sure." She walked to the podium, hoisting her messenger bag on her shoulder and clutching her tablet.

He glanced up to make sure no one else was within earshot, then continued in a softer voice. "What do you think of Steve? He applied for a TA position."

"After a question like that? From a senior in a science major? I don't know. This isn't hard stuff, Uncle Tony."

She had grown up knowing this man as Uncle Tony. He was her godfather, her mother's peer, and a longtime friend of her parents; he had known her from birth and had been over to their house for formal departmental dinner parties every few months and for more relaxed meals, birthdays, Christmas, Easter, and all the other holidays for as long as Natalia could remember.

"That's what I'm thinking now as well," confessed Professor LaVista, with a sigh. "Do you know anyone else who would be good for that spot?"

"Excuse me, Professor," came an overly loud woman's voice from the classroom doorway. "I'm looking for Natal…oh, there you are!" Betty, the biology department's secretary, who also was a regular fixture at the Doxiphus house, was out of breath, flushed, and unsuccessfully trying to compose herself.

Hearing her name, Natalia pivoted and started to walk up the steps. "What's wrong, Mrs. Bamiyan?"

"Oh, my dear, I've been looking all over for you. I thought you might be on your way to your next class. Then you weren't there, so I came back here and—"

Nat interrupted her rambling. "What's wrong?" Although Mrs. Bamiyan was as sweet as they came, she was flighty.

"It's your mother. She collapsed. She's in the ER right now."

Nat took the last fourteen steps three at a time and met the secretary at the doorway of the lecture hall. "What do you mean, she collapsed? What happened?" Nat asked more in disbelief than in panic or fear.

"I don't know, dear. Dr. Kelley just called me and told me to find you as quickly as I could. He said to get you to the ER right away."

As Natalia read the anxiety and concern on Mrs. Bamiyan's face, her stomach sank. This was for real. She knew that the secretary meant well, but she wasn't helping her feel calm.

"I'll go with you, Nat," Professor LaVista said, gently laying a warm hand on her shoulder.

"Yes, please," she stammered out.

"Come with me, dear," the secretary intoned softly. "Security is waiting to drive you over."

Natalia's mind whirled around an axis of alarm, fear, and disbelief. Her mother had collapsed? How was that possible? Her mother could lead her yoga class, and she was in excellent shape; she never let physical things slow her down. The woman was a rock—she was Nat's rock.

Mrs. Bamiyan's shoes tapped out a fast tattoo as the trio made their way through the halls to the building's main entrance. Natalia's brain started to kick into gear. "What about my dad?" Natalia asked, then remembered the answer as soon as the question was out of her mouth. *Shit! Dad is at Fermilab, outside of Chicago.*

"Dr. Kelley is contacting him now. We'll get him back here as soon as possible."

What could she do to help her mom? What should she do? Natalie had never been through anything like this before, and her world was swirling around her. Once she was in the car, she buckled her seat belt automatically. The guard quickly slipped into the driver's seat, and they set off, lights on, but no siren.

Natalia rummaged through her messenger bag and pulled out her cell phone. "I'm calling my dad," she told her godfather. She got no answer, so she texted him instead. It took her shaking hands a few tries to type out the text.

Mom in ER. She collapsed. On the way to ER w/U Tony. CALL ME!

A couple of minutes later, the car pulled up to the patient entrance of the ER. Natalia recognized Dr. Kelley, the president of University Hospital, waiting at the patient entrance. He was short, with graying curly hair and a noticeable paunch. Nat was out of the car before it had fully stopped and rushed to the entrance. Professor LaVista was close behind.

"How is she? Where is she?" Natalia asked in a rush.

"She's in trauma A. They're working on her right now. I don't know any more than that, Natalia. Come on. This way," said Dr. Kelley, who led the two of them into the building. He gave LaVista a glance and a nod.

He navigated her through the ER. It was bright, and a small child was shrieking in one of the curtained rooms. Even in her agitated state, Natalia noticed how incongruent the calmness of the ER staff was in the context of the environment they were in and the job they were doing. It was as if they saw a different world, as if they were in a different world than she was. In an instant, her world had gone from one of petty annoyance to catastrophic tumult. And she was mad at herself for losing control. Her mother would have been strong in a situation like this; she had to be as well. She heard her mother's voice in her mind: *Pull yourself together. You don't get the luxury of a meltdown. You're in charge.* Nat took a deep breath, pushed the emotions down and, spoke in a more controlled voice.

"What happened, Dr. Kelley?"

"Your mother's tech found her on the floor of her lab a little after eight this morning. We don't know what happened."

Nat's stomach started to rebel, but she ignored it.

"The medics got to her, worked on her, then transported her here. We've been working on her for about twenty minutes now. We're doing our best." Kelley stopped. There was nothing else for him to say.

"Is she dead?" Nat choked on the words.

"No," he said with great certainty. "She was stable when she came in, just unconscious."

"Can I see her?" Natalia asked, already knowing the answer but hoping otherwise.

"That's not possible now. Let the team do their work. We'll get you in as soon as we can."

Kelley walked the pair to a quiet waiting room, one reserved for families of patients in critical condition.

"I'll stay with her until Greg arrives," LaVista told Kelley.

"I'll make sure you're kept fully informed," Kelley assured them, then turned to make a hasty exit from the room.

***

Outside the waiting room, Kelley set off toward the automatic double doors that separated the ER from the rest of the hospital and pulled out his cell phone. He hit speed dial 2.

A young man answered, "Dr. Kelley's office."

"Randy, it's me. Did you get in touch with Dr. Doxiphus yet?"

"No, his line is busy. I contacted the administrator's office, and they're tracking him down now."

"Okay, transfer the call to me when it comes. Get the first flight out of Midway or O'Hare. Charter a helicopter out of DuPage if you have to. He needs to be here ASAP."

"Yes, sir. Anything else?"

"When are the grant auditors due?"

"The National Science Foundation lands at 11:45 a.m. the day after tomorrow, and the National Institutes of Health arrive at 12:23 p.m. the same day."

"Thanks."

Kelley had time to get Greg Doxiphus here and hopefully get this situation under control before he faced the auditors. Dealing with auditors was stressful enough on a good day, but having a major grant recipient lying unconscious in the ER complicated things.

No sooner had the line gone dead than his phone went off.

"Dr. Kelley," he answered.

"Alvin? It's Greg Doxiphus. What's going on with my wife?"

"Her tech found her collapsed in her lab. He called the EMTs, and they transported her here to the ER. She was stable but unconscious on arrival," he said.

"That's what my daughter just told me. Don't you have anything else?"

"The code team is working on her right now, Greg. That's all I know. My office is booking a ticket for you on the first available flight. Randy will call you. Just get yourself home. We have things covered here."

"Thanks, Alvin. I'm already on my way"

"Okay. My office will keep you updated." Kelley ended the call.

"Alvin?" a voice called. It was Dr. Mark Gilman, the trauma lead. He poked his head through the double doors.

Flustered, Kelley turned and asked, "What's Aida's status?" Mentally he was trying to put his clinician's coat back on, but he had been out of practice so long that it didn't fit him very well.

Dr. Gilman's body followed his head through the doors. A man Kelley had personally recruited and thought was unflappable, Gilman looked as confused and concerned as a first-year resident.

"She's still in AMS but is otherwise completely stable. Initial bloodwork is normal. Toxicology will be back any minute, but I expect that to come back clean. I'm sending her to imaging to rule out hemorrhagic or ischemic stroke. After that she'll need an EEG study."

"Some long-term postictal state?" Kelley posited aloud, referring to the slow recovery period seizure victims go through after an attack.

"If it is, I've never seen one like this; she should have been out of it by now. I don't have an explanation yet. As far as I can tell, she should get up and walk out of here," Gilman replied, looking at his watch.

"What now?"

"We'll move her to the neuro ICU for a full workup."

Well, at least that will get her out of the ER and into a lower-profile place.

"I'll tell the family and get them moved up to her room. Keep me in the loop on this, Mark," said Kelley as he turned back toward the private waiting room. He had gone all of two steps when his phone chirped.

"Dr. Kelley, public relations just called. Channel Seven news just contacted them about Dr. Doxiphus. They need you here."

Kelley hated this. He hated the exposure that a high-profile incident like this would bring to the hospital. "Okay, tell them I'll be there in fifteen minutes. I have to talk to the family." Sometimes he felt as though he worked for Randy, not the other way around.

3 Indeterminacy

The steady beep of the heart monitor was the only sound Natalia could hear. She clung to it and took comfort in it as the minutes dragged by. They had moved her mother to a private room an hour ago, and Nat felt steadier now that they were together. Uncle Tony had left to get something for them to eat.

When's Dad going to get here? It was a thought she returned to every minute or so when she wasn't checking on her mother, not that there was much to check. Nat sat next to her mother's bed. The nurses had changed her into a hospital gown and a diaper, started an IV, and inserted a urinary catheter. She was breathing steadily on her own and looked as though she was asleep. In a moment of hope, Nat had gently nudged her mother's arm and called to her to wake her up, but there was no response. All she could do was hold her mother's hand.

This hospital room had been set up to monitor seizure patients. It had a camera up in one corner, pointing down at the bed, and a computer cart with a laptop and an EEG machine against the far wall. A doctor was supposed to be here at any moment to hook her mother up to it.

The beeping continued, slowly and steadily, and Natalia started to notice it less. The midday sun through the window was warm on her back. It felt comforting, like her mother's warm hand, and a little of the tension that was living between her shoulders and that had climbed up her neck gave way, ever so slightly. Going from the tumult and alarm of the morning to quietly waiting had drained her, and she started to drowse off, losing count of the beeps. She was in that place between sleep and wakefulness, where disconnected memories surfaced in a jumble and ran through her head. She experienced sitting at her desk in the lecture hall, saw the trees rushing by the car window, and felt the anxiety over an upcoming exam. Soon even these faded as her sleep became deeper and she lost awareness of her surroundings.

"Natalia, wake up. The doctor is here!" Her mother's commanding voice jarred her from sleep, and she bolted upright, back into the world of her senses. She looked around, startled. "Mom?" she responded reflexively, but there was no answer. Her mother was still and quiet in the bed, the companion beeping continuing undisturbed.

There was, however, a light rapping on the doorjamb.

"Hello? Miss Doxiphus? I'm Dr. Hernandez." The woman offered her hand and a warm smile as she came into the room.

Nat took it, grateful for her gentle manner, and responded with a soft, "Hi. You're here for the EEG, right?"

Dr. Hernandez stepped over to Aida's bed and started a quick exam. "Yes, I'm going to start an EEG study so we can get a better idea of what's going on. I'm sorry it took me so long to come up. I had to handle a blunt cranial trauma." Dr. Hernandez went silent for a moment as she listened to Aida's breathing, and then she continued. "You don't ride a motorcycle, do you?"

"No, never have."

"If you ever do, make sure you wear a helmet. It's amazing how such a simple choice can affect the course of a life." Dr. Hernandez finished with a sigh and tested Aida's deep tendon reflexes by rapping a small rubber mallet on specific points on the front and back of the upper arm, near the wrists, and then ankles. She finished by stroking the handle of the reflex mallet across the bottom of Aida's foot; the toes curled downward, as expected. She then tucked the mallet into her lab coat and took out a penlight. "Has your mother ever had a seizure, even in childhood?"

"No...I mean, not that I know of, not that she's ever mentioned. My dad might know more about her childhood," Nat replied.

Dr. Hernandez clicked off the penlight she'd used to check Aida's pupillary reflex. "Do you know when your father will arrive? I'll need to talk to him about your mother's history."

"He should be here soon; he's flying back from Chicago. He was at Fermilab."

Dr. Hernandez paused and looked sympathetically at Natalia. "Your mother's imaging studies came back fine. Her brain is healthy and normal. No stroke, no physical damage at all. Are you here alone?"

"My uncle Tony's here with me. He left to get us something to eat."

"Good. We need to make sure you're okay too," Dr. Hernandez finished, using her warm smile again.

The doctor moved the EEG cart next to the bed and worked to set it up while Natalia sat quietly, not taking her eyes off the medical equipment; she massaged the back of her neck to get some of the tension out. The EEG cart didn't look all that impressive to her, considering what it did. Nat was familiar with the EEG test; she used to play with one in her mom's lab when she was on summer vacation from high school.

This test isn't for fun, though, she thought grimly.

The electrical activity in a healthy brain is coordinated into rhythmic waves that flow over the surface, or cortex, of the brain. Within moments of starting the test, Dr. Hernandez would know if anything major was wrong. The EEG was mostly used to diagnose different types of epilepsy or damage to the brain from strokes. It was also one of a collection of exams used to determine cerebral death. As Natalia's mind fixated on that last thought, she wiped the palms of her hands on her jeans.

"Nat, food's here." It took her a second to hear her godfather's voice. "Got you a steak salad and a zebra brownie." Nat liked the steak and blue cheese salad. She realized he had gone to two different restaurants to get her favorites. She loved that about him.

"Dr. Hernandez, this is my uncle Tony."

Dr. Hernandez blinked a few times, clearly not expecting "uncle Tony" to be Anthony LaVista, MD, PhD, and head of the neurology department at University Hospital. "Dr. LaVista…oh! It's a pleasure to meet you."

Uncle Tony returned the handshake awkwardly around the bag of food and drinks. "Yes, Dr. Hernandez, I remember your name from the final resident applicant list. Congratulations on getting hired. And thank you for taking care of Dr. Doxiphus. She's family, you know."

"Of course, I'll let Miss Doxiphus know as soon as I have results," Dr. Hernandez said confidently.

"Nat, let's go out to the garden to eat," LaVista suggested, exchanging a glance with Hernandez. Nat started to protest, not wanting to leave her mother's side, when Hernandez spoke up.

"Miss Doxiphus, it really would be better to have a quiet environment for the test. It'll take about an hour to calibrate the machine and run the study."

"C'mon, Nat. It'll be okay," her uncle coaxed her.

"All right. I do need to eat," Nat admitted as much to herself as the others. As they walked down the hallway, she surprised her godfather. "Did you just threaten her job?"

"No, I just let her know that this is a high-profile case."

Nat scowled her disapproval of the expression of departmental politics. She liked Dr. Hernandez.

Picking up on the reproach, LaVista continued. "Just so you know, I requested Dr. Hernandez for this. She's very good with EEGs. Not everything is as it seems at first glance, Nat."

Silently they passed through the swinging double doors on the way to the nurses' station and headed toward the elevator.

***

On any other day, it would have been a great lunch. The garden was beautiful, and the summer flowers were aromatic. The sky was clear and blue, and a gentle breeze kept the bugs down. Around them, hospital employees chatted away during their lunch hour, and families huddled in close, supportive groups.

Natalia and LaVista chewed in silence, neither of them feeling like talking. A little more than an hour had passed since they had left Aida's room. When Nat was halfway through her zebra brownie, her phone chirped.

"Hello," she mumbled.

"Hi, sweetie. I just landed. How's your mother?"

"Hi, Dad. They're doing an EEG now. Her CAT scan and MRI came back clean."

26

"How are you doing, honey? Is Uncle Tony there?"

Nat could hear her father running. "I'm okay. Yeah, he's right here. We're having lunch in the hospital garden."

"Okay, good. Stay with him. I'll meet you at the hospital after I get my bags and the car. I should be there in about an hour and fifteen minutes or so, depending on traffic. I love you."

"Drive carefully, Dad. Love you," she finished. *I don't need you in an accident too*, she thought. She crumpled up what was left of her lunch. "That was Dad. He says he'll be here in an hour or so."

"It'll be more like an hour and a half," LaVista observed, having overheard the conversation. "Your dad's a great guy, but he never estimates time well."

Natalia smirked at the truth of the comment. Her dad was an eternal optimist, always thinking he could get things done faster than he could. When Nat was younger, her mother would tell her, "Take whatever amount of time your father says it will take for him to finish whatever he's doing and double it."

Nat's phone rang again, and this time it was the general number of University Hospital. "Hello?"

"Miss Doxiphus. Hi. It's Dr. Hernandez. I have the results of your mother's EEG. Can you and Dr. LaVista come back up, please?"

"We'll be right there. Oh, and my dad just landed. He should be here in about an hour and a half."

"Okay, good. I'll meet you at the nurses' station."

When they reached the nurses' station, Dr. Hernandez was working feverishly on her laptop.

"Doctor?" Natalia said to get her attention.

Dr. Hernandez stood up. "Let's go where we can talk." The woman was moving briskly down the hall, toward the double doors. Her voice had lost its previous warmth, and she wore a guarded expression. Nat felt her lunch transform into a stone at the bottom of her stomach.

Dr. Hernandez led them to an unoccupied patient room just before the double doors, then closed the door behind them.

"Your mother's condition remains stable. She's not in any danger." She put her laptop on the adjustable patient table. "But the results are…"

"Inconclusive?" Dr. LaVista interjected.

Dr Hernandez opened her laptop; a marked-up EEG trace was already up. LaVista examined it closely, then went quiet.

"Not inconclusive, but I have no explanation, so I have to say 'inexplicable.'"

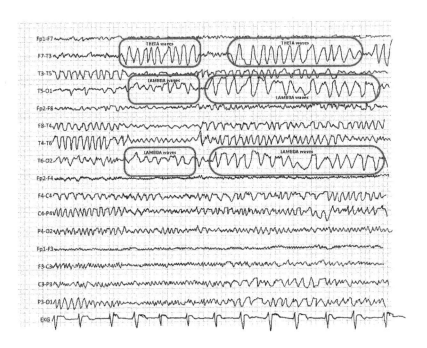

Hernandez went on as best as she could. "Dr. Doxiphus shows a great deal of lambda activity in the occipital region, which is where the vision centers of the brain are," she added for Natalia's benefit. "And there's some theta activity in the fronto-temporal region as well. Everywhere else shows organized alpha activity."

"So what does this mean?" Atypically, Natalia was struggling to keep up while her uncle was quietly considering the trace.

"You recalibrated?" he asked.

"Twice, and then I changed out machines. I sent the first one to medical equipment for diagnostics. I had just used the second one this morning, and it worked fine then," Dr. Hernandez quickly replied.

"Photic stimulation?" he asked, pointing to the lambda activity.

"That's the hard part. The lambda activity was completely unaffected by any stimuli that were presented in the visual field. The activity remained consistent with the subject's eyes closed!" Hernandez was clearly puzzled and was looking to one of the people she hoped would help her.

"Uncle Tony, what does this mean? I can see the activity, so she's not…" Nat stopped; she couldn't bring herself to say *brain dead*. "What does this mean?" she blurted, with a mixture of anxiety, frustration, and strain in her voice.

Her uncle used his professor's voice. "Okay, see all the lines that don't have the red boxes? Those leads show organized alpha activity. That's exactly what we would expect to see in a normal awake adult brain."

"Mmm-hmm…wait, but Mom's not awake," Nat managed to muster.

"Right, she's not. Now, lambda activity usually is generated when something novel and visually interesting is presented in the visual field. But that's not what's happening here. The activity is occurring independently of what's going on in the visual field."

This wasn't making sense to Natalia, and her frustration was growing.

"Lastly, there's this theta activity, which usually is associated with dreaming and sleep." LaVista had his reading glasses on now and was staring closely at the trace. "Did you get this out to the attending for interpretation?" he asked Hernandez.

"Yes, Dr. Jones has them now," Hernandez replied, looking a little relieved that she had taken all the right steps and frankly that LaVista was stumped too.

"Good, keep on it. Start a long-term study with video recording." LaVista turned to Nat. Taking her gently by the arm, he led her into the hallway.

"Nat, I don't know what this all means. Technically, those readings, that trace—it's not possible. Your mom has plenty of brain activity. There's a lot going on, and we'll find out what it is."

Hernandez entered the hallway. "Dr. Jones just called. He's in consultation room three and wants to meet with you."

"You go, Uncle Tony. I'll go sit with Mom. My dad should be here in a little while anyway," said Nat.

He gave her a quick hug and turned to follow Hernandez to consult three.

Natalia leaned against the wall for minute, hands at her head, trying to keep it together. Then she stood fully, pushed through the double doors, walked three rooms down to her mother's room.

She opened the heavy, wide door, hoping to find her dad already there, but instead she found a nurse leaning over her mother and looking between the EEG trace and her mother's eyes.

"Hi. I'm her daughter. Who are you?" Nat asked, feeling oddly suspicious. *Perhaps there's been a shift change.*

"I'm from neurology. Just checking a few things," the nurse replied.

"Dr. Hernandez and Dr. LaVista just examined my mom. What are you doing?"

The nurse moved so that her back was to Nat. She was white, with shoulder-length, shapeless, dishwater-colored hair. "I'll be done in a minute, if you can just wait outside, please," the nurse said without looking at her.

"I'm staying here with my mom. My dad is due here any minute," came the determined reply. The nurse was doing something with the IV catheter in the crook of her mother's arm. "What are you doing to my mom?" Nat demanded, surprised at how quickly her anger and frustration were rising.

"You seem exhausted, dear. Why don't you go get a cup of coffee? I'll be done in a few minutes." The nurse reached into a pocket and pulled out a blood-collection tube.

Nat practically exploded. "I told you my mom just had an exam. Why do you need to do another one?" She moved to the opposite side of the bed, her back to the window so she could face the nurse. The nurse turned away from Nat to face the EEG cart. "Why won't you face me?"

"Really, dear, it's okay. Go take a short break. I'll watch your mother."

This time, Nat did explode. "No, get the hell away from my mother, bitch!" she shouted, leaning across her mother's body to push the nurse away.

"Hey, let's all calm down," came a deep male voice from the doorway. The nurse didn't turn to look, but Nat's eyes snapped toward the stranger. A man in a medic uniform stood in the doorway. He had the solid, lean look of a swimmer and closely cropped dark-brown hair.

"What's going on?" he asked.

"I'm sorry, miss. I can do this later," the nurse said in a quiet voice, then quickly moved to leave the room. As the medic stepped aside for her, the woman kept her head down, so Nat still didn't get a clear view of her face.

She pulled herself up from her mother's bed, her pulse still pounding but starting to slow. "Thank you," she told the medic.

"What for?" he replied.

"For helping get rid of her...and who are you?" She paused, then yelled out to the duty nurse who was walking by, "Excuse me!"

"Yes?" the nurse said, entering the room.

"There was another nurse in here just now—shoulder-length dirty-blond hair, about my height. Do you know who she is? She said she was from neurology and had to examine my mom."

The nurse bit her lip and thought for a second. "That could be a lot of the nurses on staff. What did she say she was doing?" The quizzical look on the woman's face didn't reassure Nat. The duty nurse came over to check her mother's vitals and IV.

"She said she was from neurology and had to do an exam," Natalia repeated. "It looked like she was going to take a blood sample."

"Well, everything looks okay here with your mom. Let me go check the orders. I don't know everyone who works here," the nurse said, then left the room.

Nat turned to the medic again and eyed him.

"Sorry, I'm John Holden. I'm the medic who brought your mother in this morning." He grinned sheepishly, getting his first full look at Natalia as she walked around the bed. Nat's long brown hair, frazzled as it was, caught the sunlight from the window, and hues of gold, red, and auburn shone clearly. John was stopped in his tracks by the sight of sunlight shining through something wondrous. He came over to her, almost tripping. "Are you okay? You're obviously pissed off."

"Yeah, sorry about the yelling. I just didn't know...that just didn't feel right. Why are you here?"

"Why am I here?" he repeated, looking at her face. "Right, uh, I just brought in a guy who tried to put his car through a bridge column—he was drunk. Anyway, there were some odd things about your mother's call that I remembered. I already talked to 911 dispatch, and I wanted to tell the doctors too. I was going to wait until the end of my shift to file a report, but I was here anyway, so..." He paused, looking over to Aida and then back to Nat. "I'm sorry about all this."

"She's...well, the same," Nat said, turning to her mother. "I'm Natalia Doxiphus, by the way."

"Nice to meet you."

"Natalia?" called a voice full of concern from the hallway. A second later, Dr. Gregorio Doxiphus strode into the room. Nat moved to her father, whose skin glistened with a slight sheen of sweat.

"Dad." Her voice cracked as he held her for a moment.

"Sweetie, are you okay?" he said, then gave her a kiss on the forehead.

"Yeah, I'm okay," she said, and they let go of their embrace. "This is John Holden. He's the medic who brought Mom in."

Greg glanced at John and muttered, "Thank you" as he moved toward the bed.

Gregorio Doxiphus was trimly built, with a salt-and-pepper black beard and a full head of hair. He took his wife's hand and sat on the edge of the bed, stroking her face with his other hand. After a long moment, he got up and went to examine the EEG trace. He studied it for a long minute and then another.

"This doesn't make any sense, Nat. What did Uncle Tony say?" he said.

"He said there's a lot of brain activity, but basically the same thing—those readings aren't possible. But here they are. He's with other doctors now, trying to figure it out."

Sitting back on the edge of the bed, Greg leaned over and kissed his wife tenderly on the cheek and whispered, "Aida...where are you?"

4 Withdrawal

*T*urn *right, and it's fifteen steps to the double doors.* She had planned for this. The nurse walked with purpose, but not so fast as to draw attention. *Once through the doors, take thirty steps to the nurses' station and another thirty to the next set of double doors down the hallway. I'll be through the next set in a few seconds.*

The hard part about withdrawing was resisting the urge to rush or, worse, to run. The trick was to avoid being noticed, and running was a dead giveaway. The human eye is naturally drawn to movement, especially if it sticks out in a scene. It's a reflex buried deep in the primitive brain, and it served our hunting ancestors well.

She fought the urge to speed up again as she approached the nurses' station with its wide-angle camera mounted on the ceiling, but her plan had accounted for this too. She raised the clipboard in her hand. Pretending to read something off it, she strode past the station, her face clearly visible only to the clipboard.

Go through the second set of doors, then into the fourth room on the left.

The patient room was empty except for a cleaning cart, with only the afternoon sun leaking in through the drawn blinds. After making sure the door was closed, she went straight to the cart and stripped off the nurse's identity, then dropped it into a hanging laundry bag on the cart and pulled out a set of surgical scrubs. She kept the exam gloves on and dressed in smooth, quick motions. After she finished, she tucked her hair up under a surgical cap and slipped on a surgical mask. The last items she put on were an ID badge from a facilities worker and a pair of glasses with thick, dark frames.

She pulled the cart behind her to the door, listened for a moment, then slowed her breathing. She then pulled the door inward in a casual, almost careless fashion before propping it open with the cart. As she walked around to get behind it, she completed her transformation, taking on a slight hunch and a slower, tired gait. She belonged here; she was doing her job just like everyone else. She wouldn't be seen, and no one would ever see the "nurse" again either.

Pushing the cart ahead of her, she turned left and continued down the hallway, moving away from the commotion at the nurses' station. She heard the duty nurse's voice. "Who was just in 206? Did neuro have someone up here?" *Good timing.*

She plodded along to the elevator at the end of the hallway, not looking at the security camera in the corner. *Go down to LL1. Drop the cart, and go out the service entrance.* Those were the next three steps. She kept her cart—or surgical cap or something else—between her face and the cameras at every turn and never made eye contact with passersby.

Three minutes later, she made her way down the sidewalk, under the green summer trees, her stride once again purposeful. With a parking lot on one side and the back of an apartment complex on the other, there would be few eyes to see a hospital facilities woman walking to the bus stop after her shift.

When she was halfway down the block, a cab pulled up to her and stopped. Without missing a stride, she got in the back seat. One whiff told her of the countless junk food meals that had been eaten in the cab, fries stuffed into the mouth between pulls on a cigarette and slurps of coffee.

"Where to, lady?" the cab driver sneered, and she stiffened, freezing in place. She felt his eyes on her but didn't look up. Without a word, the driver reached up with a meaty, pasty white hand and flipped the meter. The doors locked automatically as the cab pulled out onto the nearly empty street.

She swallowed, trying to wet her throat. "I wasn't expecting you."

"Plans change." His eyes drifted slowly up to the mirror, then back to the road. "Sit back and enjoy the ride."

Her eyes searched the cab's interior; there was nothing for her to use to defend herself, not even a pen. She swallowed hard and sat back, her eyes drawn to his bright-red hair.

"That's right—just sit back," he said. When the cab was a few blocks away from the hospital, the driver nodded, glanced at her in the mirror with indifferent ice-blue eyes, and said, "Go ahead."

"Her EEG is similar to the observers," she said, scratching her eyebrows. "The daughter interrupted me, and I couldn't get blood or cerebrospinal fluid samples. I had to leave the sampling equipment on the cart."

The driver flashed a sharp look at her in the mirror. The terms of her mission had been clear: payment only with samples. Now with him here, she realized other terms might have changed.

"I had planned for the daughter, but a male medic intruded as well." She cursed herself for making excuses and glared out the window at the concrete dividers that were speeding by. "I was compromised; I withdrew. I got out clean." That was all there was to report. *If they don't like it, fuck them.* Dispassionate eyes met her nervous glance in the rearview mirror. He owned her right now, and they both knew it.

The cab was heading east on the interstate, toward the airport and the river. The setting sun was behind them. She felt the back seat of the car close in on her, and her pulse pounded in her ears. The hulking driver nodded again. "Acknowledged."

His large bowling-ball head swiveled with surprising ease. Determined not to cave in this time, she kept her eyes up and faced him square on. He saw this and considered it for less than an instant. He snorted and said, "Get changed. You're going to the airport." He passed a small overnight bag to her from the front seat.

She didn't feel connected to her hands as they opened the bag, but they seemed to know what they were doing. She took out the pants, blouse, vest, scarf, and shoes of a flight attendant and breathed deeply.

"Where am I going?"

"You'll find out on the plane."

She pulled off the thick-rimmed glasses and then the irritating facial prosthetics that had hidden the true shape of her cheekbones, jawline, chin, and the distance between her eyes. There were too

35

many cameras in the hospital; there was even one in the patient's room. After she pulled off the surgical cap, her hair fell free. She thought there was probably a camera here in the car as well—not that it mattered. She was used to letting people see her only as she wanted them to. She slipped into another persona as she stripped, one that liked being watched. Disguises weren't all about makeup and clothing; you simply had to give the observer just enough, and then their minds would see what you wanted them to see. People were excellent at deceiving themselves—a flaw from which she made her living.

The cab rolled into the private area of the airport, where a small jet, its engines already turning, waited on the tarmac. With its running lights on, it looked like a firefly in the quickly settling summer night. As she got out and pulled the handle on the overnight bag to pop out the wheels, the driver's burly arm shot out, his massive hand grabbing her wrist. He pulled her down so her face was inches from his, wrenching her elbow and shoulder in an effortless move. There would be no disguises to hide behind now.

"Quiet, now. Don't draw attention," he cooed to her, and then the ice returned. "Next time, you finish the job. Those are the rules."

Wincing in pain, she knew if he squeezed just a little bit harder, she'd be dealing with a fracture. But apparently that wasn't part of the job, as a few seconds later he relaxed and let go. She stood, clutching her nearly broken forearm.

"That's good," he said, grinning. "I'm glad my message got through all those masks you have."

She boarded the plane, which was empty, save for whoever was on the flight deck. A jolt of sharp pain electrified her arm as she pulled up the aircraft door. "Okay, asshole. Message delivered," she admitted.

She sat down and strapped herself in. A few minutes later, the plane moved to the runway and took off. As soon as they were in the air, she unbuckled and walked over to a table in the middle of the cabin. On it was a tray with a flat rectangle of modeling clay. A message had been cut into the soft clay. It read:

Heard your report. I'm disappointed you were unable to retrieve samples, but you made the right choice to withdraw. You'll be staying in residence 32 until contacted.

She grabbed the thin slab of clay and mashed it into a ball, obliterating the message. Residence 32 was in Argentina, and it meant another persona, one that particularly suited her, and at least it meant no prosthetics. This turn of events brought a soft grin to her supple face. She got herself a drink and settled in for the long night flight to South America.

5 The Crucifix and the Ice Pick

Natalia Doxiphus strained to open one eye as she swiped at the buzzing phone on the small table. She missed and knocked it to the floor, where its vibrations were amplified and irritated her ears like a persistent mosquito.

"Son of a bitch," she grumbled.

She sat up, grabbed the phone from the floor, and silenced the alarm. On a regular day, she'd be waking up now to get ready for class, but here she was, on a cot in her mother's hospital room. Her father was in the recliner, his feet up. Though bloodshot and dark ringed, his eyes were alert. The two ended up spending the night in her mother's hospital room, both agreeing that after the incident with the nurse and John Holden's news that they wouldn't leave her alone.

"Morning," Natalia offered.

"Morning, sweetie," he said, somehow managing a slight smile for her.

Her eyes went immediately to her mother, but she didn't see any change. "How's Mom?"

"I watched her all night. She's the same, stable but nonresponsive." Greg sighed, shifting in his chair to relieve the stiffness from the night in the recliner.

"Did they come up with any ideas?"

Her father shook his head. "Not yet. Tony, Dr. Jones, and Dr. Hernandez have been in a few times, but nothing yet. The next test they want to do is an fMRI, a functional magnetic resonance image, but the machine is down for maintenance, so it'll be a day before that can be done," he said, dejection coloring his voice.

Nat stood and stretched out a knot in her lower back. "What'll that tell us?"

"The fMRI shows blood flow in the brain. When an area of the brain is active, the blood flow to it increases. It'll tell us which areas are working and can respond to stimuli." Nat knew it wasn't the explanation Uncle Tony would've given, but her dad was a high-energy-particle physicist, not a neuroscientist. Looking back at her, he added, "Get cleaned up. I'll order us breakfast."

Feeling only slightly less fried than she did last night, Nat excused herself to go to the bathroom and splash some cold water on her face. The air in the small room was heavy with the fumes of hospital-strength disinfectant, and the sound of the toilet flushing echoed off the tile. She made her way to the sink and found the eyes staring back at her in the mirror looked only marginally better than her father's. She then ran the cold water and soaked her face and neck. The water shocked her a little and brought her fully awake. She dug into her bag for a hairbrush and some makeup to make the best of things and wished she could brush her teeth.

In the room, breakfast had arrived: an egg, sausage, and cheese breakfast sandwich and coffee for her, and a container of oatmeal and a cup of tea for him. They ate for a moment in silence, drawing strength from being together and sharing a meal. Unlike the habits of most contemporary families, the Doxiphuses ate as many meals together as possible, and despite the surroundings and situation, this simple act was the most normal thing that had happened in the past twenty-four hours.

"The head of hospital security came by, too, asking about that strange nurse," Greg said, absently waving his plastic spoon over his oatmeal.

"Did they find out anything about her?" Nat asked.

"No, they didn't have any news. They're just starting to review the security tapes now. They were concerned she might be stealing drugs from patients' rooms." He paused to take a sip of tea. "Hey, have you seen your mother's crucifix? I looked everywhere, and it's not with her clothes or in her purse. Did you see it on her when she came in?"

"I don't think so, but I was pretty upset. I wasn't looking for it."

"I'm still fuzzy on what happened. Tell me again, please?" her father asked.

"A nurse came in here yesterday afternoon, a little before you arrived. I didn't recognize her, and she was acting shifty. She was doing something with mom. She wanted me to leave the room, and I kind of lost it." Nat looked out vacantly, searching for the reason she had reacted so aggressively.

"So I heard. What was she doing that made you so upset?" he replied as he put down the empty oatmeal container.

"She said it was a neuro exam. She was touching Mom and looking in her eyes with a light." The anger rose in her voice as she relived the incident. "She was looking at Mom's EEG and fiddling with the IV...but what got me was that she was trying to get rid of me and she wouldn't look at me. I never got a clear look at her face." Nat was leaning forward in her chair, lips pursed and eyes flaring.

"Take it easy," Greg said in a steady tone, "I'm glad you were here."

Nat took a moment and settled back into her chair. "When the medic, John, came in then, she left. I asked the duty nurse to check Mom and asked if she knew who the other nurse was. No one had seen her before, and they haven't seen her since."

Greg ran his hand through his hair and sighed heavily again. "I guess I really don't care who she is or where she went." His voice was rough and cracked. "We have enough to worry about here."

He turned to look again at his wife and silently took her right hand in his. A long silence stretched in the room, and Nat saw her father's chin start to droop toward his chest. Thinking he was finally giving in to exhaustion and would fall out of his chair, she got up to go to him, but he spoke before she could reach him, his eyes still closed and his head slightly drooped. Nat recognized his posture; she'd seen him do this countless times in his office at home when he was puzzling things out.

"What do you think about what the medic said? About how your mother was found or the timing of events in the lab tech's story being off?" he asked.

"I dunno, Dad. This whole thing doesn't make any sense."

Looking up at her, he nodded and paused, then looked out into space.

"Dad? What is it? What do you think?"

"Oh…sorry." He shook his head slightly and blinked hard. "I don't know what to think either, but I'd sure like to talk to the lab tech."

In the hallway, the sounds of another day in the hospital were starting to pick up. Breakfast was being delivered to patients' rooms, and visitors were arriving.

"The lab…we haven't checked the lab for Mom's necklace," Nat said in a hopeful tone.

"That's true. If you could go check, maybe we could…"

"Close the loop on one thing," she finished for him.

Nat crumpled her breakfast-sandwich wrapper and stuffed it into the paper bag, along with her coffee cup, ending the peace of the meal. "Trash?" she said, extending the open bag for her father to dump the remains of his breakfast.

"Here. You need the lab keys." He reached into his coat pocket for them. "I'll call security to meet you there."

She started to protest, but he gently said, "Sweetheart, it's for me. I'd feel better if someone were there with you. Please?"

Nat conceded to his fatherly concern, knowing he was feeling shaken and vulnerable too.

"Okay, Dad. I'll call you from the lab."

He hugged her. "I'll call you if there's any news."

***

Fifteen minutes later, Nat arrived at the lab and, not seeing campus security, let herself in. She was glad to have something to do. The lab was quiet, and though the lights were off, the room was almost too bright as the morning sun streamed in the eastern windows and cast brilliant rectangles across the gray countertops of the lab benches and the white linoleum floor. The lab benches stretched to her left about twenty feet or so, and her mother's office was diagonally across the lab from the door through which she had just entered. She started walking along the length of the lab bench, searching for her mother's heirloom necklace, and was halfway down when the click of the closing door made her jump. She spun around to see a man in a campus security uniform.

41

"Sorry, miss. I didn't mean ta spook ya like that," he said, flicking on the lights.

"No, that's okay. Um, I'm okay. Thanks for coming" was all she could muster.

"My name's Bernie." He smiled but didn't extend a hand. "I was the first one on the scene here yesterday, besides the lab tech. I was told to come here to help you, but I see you didn't need any help getting in...so what do you need me to do?"

Finally, someone with some answers. "Can you show me where my mother was found? I'm looking for her necklace. She always wears it."

"Sure. Well, when I got here, she was lying in the aisle, between the two benches." He moved around the end of the first bench and started down the central aisle. Nat followed.

"The lab tech was standing here, looking at her. He was seriously spooked."

Nat squatted to search the floor in the general area Bernie had shown her but found nothing. "Lemme give you a hand. What does the necklace look like?" he said.

"It's a gold crucifix, about an inch and a half long, on a gold chain," she said, standing up.

Bernie walked to the end of the aisle and started his search, crouching as well to get a better view of the floor and the kick space under the benches.

"What did the lab tech say about what happened?"

Bernie duck-walked down the aisle. "He said he got in at eight, and Dr. Doxiphus was in her office. He left for a few minutes, came back, and found her lying here in the aisle. He called 911 and waited."

Several old dust-covered moving boxes sat atop the bench next to where her mother had been found. Nat knew they weren't important to her mother, as they were still tightly sealed. "I'm going to look around the lab and check her office. Can you keep looking here?" she asked the guard.

"Sure, I'll check the hallway too. Maybe it fell off when the medics took her to the elevator."

Nat went to the opposite end of the aisle and walked slowly, swinging her gaze around, hoping to see a glint of gold. Not seeing

42

anything, she moved on to her mother's office. The office had been built at her mother's request when she had acquired this lab. It had windows from about waist height up to the ceiling. The door had been built to match—wood on bottom, glass on top. Like everything else in her mother's life, the space was warm and welcoming, with a few plants and neat as a pin. The only thing out of place was the open desk drawer where her mother kept her purse while at work. Security had brought it to the hospital room last night. Finding nothing, Nat left the office and closed the door behind her.

"I didn't find anything out here, Miss Doxiphus," Bernie said as he stood up. "I'm gonna check the hallway now."

"Thanks. I'll keep looking in here."

To the right, out of the office, Nat spied a different set of rooms that were on a raised platform. This space also had been custom built to house her mother's work. She stepped onto the platform and the insulating black tiles. They weren't rubber, but Nat always thought of them that way, as their purpose was to help electrically isolate the platform. Before her was a thick but surprisingly light composite door with a sign that read TMD/TDS, but the common name for it was the "stim room." It had no lock and easily swung open at her tug. The inside was dark except for the glow from a few small LEDs. She flicked the light switch; the cramped space felt stifling. The outer room she now stood in was small—no more than two people could fit in here comfortably. Most of the space was occupied by a console, a chair, and racks of servers, their onboard fans whirring madly away as they emitted loud beeps. Aside from a weak fluorescent light overhead, the only source of illumination was a drafting lamp attached to the side of the console.

Beyond the console was a window into another room that held the actual transcranial magnetic stimulation/transcranial direct stimulation equipment. In contrast to her mother's office, this room didn't look like much, its spare contents consisting of a treatment chair procured from the college of dentistry, a table, and some shelves and equipment. In the corner of the room was a device on the end of an extension arm that looked like a large figure eight or an infinity sign, depending on which way it was oriented. This was the magnetic coil of the TMS part of the lab. On a shelf behind the chair were sets of what looked like crude, bulky hairnets that had wires attached, like the EEG sensor caps back at the hospital. This was the tDCS part.

Hovering over the chair, suspended by a strong support arm that grew out of the ceiling, was a squat tube with an opening at the end. This new device was the focus of her mother's work. Although her father was deeply involved with this project as well, her mother was the principal investigator.

Nat's eyes drifted down from the tube-shaped device and rested on the chair. Then a flash from the table caught her eye. Eagerly she reached out and pulled on the door handle, but the door didn't budge. She went to pull again; this time she put a foot forward so she could put her weight into it and stepped on a small foil mat that was different than the rest of the rubber floor. Then she remembered. *Right, both feet on the mat, then a hand on the handle.* This process completed a grounding circuit to ensure no static electricity was brought into the inner room. There was a slight click as the latch released, and the door easily swung open.

Nat strode into the room. There, on the table next to the treatment chair, was the small crucifix on its chain. Reaching out to pick it up, she brushed a tissue aside, and underneath were a pair of her mother's earrings. *This is where she was. What the hell?* After scooping up the necklace and earrings, she tucked them into the pocket of her jeans and headed to the outer room and to the lab, agitated and suspicious.

"Whaddaya mean, I'm not allowed to be in here? I work here." A scrawny man in a T-shirt and jeans was waving his hands and yelling at the security guard. Bernie was in the doorway, stopping the man from entering the lab.

"I know you work here, Bill. I was here yesterday with you when the medics came for Dr. Doxiphus." Bernie tried to calm the man. "But the lab is sealed. Dr. Kelley's orders."

Bill's head turned sharply toward Nat as she came through the stim room door. "Then what's she doing in here?"

The spark of Nat's suspicion flared into a full flame as she locked on to Bill's eyes and advanced on him. "I'm in here looking for this!" she said, pulling the crucifix from her pocket. "I found it along with her earrings, on the table right next to the chair in there!" The accusation hung in the air as she pointed behind her. "She was in that room, in that chair. That's where she took these off, and she would've picked them up before she left!"

Bill had gone silent at the onslaught, the color draining from his face.

Bernie broke the silence, also fixing Bill with a cold stare. "What happened here yesterday, Bill?"

Cornered, Bill found his resolve and fired back. "What the hell's going on here now is what I want to know," he said, staring down the guard. "I just came here to check on the lab, which I have a responsibility to do, and you two are accusing me? What is this, some goddamn inquisition? I told you everything yesterday." Then he rounded on Nat. "Your mother was in here before me yesterday. She could've been in the stim room before I got here."

The guard looked at Natalia; he could see she was seething, but she was taken aback by the lab tech's argument and went silent.

"All right, Bill. Take it easy. No one's accusing you of anything, and it's my responsibility to ask questions."

Mollified by the guard's response, Bill backed down as well.

"Thank you. Now, Bill, for Miss Doxiphus's sake, 'cuz she wasn't here yesterday, could you please tell her what happened?"

"Yeah, sure. I'm sorry about your mom. She's really great to work for, and I'm worried about her too." Bill was looking at the floor now. "So I came in right at eight a.m., and your mom was in her office. She looked fine and waved hi." He looked up at Nat. "I dropped my stuff on my chair, then went to use the men's room and grab a cup of coffee. When I got back at ten after eight, she was lying there on the floor," he finished, pointing to the same spot Bernie had, in the aisle between the lab benches.

"Why would she be there?" Nat asked in a controlled voice.

"I dunno. Maybe she was working on something."

"Really? There's nothing in that area except sealed, dusty moving boxes." *This is going nowhere*, thought Nat. Having lost her patience, she blurted, "Did you see her in the stim room? Were you in there with her?" Her voice was rising again.

Bill was just about to respond when his cell phone went off, filling the lab with the opening riff from "Highway to Hell."

45

Seizing the opportunity to separate the two of them, Bernie broke in. "Why don't you take that in the hall?" Not waiting for a response, he herded Bill out of the lab.

"Miss Doxiphus, you can't just go accusing him like that," he said when he returned.

"The hell I can't! My mother was in that room, and she wouldn't have left her jewelry there. That little rat bastard knows something that he's not telling."

"Okay, she was in there. Maybe she felt sick and got up in a hurry to get to the phone to call for help."

"The phone in her office is a lot closer to the stim room than the one here by the door," she pointed out to the guard, which stopped him.

"All right, look, I gotta call this in. This is all way beyond me." Bernie grabbed his radio off his belt and took a few steps away to start the call.

Nat looked around, then remembered she should call her father. She walked away from the guard and the main lab door, back toward the stim room, and hit the speed dial for her father. "Dad? I found Mom's necklace and her gold earrings too…on the table next to the chair in the stim room…yeah, the guard's here. The lab tech showed up too, but he didn't have any new answers. We kinda got into it…I'm okay…he's in the hallway now. He got a call, and the guard separated us."

There was more she wanted to say, but the lab was so quiet, there would be no way to keep the guard from overhearing her side of the conversation. She started for the office to get some privacy, and then she stopped in her tracks. "I'll call you back. I need to check something."

Nat spun on her heels and went back into the stim room. Seated at the console, she noticed again that the fan noise in there was annoyingly loud. *The servers are still on*, she thought. *That's why it's so hot in here.* She turned the chair around and faced the dark console screen and keyboard. *What if…?* She nudged the mouse, and the console screen woke up. The lock screen displayed a password prompt for the logged-on user, BillF. Nat let out a hushed breath. "Got him!"

But she knew she needed more. Looking around the console, she found pens, and in the glistening clean garbage can was a coffee cup with two or three swallows of congealed gray coffee still in the bottom. *This place really has been sealed. The trash cans are supposed to be emptied every night; Mom put in a special request for that.*

Then something caught her eye. On the wall, a spiral-bound notebook hung from a pushpin, along with pencil. She plucked it off the wall and flipped through the pages. This was the paper log of the sessions. Her mother insisted on keeping a hard-copy log in case the hard drives failed. Each page was filled with the start times, each sessions purpose, who the subject was, and, in the last field, a coded summary of the results. The entries ended about a third of the way through the notebook. *Here it is. This is where yesterday should be.* But she found…"Nothing…damn!" Exasperated, Nat dropped the notebook onto the console surface, which was illuminated by the light of the drafting lamp. She sat for a moment, then decided to check again. In the more direct light of the drafting lamp, she leafed through the pages to yesterday and saw that the paper immediately below the last entry was roughened, and eraser shavings clung to the exposed paper fibers.

She bolted back into the lab to get a better look at the log paper and to share this new information with security. "Bernie, you need to see this! The stim room console is locked. It shows user BillF as having logged on, and something was erased from the paper log."

The fiftyish guard was on the campus phone, deep in conversation, and held up a hand to Natalia. "Just a minute, please."

Wanting better light, Nat hurried over to the eastern windows for the best of the morning sun. Holding the last page at an angle to the sunlight, she saw…*there!* She couldn't make out what had been written, but something had been there and then was harshly erased. She took the pencil and lightly went over the impressions, like she had with "secret" messages with her friends in second grade. The handwriting showed up clearly now, and it wasn't her mother's.

CALIBRATION RUN, SUBJECT A. DOXIPHUS, START 07:10

The results field was empty. She ran to the door just as Bernie hung up the phone. "My supervisor is on her way. What were you saying just now?"

"We've gotta stop him!" Nat yanked the lab door open and burst out of the lab, looking one way and then the other, but found the hallway empty.

***

"I didn't sign up for this shit! It wasn't supposed to be like this!" Bill Fahy squawked in a hoarse whisper into his phone as he made his way down the central stairwell of building 87.

"Keep quiet and keep moving. It'll be okay," said the man's voice on the other end of what Bill considered his lifeline.

"Fuck you, man! It will not be *okay*! They're gonna find the console and logs and call the cops. I'm screwed!"

"And what crime did you commit? The device malfunctioned—that's all. Did you talk to any police?"

Bill rushed out into the late morning through a side door and started walking more slowly down the sidewalk. "No, I didn't talk to any cops."

"So no giving of false information to the police, and a piece of highly experimental equipment went haywire, so what? You need to take it easy. Don't forget your compensation."

That calmed Bill down a bit—just thinking of what he could do with five grand in cash. *I'll throw one helluva party and maybe even spring for a few strippers. The guys will love that shit. Have to pay off the bookie, but this would take care of that too.* Bill continued to walk down the street, passing parked cars. Up ahead he spotted a University City Police unit; the officer was sitting in the driver's seat.

"There's a cop car up ahead. What should I do? Turn around?"

"No, that would draw attention. Just keep going and act natural. It'll be okay."

As he came up behind the unit, Bill saw that the cop was looking out the window and talking on his phone.

"Did he see you?"

48

"Nah, the fat bastard was yapping on his phone and looking out the window. Probably talking to his cop buddies." Bill's spirits buoyed after having walked right past the cop. He continued down the sidewalk with a spring in his step.

"See? I told you it would be okay. Now just keep going. Don't go home. Be at The Jester at seven p.m."

***

In the University City Police unit Bill had just passed, the officer lowered the phone and dropped it on the seat. He cracked the knuckles of his large, pasty white hands while he watched the scrawny man in the T-shirt saunter down the street.

"He's a liability now," the burly redheaded officer said, apparently to no one. He waited a moment and then said, "Understood."

***

Bill passed a dozen or so more cars and reached his old Toyota. Feeling relieved at reaching his car, he hopped in and pulled out his phone to text his friend.

Need a backup Jester 7 pm

Bill reassured himself. *This was some scary shit, all right. Dr. D wasn't supposed to be in a coma or whatever. But at least she's not dead, and I can blame it all on the machine.*

He thought about the evidence that had been left behind; the console was still on, and he was logged in. *Well, no one else has my password, and it's my job to be logged in to that machine. At least I took care of the paper log and the vomit in the can.*

He started to feel better about his situation. He really hadn't done anything wrong after all, and for what he did do, he wouldn't get caught. He smiled as he put his phone away; it was dangerous to drive and text at the same time. *In a few hours I get five grand! Hell, yes! Five grand coming, in cash. Yeah, life is getting pretty good for*

49

Bill. Time for a little celebration. He reached up under the dash and pulled out a joint, then sparked it up as he drove away.

***

The Jester stood in the middle of a triangular-shaped parking lot. Across the street was an Italian restaurant with picnic tables for eating outside on summer nights like this. The grass was brown and dry here; lawn sprinklers weren't really an investment for a bar. Across the parking lot next to The Jester was a do-it-yourself carwash, the white paint starting to peel off the cinder block. The bar was in an older neighborhood with prison-block-like storage buildings and 1950s-era houses. Bill walked past a big Harley that was in front of the bar, wondering if he could get himself one of those—used, of course—with all the cash he was about to collect. Striding along the wooden porch, he looked up at a thirty-year-old neon sign that lit up one letter at a time, T-H-E J-E-S-T-E-R, with a laughing guy in a clown hat. Under the sign was the rickety screen door of Bill's favorite dive.

Inside the bar, the air was murky with cigarette smoke, and peanut shells crunched underfoot as Bill walked over to the bar and took a seat on a stool in the middle. He scanned the darkened room for his friend but didn't see him yet. *Figures he'd be late.* Nodding to the bartender, he ordered a beer, lit a smoke, and settled in to wait for whoever was bringing the money. It only bothered him a little that he didn't know what the person looked like or what to expect. He remembered this whole thing had started here, in this bar, when a woman with shoulder-length dishwater hair and sweet eyes had said she had seen him around the university and offered to buy him a few shots.

"So I know you work in the Doxiphus lab. They're so smart! You must be pretty smart too, huh?" she'd said, those sapphire eyes eagerly gazing into his.

"Well, yeah, I do okay." He grinned and felt hot, uncertain if it was because of the shots or the girl.

"What do you do there?" she said, resting her head on her hands and leaning forward across the table.

50

"I help Dr. D—Dr. Doxiphus, that is. She and her husband are working on this new device, it's a combined brain scanner and stimulator." He took a long drag of his smoke, hoping he looked a little like Bogart. "It gets pretty technical, but I run the computers, manage the lab, and help run the device."

"You're really important to the lab, then."

After three more rounds, they went out to his car for some weed. She asked him if he wanted to make some easy cash. She said if he could fry the machine, she'd get him five thousand in cash. Nothing big, just break the machine so it would be out of commission for a good long while.

"Why do ya want that?" Bill asked.

"It's just business," she purred as she gently stroked the side of his neck.

"Sure. No one gets hurt, right?" he asked, the last vestiges of his reason quickly slipping away to greed and desire.

"No one gets hurt. You can even have some help. Call this number if you run into trouble." She slid a piece of paper and her hand fully into his front jeans pocket. Never having been one to keep his zipper up when the opportunity arose, Bill was all hers from that moment on.

She left later that night, and he hadn't seen her since. He had called the number the next day to make sure it was all real, and he was told to look in the trunk of his car, where he found a deposit of five hundred dollars. Now here he was, two weeks later, the job done and waiting for the rest of his money.

It was 7:30 now, and The Jester was starting to fill up. Bill was on his third beer. A band was getting ready, and the bouncer was breaking up some ice and changing out the kegs. Bill had been watching the door for his friend, but he hadn't shown, and no one else had approached him either. The table behind him, swarming with bikers, was getting kind of loud, and he had just made up his mind to find a quieter spot to enjoy the band. As he stood up, draining the last of his beer, he heard angry voices and threats.

"You asshole!"

Bill spewed that last swallow of beer as a crushing weight pinned him against the rounded edge of the bar, which caught him just under the rib cage. Reacting instinctively, he pushed hard with his legs

51

against the bar to get the weight off him. Spinning around, he saw the men at the table behind him had erupted into a fight. One of them was reaching for something in his back waistband.

An elbow came out of nowhere and caught Bill in the right eye and cheek, sending a jolt of pain through his head and down his back. He barely could see through his good eye as it welled up with tears. Then, with blind, desperate swings, he actually connected with something hard. The impact made the bones in his hand feel as though they'd shattered.

"He's got a gun!" someone shouted.

Hearing the shout, Bill tried to turn to get to the door. Another blind shove and he was pinned again, this time feeling the edge of the bar against his back. And then he heard a sickening crunch accompanied by a sledgehammer blow right in the middle of his chest. He stopped and collapsed, struggling to breathe, and in his last moments he felt excruciating pain. Struggling to lift his head, he looked down with his good eye at the handle of an ice pick sticking straight out of the middle of his chest. Through his chokes, all he managed to say was, "There's no blood."

***

The Jester was painted red and blue with flashing lights as Medic 82 turned the corner, sirens blaring. It was 7:40 p.m., and things were already hopping for John and Megan.

"A little early for a bar fight," he told Megan.

"Must have been one helluva fight!"

Even from a block away, they saw a sizable crowd in the parking lot of The Jester being contained by University City blue and whites.

"I'll get the chest kit and make sure the scene is secure," John said. "This guy probably has a punctured lung. Get the trauma kits onto the gurney. There'll be broken bones and lacerations by the looks of this crowd."

John leapt from Medic 82 as soon as it was close to stopping. In the distance, he heard the sirens of another ambulance on its way to The Jester. He had already put on his gloves and made sure he had a mask and protective glasses in his pocket. *There might be aerosolized blood*, he thought. After grabbing the chest kit from the back of Medic 82, he made his way to the door of The Jester, the police waving him in.

"Is the scene safe?" he asked the uniform at the door, a newly minted rookie all clean and polished.

"You can slow down. You're good. We got everyone out and separated the suspects."

"The chest wound?"

The officer turned to John. "No rush. He's not going anywhere."

Inside, two other officers stood over a scrawny man who had what looked like the handle of an ice pick protruding from his chest. Blood had saturated the man's T-shirt and was pooling on the floor around the body.

"He wasn't breathing when we arrived, and well…I couldn't start CPR," the younger of the two officers explained to John, who approached the body. He crouched next to the victim to check for pulse and breathing. An unnecessary step, but he had to make it official. As he stood and turned toward the two officers, the rubber sole of his shoe stuck slightly and made a soft *tick* when he lifted his foot from the pool of coagulating blood.

He had seen his share of death. It was never the clean, sanitized version you see in the media. A body twitched while it cooled, and wet stickiness crept out, forming a scarlet halo of oxygenated blood on the floor or ground that pushed the everyday world away from the body. Now the acrid odor of the man's urine climbed up John's nostrils and mixed with the thick iron smell of the blood, nauseating him.

"There's nothing we can do here; you guys need to call the MEs." He keyed his radio. "Medic 82 to all responders. Start triaging the crowd outside the bar."

"What about the chest wound?" Megan said through the radio.

"It's a fatality."

The younger officer moved a few paces away and was on his radio. They needed the forensics team for the scene and the county medical examiner to collect the body.

John turned his focus from the wound to the man's face and got a shock. "I know this guy. His name's Bill. I just talked to him yesterday." The surprise in his voice made his declaration louder than intended. It was easier to see a stranger's dead face. That made

53

sense; you'd never seen the face alive, so there was no reconciliation needed between your memories and what you were staring at. But, seasoned as he was, John hadn't gotten past the shock of looking at what he remembered as an animated living face, which now was not.

"Yeah, we've been looking for him since this afternoon as a favor to university security. Seems he was involved in some sort of lab accident that left a woman in a coma," commented the older officer. "Not gonna be much use now."

Focusing on the wound again, John asked the older officer, "How'd this get here?"

The officer crouched next to John. "Pretty simple. A bar fight broke out. This guy caught the bouncer in the back of the head with a fist. The bouncer, who'd been breaking up ice, spun around, heard someone shout 'He's got a gun!' and skewered him in self-defense."

"Where's the bouncer? I should take a look at him."

The older officer pointed to a table in the corner next to the bandstand, his eyes still fixed on the friendly end of the ice pick. John looked up and saw a burly redheaded officer with pasty white skin taking a statement from a large man in a Jester staff shirt.

6 Too Much Information

"Here. Hold this on that lump," John told the bouncer, handing over an instant ice pack.

"That guy was skinny, but he sure nailed me." The man winced as he put the ice pack on the goose egg that had grown from the back of his head. "Thought he hit me with something metal...like the butt of a gun."

After the police had finished taking the bouncer's statement, they released him to Medic 82. He sat on the rear deck of the vehicle while John checked him and cleaned him up. Around them, insects swarmed in the lights of all the emergency vehicles.

"You really should go to the ER and have the doctors take a look at you."

"Nah, I've been whacked on the head plenty of times. This isn't even the worst." The bouncer grimaced as he shifted the ice pack.

"Okay, but I'll need you to sign a form stating you were advised to go to the hospital but chose not to."

"Yeah, sure. No problem."

Ten minutes later, the bouncer had left The Jester with his girlfriend. She insisted on driving, and John saw the man at least had the good sense to listen to her. The crime-scene investigation team was working the site, and the ME van hadn't arrived yet. Though most of the bar's patrons were long gone, John had kept Medic 82 at the scene under the pretense of taking inventory of their supplies after the call. Megan had ridden along with another unit that was taking a patient to the ER, letting him avoid any questions about the delay.

John kept an eye on the bar door, waiting for the burly redheaded cop to come out. Soon, three officers emerged, and John's target was among them. He caught the cop's attention, who then waited for John at the bar door while the others went to their vehicles. John strode across the parking lot toward the officer, who nodded and spoke first. "Hey. How's it going?"

"I just finished cleaning up the bouncer; he went home with his girlfriend. He must have had a good story for you guys not to hold him."

The officer swatted a mosquito away and muttered, "Damn things," then turned to look at John full on. "We have corroborating stories from at least six sober witnesses, plus the security video. A bar fight breaks out, someone thinks someone has a gun, and then the bouncer, Mr. Rimer, gets involved. He takes one to the head, spins around, and defends himself. Pretty clear-cut case. We contacted the DA's office on this. They advised us to take a sworn statement and send him home."

John nodded and raised his eyebrows as he approached the question he really wanted answered. He knew he didn't have the right to ask, at least not until the next of kin was notified.

"What about the victim?"

"Unlucky bastard. Hell of a way to die. His name's..." The cop reached into his breast pocket and took out a small notebook, flipped through a few pages, and squinted in the dim light. "Bill Fahy."

"Notified the family yet?"

"No. We're trying to track them down now," the cop said.

John scratched the back of his head. "The weird thing is that I just talked to Fahy yesterday at the university labs."

"Really? What for?" the cop said, clearly interested.

"He works...worked in a lab there. My partner and I were responding to a call about a collapsed woman. Turned out to be Dr. Aida Doxiphus, the lab director, and this guy was her lab tech."

"What happened to her?" The cop had his notebook out again, pencil hovering over the paper.

"We couldn't really tell. Some sort of AMS—that's altered mental state—possibly a seizure. Anyway, this guy, Bill was there, acting squirrelly, like he was scared."

56

"Did he say what he was afraid of?" The pencil was scratching across the page.

"No, he didn't say. He just went pale. My partner had to sit him down to keep him from keeling over. I think there was more going on, because the whole situation was...well, it just didn't make sense. The way we found Dr. Doxiphus, with her arms and legs straight and at her sides, like she had just lain down. And the timing of his story didn't add up. He said he called 911 at 8:15, but we didn't get toned out till 8:25, and 911 never takes more than a minute to roll a medic unit."

"So you think he was involved somehow?" The pencil had stopped scratching; the cop's icy-blue eyes transfixed John.

"I don't see how," John replied, breaking the uncomfortable eye contact.

The cop looked back down at his notebook and began writing again. Without looking up he asked, "Have you told anyone else this?"

"Yeah, I did, at the end of my shift yesterday. I was at University Hospital, and I needed to report this to the doctors and family." John gave a sudden jerk, and his right hand went up to his left shoulder. "What the...? Felt like someone pinched me." He looked around, but there was no one else there besides the two of them. "Must be some damn big mosquito."

The cop was silent and still, though his eyes raked the parking lot. "You told the family about this before reporting it to the police?"

Hearing the accusation in the officer's voice, John hesitated. What had started out as a professional conversation had taken an unpleasant turn. "Campus security was there, as well as University City police. We were there to take care of the patient, not run an investigation. That's your job." John chewed out the last words; he didn't respond well to being muscled.

"You know what? You're right. Sorry," the cop said in a more congenial tone, then tucked his notebook away. "Anything else? How's she now?"

A feeling of unease had settled on John in the past few seconds after that pinch. "I don't know. I can't really find out. I'm not family...patient confidentiality and all that."

"Sure, of course." The cop gave a smile that didn't move beyond his mouth. "Gimme a minute. I need to talk to the shift commander about this. What's your name?"

He felt that sickening feeling he always got on roller coasters when they went through a negative G turn. *Damn!* He couldn't refuse to answer, and the police could get his name with a single call to dispatch anyway. "John Holden. I gotta get back to my unit and pick up my partner."

"This'll only take a few minutes. Can you come with me, please?" Though it was phrased as a request, John knew it wasn't. The cop held the door open for him, and the two of them went back into The Jester. The bulky man made his way over to the shift commander. He was the only officer in the room not in uniform; his polo shirt partially covered the badge and gun on his belt. John took a seat at a table about six feet away, close enough to hear but far enough away to allow the illusion of privacy.

"Sir? Has next of kin been located?" the redheaded cop began.

"Not yet. Why? You have something?"

"Yessir, actually I do. The responding medic ID'd the deceased as a lab tech over at the university. He knew the deceased from a call he had there yesterday. Turns out it was for the deceased's boss, Dr. Aida Doxiphus. She's in the hospital, and I thought I could go over and notify the family of tonight's events and try to get a statement from the family, since they knew him."

"Thanks, but not your job tonight. I want a senior detective to handle the doctors and university. I think Fitzsimmons is on tomorrow. Tell you what, though...you can ride along with Fitzsimmons since you came up with this."

"Well, thank you, sir," the cop managed with a modicum of sincerity.

At least I'm not going to be arrested tonight, John thought. He heard the officer snap off another "yessir," and then he turned toward John, his face slightly red from the vote of no confidence his boss had given him. He walked the few feet over to where John sat.

"Shift commander says you're free to go, and to thank you for bringing this to our attention."

John was puzzled at the lack of forthrightness on the part of the officer to his superior, but at this point he just wanted to get out of

58

there. "No problem. Glad to help," he said, and wondered if he was lying.

As he walked back to Medic 82, he still felt the weight of the man's eyes on him. *That didn't go as expected.* As he climbed back into the unit and closed the door, Natalia's face leapt unbidden to the front of his mind along with the urge to check on her and make sure she and her family were okay. Somehow he felt he had just put them all in danger.

"Shit! What did I just do?" Frustrated with himself, he started Medic 82 and pulled out of the parking lot.

The redheaded cop stood in front of The Jester and watched the ambulance pull out. He didn't move for a good minute or so before going to his patrol car. He checked to make sure his radio was off and the dash cam was powered down as well. Touching a finger to his ear, he said, "The problem has been eliminated as planned. Holden, the medic, noticed the sloppiness of the first job. Unfortunately, he was also on the scene tonight and made the connection between Fahy and Doxiphus. This risk needs to be mitigated." He paused, still holding his hand to his ear, and said, "Acknowledged. I'll report back in about an hour." He started his unit and pulled out of the lot, following the route of Medic 82.

7 Messages

Illuminated by the copper glow of a single sodium-vapor streetlight, the one- and two-story brick storefronts from nearly a century ago stood around a potholed intersection in mute testimony of unrelenting decay. John knew this part of town well, and though his eyes saw the blanched colors of the red and brown buildings and the summer green leaves sapped of their vitality by the light from the lamp, his mind filled in the normal daytime image it was more familiar and comfortable with.

Medic 82 was stopped at the deserted intersection, waiting for the light to change. Fifteen blocks ahead was University Hospital. Catercorner from him, a dim yellow light shone through steel bars that covered the grimy windows of a packaged goods store, the only business that had survived here.

Why am I waiting? No one else is here. 'Cuz it's the law, he answered himself. He didn't feel like tempting fate, not after that almost run-in with the cop at The Jester thirty minutes ago. So he sat, focused on the holes in the street where the blacktop had worn away, exposing the original paving bricks, while, to his left, a figure slowly approached from the shadows. He reached over to rub the spot on his left shoulder where he had been...*pinched*—that was the only word he could think of. *What the hell was that, anyway?* The shadowed figure was about five steps from the driver's-side window. It swiftly raised an arm, pointing at John.

John blinked. There in front of him, and off to the right of Medic 82, stood a white lab-coated Aida Doxiphus. She was mouthing words and moving her arms frantically, as if pushing something down to her left.

The message was clear: "*Get down!*"

He looked at her in stunned silence. Then he caught a flicker of movement on his left, and alarms went off in his head. He threw himself down on his right side, the arm of the seat digging into his ribs as shattered glass sprayed him and the unmistakable staccato popping of gunfire reverberated through the cab. The first shot had taken out the glass. Two more followed a second later.

"*Go!*"

Lying stunned in the dark cab, John slammed his foot on the gas. The sudden acceleration pushed him backward as the roaring engine and screaming tires blocked out the sound of any other shots. With one hand on the wheel, he pulled himself upright. Shards of shattered glass cut him as they slid under his shirt. Ignoring the pain, he glanced in the right-side mirror, looking for the woman in the white lab coat who couldn't possibly have been there but had been. He stood up on the brakes. He couldn't leave her there in the street with the shooter feet away. He threw the vehicle into park and jumped out into the live fire zone. It wasn't the first time he had done this, but it was never a smart thing to do.

Go, go, go! Moving targets are harder to hit than stationary ones, yelled the drill sergeant in his head. He rounded the back end of Medic 82. Off to his left, he caught a dark flash of movement heading into an alleyway on the far side of the unit. After scanning the intersection for the white lab coat, he went to the passenger side of the vehicle and up to the front bumper. The woman wasn't in the street or in any of the doorways. *Where the hell did she go?* John circled around the front of the unit and got back in the driver's seat, the broken glass from the window crunching under his feet. He sat there for a few seconds trying to make sense of all this. *She can't be here—she's lying in a hospital bed.*

His eyes ping-ponged between the two side mirrors, but he saw nothing other than empty intersection. Unless the shooter could fly, he or she was nearby. John's best bet was to get clear of the area as quickly as possible and head to the hospital, where Aida Doxiphus had to be.

Lights, sirens, radio! He ordered himself as the speedometer rocketed past fifty-five. The hospital was about ten blocks away now. As he hurtled toward the next traffic light, his brain seized on the traffic that was crossing. *Shit!* He slammed on the brakes, the tires screaming against the pavement. Medic 82 jerked to a stop, throwing John against his seat belt and then back in his seat.

He grabbed the handset. "Medic 82 to KEA571. I've just been fired at. Corner of Claremont and Thirty-Third Street."

"Medic 82, are you injured?"

"No, I'm about ten blocks from University Hospital. I'm heading there. Have any units meet me at the ER entrance." He killed the lights and sirens, which looked odd on an ambulance that had just come to a screeching stop at a traffic light.

"Acknowledged, Medic 82."

John's head was on a swivel, scanning ahead, right, left, in the rearview mirror, hunting for any more threats. Now that he was closer to the university, the lighting was better, and the traffic, both foot and vehicle, were heavier. All he saw were college kids bar hopping, a street musician on the corner, a line outside a club, and people eating at a sidewalk café. All eyes stared at him in amazement through the shot-out window.

A normal summer night, my ass! John's brain was wrestling with the impossible. He had just seen someone he knew—*knew*—he couldn't have, and someone had just tried to kill him.

Okay, the immediate threat has passed. You're okay...now get to the hospital. Get back to reality.

He was six blocks from the hospital now; the large blue-and-white backlit letters on the central tower of the medical complex grew in his field of vision. *Get there. Get to safety.* And then another thought crept into the spotlight of his attention. Alarm ran through him again, and his hand shot to his shirt pocket. The glass from the bullet-shattered window cut his fingers as he fished around for his phone.

He hit speed dial 3.

"University Hospital," the operator intoned.

"My name's John Holden. I'm a University City medic. I need to talk to Dr. Gregorio Doxiphus. It's urgent."

"I can take your number and have him contact you, or would you like to leave a message?"

"No! I don't wanna leave a damn mess—" He bit off the rest of his words and paused for a beat before continuing. "Sorry. Can you put me through to his mobile number? I'm on route to the hospital now. This really is an emergency. It's regarding his wife."

That last part got the operator's attention. The news about Aida had traveled quickly across campus.

"Hold on. I'll transfer you."

***

Night again, thought Greg Doxiphus as he lay on a cot in his wife's hospital room. He had dozed for maybe an hour; then anxiety and discomfort had goaded him back to wakefulness with cruel ease. He sat up and glanced at his wife and saw the gold crucifix slowly rise and fall with each breath. It was an heirloom on her mother's side of the family from four generations back. Nat, who would be the next recipient of that treasure, was in a recliner, curled up in a blanket with a pillow, her eyes closed.

Massaging the dull throbbing in his forehead, he lay back down. Through the window he saw the constellation Cygnus rise in the darkening blue sky. It looked to him more like a cross, like Aida's crucifix. *Thank God Nat found that.*

She had called to fill him in on the lab tech and what she had found. He immediately had contacted the office of the president. It wasn't a pleasant conversation, he recalled.

"Greg, you're upset about Aida, and the university will do everything we can in this matter, but I don't know if we need to involve the police. The situation doesn't look that suspicious," Kelley had equivocated over the phone. "It was that man's job to be there and use that equipment."

"I'd hardly call lying about the timing of events open and honest communication, Alvin!" Greg had shot back. "I realize that this is grant-review time, but you must realize I *will do* whatever must be done to take care of my family."

Deneb, the bright star at the tail of the swan, or short end of the cross, blinked at him. He hadn't needed to finish the statement to Kelley. *I guess in the end, he saw that it would be quieter for his office to run this all through security to the police than if I did it myself,* Greg thought.

He closed his eyes again, trying to think, but his mind was in a thick fog and as fluid as cold oatmeal. Soon he started to drift off again.

"Greg!" he heard Aida call in alarm.

"Aida?" In a spasm of hope, he shot up from the cot. Nat sat up, her eyes snapping open.

"Dad! I just heard Mom again. She sounded scared. Is she awake? Is she okay?"

Greg was hunched over the bed, his eyes switching back and forth from his wife to the EEG. "No...no, she's not awake, but I heard her too. Wait, what do you mean 'again'?"

"Yesterday, before you got here, I thought I heard Mom tell me to wake up because Dr. Hernandez was here."

Greg paused and looked at his daughter, trying to understand what she had just told him. More important, he was trying to understand what it meant. A loud knock at the door interrupted any questions he might have asked.

"Dr. Doxiphus?" said a louder-than-normal voice. A hulking redheaded police officer step into the room. The cop looked at Greg, then Aida, then Nat, and gave a suggestion of a smile as he took a few more steps into the room. "Dr. Gregorio Doxiphus?"

"Yes, how can I help you? Has my wife's lab tech been found?"

"Well, yeah, he has, but there's been an incident. He got mixed up in a fight at a bar a few hours ago. He didn't start it, and it wasn't his fault, but in the course of the fight, he was stabbed in the chest and died."

"Oh my God!" said Nat, clasping a hand to her mouth.

"What happened in your lab is—" the cop continued.

"My *wife's* lab," Greg corrected him.

The cop moved closer to them now, his voice lowering to a conversational level. "Right, your wife's lab. This is now part of a police investigation, and I need to ask you both a few questions." He took out his notebook and pencil while his gaze settled on Aida. "I know this is a difficult time, so I'll be as quick as I can." He shifted his considerable weight to his right leg, then slid his left out and settled into a stance. "When was the last time either of you saw Mr. Fahy?"

"I haven't seen him in weeks. I've been out of town," said Greg.

"Today around noon, in my mom's lab, but campus security knows about that," Nat interjected. "President Kelley's office contacted the police, didn't they?"

"They did, and we got the full copy of that report, but this has to be for the record now." The cop looked at Nat over the top of his notebook. He shifted his weight to his left leg and drew in his right, then shifted his left leg out again, resuming his stance. Greg turned his head to follow him.

"Do you know if he was involved with drugs?" the cop continued.

"No, not that I know of," Greg said. "My wife never mentioned anything about that. The university does a full background check and drug tests on all employees. I know nothing turned up there."

The cop repeated his shifting motion and inched his stance toward the head of the bed; Greg's eyes stayed on him. Aida was directly between them now, and the darkened doorway to the bathroom framed the barrel-chested figure.

"What can you tell me about your wife's condition?"

Nat stood at the foot of the bed, her arms crossed, watching the cop.

Greg's gaze darted down to his wife and then to Nat, who shook her head almost imperceptibly, then back to the cop and the monitors. "Well, I'm not a medical doctor, but she's stable."

The cop glanced at monitors. "What does this EEG trace indicate?"

Greg gave the cop a quizzical look and didn't answer. A moment later, his cell phone rang, interrupting the silence.

"Hello? This is Dr. Doxiphus."

"Dr. Doxiphus, it's John Holden, I need to talk to you in person right now. Your lab tech was just killed."

"Actually, he was my wife's lab tech," Greg replied. The cop had inched closer to the EEG readout, but at Greg's reply he turned to focus on the phone conversation. "Excuse me," Greg continued, "but I can't talk right now. There's an officer with us in the hospital room, taking our statement. I think he's nearly done," Greg said to John and the cop.

"Is the officer a big pale guy with red buzz-cut hair?" John asked.

"Yes, but I don't see how that's relevant."

"Don't react to this, but he's not supposed to be there until tomorrow morning, and he's supposed to be with a detective, not by himself. Can you find a way to get rid of him and call for help?"

"Yes, I think so," Greg managed to say despite the growing constriction in his throat.

"Good. Do it. Someone just tried to kill me, so it stands to reason that the three of you are in danger too."

"Yes, I see," Greg's voice quavered as he looked at the floor, subconsciously intending to exclude the cop from the conversation. "I think you're right. Thank you. Hang on." He put the phone on the tray table but didn't end the call. *What the hell do I do now?*

When Greg looked back up, the huge redheaded man asked, "What's going on here, Doctor?" But Greg's eyes were looking just past the man, into the bathroom. There, stabbing her finger in the air at the cop, was his wife. Her mouth was moving as though she were trying to tell him something, but no sound came out. He looked back down at his wife, in the bed before him, then back to his wife standing in the bathroom door. A short, sharp intake of breath from Nat pulled his attention to his daughter; her eyes were fixed on the bathroom door too. He looked back to the door. Aida was gesticulating frantically as she screamed soundless words at him. This time he caught what she was saying.

"Greg! Grab Nat and get out! He's dangerous."

In a moment of awakening, Greg understood the look Nat had given the cop, and he understood his own anxiety regarding this man and this situation. *He's a threat. He's involved in this all somehow.* Greg froze. The cop's stare focused on him while his hand drifted toward his gun belt.

The radio handset on the cop's shoulder blared, "Unit 21 to KEA571. I'm at University Hospital ER in response to shots fired on an ambulance. Medic 82 is here. Only minor injuries, though the medic is a little shaken. Requesting additional units, CSI and shift commander on-site. Over." Greg and Nat flinched, startled at the harsh sound. Greg blinked, and Aida was gone from the bathroom doorway.

The cop's hand stopped its motion toward his gun belt and reached for the radio handset. "Unit 54, KEA571. I'm at the hospital now. I'll meet unit 21 and the ambulance downstairs." He turned quickly and left the room.

John's tiny voice yelled at them from Greg's phone, like some Lilliputian trying to get Gulliver's attention. "Dr. Doxiphus! Natalia! Hello!"

A shaken Gregorio Doxiphus picked up his phone. "I'm here, John. The officer got a call about an ambulance shooting, and I assume that was you. He's heading to the ER entrance now. You need to be careful."

"There's already another unit here," John said, "and more on the way. Don't worry about me. I can avoid him. Listen, I didn't get a chance to tell you before, and I don't think you're gonna believe this, but I saw your wife a few seconds before I was shot at. She was standing in the street off to the right of my vehicle. She told me to get down."

Aida, wherever you are. You're looking out for him too. "Yes, I believe you, John. Natalia and I just saw her too. She was trying to warn us about that officer...no, she's not awake; she's lying here in bed."

Nat was pacing from the window to the door, checking the hallway for signs of the cop and looking out the window at the parking lot by the ER entrance. "I see John's ambulance, Dad, and three...no, four police cruisers."

"We can see the police cars and your ambulance from Aida's hospital room," Greg said.

"I'm busy with the police right now," John continued. "I can't come up there yet, and you shouldn't leave the room. Stay there, and I'll come up to you as soon as I can."

"Okay, John," said Greg. "Thank you."

***

The redheaded police officer stepped out of the elevator onto the first floor. In front of him was a sign printed in large red letters that read EMERGENCY with an arrow that pointed to the left. He turned right and headed down the hallway toward the main entrance.

Holden's still alive, and the Doxiphuses know. They fucking know. She must be helping them somehow. He had parked his unit out on the street, avoiding the security cameras that constantly scanned the parking structure. Once he was through the main doors, he turned left and headed down the hill to street level. Red and blue lights strobed, casting flickering shadows in the night, but he was far enough away that he wouldn't be seen. His cruiser was half a block away.

He sat in his car for a minute. He had been on countless operations and had seen his share of things going to hell. But never like this, never so quickly. Discipline kicked in. *Time to report.* He touched his ear. "The medic is still alive, and I've been compromised in the eyes of the husband and the daughter...I need extraction." *Shit!*

He started the car and, without lights or siren, pulled away into the night.

***

"...compromised in the eyes of the husband and the daughter...I need extraction." The voice came from a speaker that was sitting on an ostentatious, hand-carved mahogany desk. *This is out of control. The whole damn thing is a liability now,* Jerome Gilden thought.

Gilden muted the speakerphone and turned to his assistant. "We need more control over this situation. We need her moved here."

"How do you want to handle that?" the assistant asked.

In reply, Gilden took out his personal phone and dialed. "Hi, it's me. Listen, our assets have made a mess of this. You were right...I know...how soon do you think you can get her moved here? Good...okay." He replaced the phone in his suit jacket pocket.

"What do you want to do about the asset?" asked the assistant.

Gilden grabbed a few almonds from a dish on the desk and popped them into his mouth. He chewed for a moment, then said, "Bring him to me."

The assistant's thumbs went flying across the screen of his mobile device. After a few seconds, it vibrated softly with a response.

"The corner of Vale and Hamilton in thirty minutes."

Gilden hit the now-unmuted the phone. "Vale and Hamilton, thirty minutes." Then he hung up. *That tool is losing its edge*, he thought as he glared at the speakerphone.

8 Eternity and a Day

John Holden sat on a bench outside the ER entrance, trying to fake his way through another police interview. Thankfully, this was with the older officer from The Jester and not that redheaded man he had the run in with.

"You've had a helluva night—first the stabbing death, and then you get shot at. I just spoke to the shift commander. He's still at the bar, wrapping up the scene and the paperwork. He told me to get your statement and then take your vehicle in as evidence. Maybe ballistics can get something off the slugs, if they can find them."

John looked at the shot-out driver's-side window of Medic 82. None of the other windows had been broken, so the bullets didn't make it to the windshield or the passenger side window; they had to be buried somewhere in the interior. Maybe the forensics team could pull something out, though he doubted it. More than likely the slugs were squashed flat against the steel frame of the vehicle.

"I haven't seen a night like this since I was in the service," said John. He held a double layer of four-by-four gauze against the scratches the broken glass had left on his neck. They were superficial, but he couldn't leave an open wound unattended.

The officer gave him a knowing look. "Over in the Gulf?" he asked.

"Yeah. Navy. I did a short tour there, but mostly in Guam and Southeast Asia as a rescue swimmer."

"Well, you're one heroic SOB then, jumping into dangerous waters just to save people."

He shrugged in reply. John didn't like to think of himself that way. It was just a job he had done, and he liked to think there were plenty of others who would do the same.

The officer returned to the statement. "Lemme read this back to you to make sure I have it straight. You're proceeding from the crime scene at The Jester to University Hospital. You're stopped at the corner of Claremont and Thirty-Third, waiting for the light to change, and an unknown assailant walks up on your left-hand blind side and fires three shots."

"Yeah, the first one broke out the driver's-side window. Then he got off two more."

"Then you leave the intersection at a high rate of speed toward the ER and radio in. Did you do anything else?" the cop asked.

"I think I scared the crap out of some college kids and diners at that outdoor café on Claremont." John felt a brief pang at not telling the whole truth here, but as far as he was concerned, he had people to protect now, and there was a problem inside University City Police. Besides, he felt his phone calls were still a protected form of communication, despite what the NSA might think.

"I'll have to send a unit to try and find some witnesses for statements, but I wouldn't worry about it. Did you get a look at the shooter?"

"No. He came at me from the blind spot in the mirror."

"So if the shooter was approaching from your blind spot, how did you know to duck?" the officer questioned.

"I dunno," John stalled, and there was that pang again. "I must have caught him in my peripheral vision, and reflexes kicked in. You know, once in combat…" That sounded like a reasonable story, and it certainly would look better in a police report than the truth. In any case, there was no evidence to the contrary, and he hoped there were no other witnesses to the events at the intersection of Claremont and Thirty-Third.

A county tow truck had pulled into the hospital parking lot while John and the officer were talking. Medic 82 was pulled in close to the building, and the tow truck couldn't get around to the front to hook it up. The driver got out of the tow truck and headed toward John, gawking at the shot-out window and glass across the seats. "Hey, are you the one responsible for this mess?"

71

"That's me."

"Can you get it turned around for me?"

"I'm still busy here." John gestured toward the officer. "The keys are in a magnetic box under the dash. Help yourself." The driver waved his thanks and headed to Medic 82.

John dabbed his neck and looked at the gauze. *I've been worse.* "Do you have everything you need? I'd like to get checked out. Maybe rest for a bit," he lied to the officer for a third time.

"Yeah, I'm good," said the officer, flipping through his notes. "We'll let you know if we find anything. You be careful." And he headed off.

John hadn't seen any sign of the redheaded cop, but being the cautious sort, he scanned the parking lot one last time. Nothing but cruisers, police officers, and one sorry-looking vehicle being hoisted onto the back of the tow truck. *Damn good rig*, he thought before turning to walk to the emergency room entrance at a fast clip. He had other people to see.

***

"What did John say?" Nat asked her father.

"He said someone just tried to kill him, and he saw your mother. She was warning him somehow. I'm pretty sure she saved his life." Greg's head was reeling as he tried to make sense of all this but knew he was failing miserably. Lack of sleep and stress took their toll on the higher cognitive functions first. "He said he thinks we might all be in danger. He's tied up with the police right now, but he'll come up here as soon as he can. We need to stay here with your mother."

"Well, yeah, where else would we go?" she said, and then she snapped, mostly at the situation. "What the hell is going on here, Dad? How could we both see Mom in the bathroom when she's lying right in front of us? And the cop and the nurse, someone trying to kill John, and that tech who lied, and now…" It tumbled out of her, and tears welled in her eyes, her voice choking off in a higher pitch. "He's dead."

Greg went over to her and held her. As strong and independent as Nat was, at this moment she was his little girl again, and she was frightened and hurting. She needed her father, and he needed her.

"I don't know, honey. I don't have any answers," he said softly through his own tears. She tucked her head against his chest, and he looked at his wife. "But the three of us need to get out of here."

A moment later, her tears subsided, and her composure returned as she considered the possibility of danger to them. "Where could we take her?" she asked. "And how would we get her there? She's…catatonic, Dad."

His shoulders slumping, Greg sat down and shook his head. "I don't know," he said in a long, defeated breath. "Let's just take this one step at a time. John should be up here soon."

***

A few minutes later, John stepped out of the elevator on Aida's floor. He actually did have to stop in the ER, and he was sporting a fresh dressing on his neck over some steri-strips that held a few of his wounds closed. The scratches on his chest had been cleaned and dressed too, but those were nothing serious and only needed Band-Aids. He trotted down the hallway, passed the nurses' station, and went through the double doors. A few yards ahead, he spotted a campus security guard sitting outside Aida Doxiphus's room. The guard raised a hand to stop him.

"Hang on. Are you family?" The guard leveled a stare at him.

"No, I'm the EMT who brought Dr. Doxiphus in, and—"

The guard cut him off. "Sorry, son. I can't let you in there." He stepped in front of the doorway, blocking John.

With a click, the door opened, and Greg's face appeared. "John, we thought we heard you." He turned to the guard. "It's all right. I asked him to come." As a precaution, Greg closed the door behind John. What they had to talk about was only for the four of them.

"Did the cop come back?" John asked.

"No, he left when he heard the call for a senior officer and backup to meet you down at the ER," Nat said. *He was hurt worse than he let on*, she thought, seeing the bandage on his neck. *Thank God he's okay.*

73

"I haven't seen him since I left The Jester." John untensed a bit at seeing the Doxiphus family safe.

"The what?" asked Greg.

"Sorry. The bar where the lab tech got an ice pick through the heart. That's where I heard the redheaded cop ask the shift commander if he could come over here and get a statement from you, but his commander denied the request and said a detective would come here tomorrow. The cop griped about it, and the commander gave permission for the cop to ride along with the detective. He was under orders not to come here tonight and not by himself."

"So why was he here?" Greg asked, knowing no one had an answer. He sighed. "Tell me about when you saw my wife."

"How did I see her?" John said. "I mean, how is that possible?"

"Just tell us what happened. We have to start with the what before we can figure out the how." Professor Doxiphus was on more familiar ground now, as long as he thought about this as a puzzle to be solved.

"I was on my way here from The Jester to pick up my partner. I had just had a run-in with the cop at the bar. He had pretty much threatened me when I told him about the unusual way we'd found Dr. Doxiph...I mean, your wife."

"It's okay. Call her Aida, and you can call me Greg. It gets a little confusing sometimes with two doctors in the house." Greg gave a little smile; John appreciated the gesture.

"So I was waiting at a light, and then I just saw her, Aida, standing not six feet off to the front right of the rig at the edge of headlights. She was motioning with both arms for me to get down. I think she was speaking too because I heard a voice saying 'Get down,' and then the gunshots came. The voice said 'Go!' and I slammed on the gas. I called it in to dispatch, then called you."

"How was she dressed?" Greg asked.

"Just like she was when I found her on the floor in the lab, white lab coat, tan skirt, white blouse." He had missed that detail before, but with the shock of seeing Aida and being shot at, that was no surprise. "You saw her too? Where? How?"

"She was there, in the bathroom," said Nat, pointing. She recounted the incident to John while Greg sat down and let his eyes close and chin droop slightly. John listened to her without interruption. He looked over to where she was pointing once, but still on guard, he swept his head across the room from the windows to the hallway door to Aida and Greg and back again.

A light rap came at the door.

"Greg? It's Alvin and Beverly Michelson."

"Come in," Greg said.

Kelley looked slightly rumpled in contrast to Dr. Beverly Michelson's smoothly pressed slacks, blouse, three-hundred-dollar haircut, and thousand-dollar shoes. Michelson was a thin blonde, but despite being Greg and Aida's age, she looked haggard and fifteen years older than them.

"Beverly reached out to me offering to help," Kelley told Greg.

"Hi, Greg," she said with a sympathetic smile and an *Oh, you poor dear* look as she wrapped his hand in both of hers.

"Hello, Beverly. You remember my daughter, Natalia, and this is John Holden, a friend of the family."

She gave Nat and John a quick nod and went straight to Aida. She whipped on a set of reading glasses to examine the live EEG trace on the screen. "How long has she been in this state?"

"Since yesterday morning. We're estimating forty to forty-three hours," Greg answered.

Michelson left the monitor and pulled out the paper copies of the traces, which were piling up in a tray beneath the cart. She quickly leafed through them.

"Greg, a word, if I may?" Kelley nodded toward the hallway. Greg followed him to the door, then leaned against it with one hand; he wasn't leaving this room.

Kelley acquiesced. "Greg, we're receiving more attention here than we'd like, and we're not really making any progress with helping Aida. I'd like you to consider moving her to Beverly's facility. She's already promised full access to all the prototype equipment, scanners, and stimulators there. We won't see that kind of equipment for years." He paused for a moment and continued in an even softer voice. "It's a secure medical facility. She'll be safer there, given what's been happening. I hate to say it, but a publicly accessible university hospital isn't built to keep people out."

Greg wanted to snap at him, to tell him that if he had gotten the police involved earlier perhaps the incident with the nurse and the

75

death of the lab tech could have been prevented. And he knew Alvin Kelley's mind. The man would be trying to minimize the university's exposure with the grant reviewers here.

"Greg," Michelson said softly, and he gave a start. He'd been so intent on Kelley that he hadn't noticed her come over to them. "We'll devote all resources at my facility to Aida. It's the best possible chance of diagnosing her condition."

Seeing the opportunity, Greg calmed down. He realized that even a guard at the door wouldn't have stopped a nurse with proper ID, and having armed police at every entrance to the hospital wasn't practical either. Still, this seemed a little too convenient.

"I appreciate the offer, and it does make sense," Greg said. "Thank you, Beverly. On the other hand, this is our home here, and if this turns into a long-term situation, Nat and I will be able to manage easier here than in Washington state. I just need some time. Can you give us until the morning to think about it?"

"Moving would be the best thing for her, and—" Kelley started to press, but Michelson cut him off.

"Of course, Greg. I'll be staying here in the doctors' residence. I'll go through Aida's records tonight. You can contact me there if you need anything."

Taking his cue from Michelson, Kelley eased up. "Just let me know when you make your decision. We'll do everything we can to support you."

Kelley and Michelson stepped into the hallway. The door latched behind them before they were four steps away.

"Greg needs to sleep, Alvin. He's exhausting himself standing vigil over her night and day. He won't be of much use to her in that condition. He isn't thinking clearly," Michelson commented as they made their way to the nurses' station.

"The local press and the NIH are starting to ask questions, and I can only shield them and the university for so long."

He has a one-track mind, Michelson thought as she listened to Kelley. She was silent as they passed the nurses' station. She knew where this train of thought would lead him and what he would say next; he just needed to get there on his own. Men like Alvin were so easy to manipulate—they just had to think the idea was theirs.

"I'll authorize her transfer in the morning without Greg's permission if I have to. It's best for her, their careers, and the university."

Michelson considered him dispassionately and thought, *How easily people justify actions that support their own interests.* Then she smiled at him. "You're right. It's best for all of them. If you'll excuse me, I'll start making the arrangements."

***

"Dad, we need to do whatever's best for Mom," Nat reasoned with her father. "We can manage there. They'll take care of us too."

"You're right," Greg agreed. "But I've always been a little suspicious of how Beverly gets her funding and the work she does there. They're not a public institution, so they don't have to be as transparent with their finances as the university does. And there's something bigger going on here that we don't understand yet."

"Um…let me step out so you both can talk this through." John stood, looking a little uncomfortable.

"No, please stay. You're part of this as well now. My wife protected you too. I think our chances of helping her and figuring this all out are best if we stay together." Greg looked between the two of them for agreement. After they nodded, he sighed and was quiet for a moment. "But we have to get out of here. I'll call Alvin and authorize the transfer." He picked up his cell phone from the tray table. "The damn battery is dead," he said, annoyed. "I'll call from the nurses' station. I want to talk to them about the prep for transport anyway."

"I'll run home and throw a bag together for us," Nat said.

"Can you hang on for a few minutes? It'd be better to have the two of you stay here until I get back," Greg said over his shoulder, then closed the door behind him.

Greg's legs were slowed by the constant ache of exhaustion and the reluctance he felt at trusting Beverly Michelson. It seemed he had nothing but bad options before him, and this was the least of all evils. He didn't like it, but he didn't see any other way out. He pushed his way through the double doors and was out of sight of the guard at his wife's room, as well as the nurses' station. An elderly man, dressed in a black turtleneck and black pants, walked toward him. His eyes were bright behind wire-framed glasses as he strode energetically toward Greg, who caught the man's eye and received a warm smile.

"Dr. Doxiphus? Excuse me, but may I have a word with you?" the man asked, stopping a few feet from Greg.

"I'm sorry, Father. Not right now. I have to make a phone call about my wife," Greg replied, thinking the man to be a priest. Who else would be here at this hour and dressed that way?

"Yes, I know, and that would be a grave mistake," the gentlemen said with complete conviction. Calmly he continued, *"Gia Mia aioniótita kai mia méra." For eternity and a day.*

That stopped Greg dead in his tracks. "What did you say?"

"That's the vow your wife had inscribed in Greek inside your wedding ring. She's holding to that vow." The man waited patiently for a moment as he watched the disbelief that had washed across Greg's face transform into a mixture of curiosity and doubt.

"Is there somewhere we can talk in private?" the man asked.

Greg gestured to the men's room. The lights flickered to life as they entered, and the man led Greg to the back of the room, as far from the door as possible.

"My name is Matthew, and I can help your wife, you, your daughter, and Mr. Holden," the man began, his gentle confidence calming Greg's obvious alarm.

"How do you know all this?" demanded Greg, though in the back of his mind, he already knew the answer.

The corners of Matthew's mouth twitched in a slight grin. *No matter how many times I see this moment*, he thought, *it retains its wonder. In hope, the mind asks a question it already knows the answer to but hasn't yet accepted. But through that hope, it is ready and only needs the slightest nudge to start believing. The dawning of awareness.*

"She told me. Your wife is very much alive and active, Gregorio." Again he watched as relief started to crack the stone wall of disbelief that was Greg's expression. "Her attention is...well...not focused on this world, not in the way you see it right now. Please, will you allow me to be of assistance?"

Greg reached out and put both hands on Matthew's shoulders, hung his head, and let a few tears release the stress from his body.

9 Certainty

Gregorio Doxiphus ran some cold water in the sink, scooped it, and splashed it on his face. The water got his collar and shirt wet as it dripped down along his neck, but the spreading chill helped revive him. Through more alert eyes, he looked at Matthew's reflection in the mirror. Matthew's face and balding head were well tanned, and Greg got the impression that the man regularly shaved the short gray stubble that wrapped around the back of his head and over his ears. Matthew stood there, waiting for Greg.

"Okay, tell me what's going on with my wife." Greg tore off some paper towels and patted his face and hands while turning to face Matthew.

Without pretense or drama, Matthew answered, "Dr. Doxiphus, there's a very narrow window of opportunity to get your wife out of this hospital and to a place of safety. It is her wish that you, your daughter, and the paramedic accompany her. There isn't time for me to fully answer your questions beyond what I've already said—that she's alive and active. You've all seen her, haven't you? She can be returned to you, but the four of you have to get out of here now."

"To where? Who do we need to be kept safe from?"

"Safe from the people who employ the police officer you recently met and the nurse who your daughter deflected...from those who arranged to have your wife's lab technician killed, the same people who tried to murder Mr. Holden, the same people who are now trying to isolate your wife and study her..."

That fits better than anything I've been able to come up with, Greg thought. "Okay, I believe you. Aida's been..."—he fumbled for the words to explain what he understood to be happening—"…in contact with you, and somehow this whole set of events is being orchestrated. How do we get out of here?"

He's grasping this very well. "There's a white ambulance in the emergency entrance parking lot. You must get your wife and the three of you to the vehicle, but don't draw unnecessary attention to yourselves," Matthew said, and looked at his watch. "I *must* leave now. We'll talk more later." He took a few steps toward the door, then turned back to Greg and said, "One more thing: turn left."

Greg stood quietly for a moment, trying to puzzle out how to move his wife out of the hospital and into an ambulance and drive away without drawing attention. *Would John be willing to do this?* Something told him that yes, he would, but it had to be his decision. *You just don't move a patient who's being watched around the clock without a doctor's ord*—his head snapped up as he realized all the pieces were already in place. Greg quickly left the men's room and turned left. He strode down the hallway feeling better than he had for days. There finally was something he could do to help his wife and protect his family. At the end of the dim hallway, the light of the nurses' station awaited him.

***

Matthew walked calmly toward the main entrance of the hospital, hoping Greg would accept his offer of help. He knew Greg was a strong man and accustomed to doing things for himself. Pride was a difficult force to overcome in anyone who was trying to protect his or her family. But with just a few words, Matthew had given him the ability to do just that. He had only to come to that conclusion on his own; however, given his present state, that was an uncertain outcome.

As Matthew left the hospital, the cell phone in his pocket rang. Now he would find out. "Hello…that's good. Please make sure everything is ready for our arrival. She'll be weak, and we won't have much time."

For the first time in two days, Matthew smiled too.

***

"Excuse me," Greg said to the nurse behind the desk. "My wife is going to be moved to a private facility. I understand the ambulance is ready. She needs to be prepped for the trip."

"Oh, okay," the nurse said, a little surprised. She looked up from the row of monitors in front of her. "Dr. Kelley told us to prep your wife in the morning, Dr. Doxiphus, but we can do it now. Just give me a few minutes to get some help. You've already told Dr. Kelley you've agreed to move her?"

Kelley was going to order the move without my approval, Greg realized, and he knew the nurse would have to report everything as well. "Yes, I already let him know. He's been very supportive," Greg lied. "I just needed a few minutes alone. Clearly this is the best thing to do for her. Thank you very much." Without realizing it, he smiled and looked relieved.

"Of course, Doctor. We'll be there in a few minutes," the nurse said, then picked up the phone to request assistance. Greg nodded to her, then headed back to the room.

***

"Nat, John," said Greg as he closed the door behind him. "We're leaving, all four of us. John, I hope you'll forgive the presumption, but the transport ambulance is already downstairs in the emergency lot. I don't know where we're going or exactly what's going on, but—"

John cut him off. "So we're not going to Beverly Michelson's facility? Good. Greg, your wife saved my life. In the past two days, I've seen things I can't explain, and things that I can, and I'm more scared by the things that I can. I'm in." He had people to protect and help; this was his job, and it was what he had always done.

"That was fast, though. Did they just have an ambulance waiting downstairs?" said Nat.

Greg shook his head. "They didn't, but someone else did."

"What do you mean, Dad? Who has an ambulance ready?"

"It's someone your mother's been in contact with. His name is Matthew. Your mom evidently trusts him. I believe he's here to help us…all of us. I don't have much in the way of answers yet, but he seems to."

81

Seeing the determination and surety on her father's face, Nat thought better of asking any more questions for the time being. "Okay, let's go," she said, standing up. "Can I run home and get some stuff?"

Greg moved around the room and started to gather their belongings. "No. Matthew said we have to get her out of here and into the ambulance right away and without attracting attention to ourselves. I just asked the nurses to prep your mother for transport. They'll be here any minute, so there's no time to go home and pack." He stopped and added, "Don't worry. Like you said, we can manage."

Nat joined her father, picking up the clothing and effects that had made their way into the hospital room the past few days and crammed them into her backpack and messenger bag. While the two were busy collecting their things, John went over to Aida and started to remove the EEG and EKG leads.

Suddenly the door opened, startling them all. The nurse and an aide came into the room, pulling a gurney behind them to prep their patient for transport.

"Oh, good, you're still here," said the nurse when she saw John. "We can use an extra set of hands." John was the expert in the room on packaging a patient for transport, and the nurse knew that. In a few minutes the job was complete, and the nurse and aide left the room.

"So far, so good." Greg looked at his wife—who was practically mummified in blankets, tubes, and equipment—and thought she would be too warm, especially on a summer night. "Won't she overheat?" he asked John.

"She can't tell us if she's too cold, but we'll be able to tell if she's too hot. She's not moving around, so she's not generating a lot of body heat. This is standard care, Dr. Doxiphus. It helps protect against shock."

Greg nodded. "That makes sense."

"Okay, stuff's all packed up," said Nat. "Now what?"

"Well, uh, now…," her father started, but he trailed off.

Seeing the lost expression on Greg's face, John realized the man didn't know what to do next or what was about to happen. *I have to get them all out of this hospital*, he thought. "The nurse and the

82

doctor will come back in. The doctor will check Aida and release her for transport. There'll be papers to sign, and we'll take your mother downstairs to the emergency entrance."

"What about the ambulance?" asked Nat.

"Yeah, I should get downstairs and get the rig ready to go. I guess I'm driving. I'm not needed for the release papers anyway, and it would look better if I were with the ambulance."

"What if someone starts asking questions?" Nat asked. "What do we say?"

This time it was her father who answered. "I don't think there'll be any questions. We're doing exactly what everyone expects us to do. We just have to hope Kelley or Michelson don't show up."

On that uneasy thought, John went ahead while Nat and Greg waited in the hospital room. A few minutes later, a bleary-eyed resident came in and did a quick inspection of Aida; then he scrawled his signature on the release papers. "Have a safe trip to Washington, Dr. Doxiphus," he said shaking Greg's hand. "I hope you can find some answers there."

***

The automatic ER doors swung inward toward John as he stepped out of the building. Across the lot, parked in a corner slot, sat a white ambulance with blue-and-red striping and yellow plates with red lettering that he wasn't familiar with. *That must be our ride*, he thought as he walked to the vehicle. The door was open, which wasn't too much of a surprise, but the note he found taped to the steering wheel was:

Your skills as a medic and your military training will be required in the coming days. They need you. The keys are where you usually leave them.

"Well, someone expected me to be the one to find this," he said to himself, then crumpled the note in his pocket. He reached under the dash and found a magnetic box with the keys. The engine started easily. *Seems like the rig is in good shape*, he thought. *Hope it's well stocked.* After slipping it into gear, he rolled toward the ER entrance,

83

where the Doxiphus family had just emerged. The nurse and aide were handling the gurney.

The ambulance pulled a quick turn around and backed up toward the entrance. John had done this so many times that he didn't even need to look at the painted guidelines to let him know he was dead on target. He stopped, killed the engine, and hopped out as someone opened the ambulance's rear doors.

Nat and her father stood on the apron, holding their bags and a backpack. They were both silent and a little stiff—not that the hospital staff noticed, and if they did, well, their behavior wasn't anything out of the ordinary. Given what the two of them had been through, it was amazing they were still standing at all.

As John helped load Aida into the ambulance, the nurse looked around and asked, "Where's your partner? There need to be two medics for a transport, especially a long one like this."

"She's at station eighty-two, getting our things together. I'm gonna swing by and pick her up," he replied, hoping the lie would work.

"The protocol calls for two before we can let you leave. Can someone bring her over here?" she said.

"Our gear is at the station, no sense in her hauling it all over here. It's only five minutes away," he said.

"Doctor Kelley authorized this transfer himself. Is there a problem?" Greg intervened. The nurse didn't like it, but she conceded, as this was above her level.

John helped Greg into the back of the unit and quickly closed the doors. He told Nat to get in the front, and then he stepped around the front of the vehicle to avoid any further questions from the nurse. He climbed into the driver's side and gave a quick chirp on the sirens to let anyone around them know they were about to roll. A moment later, they headed out of the parking lot toward the street.

"Okay, Greg. I'm driving, but I don't know where I'm going." For a second, John thought that he should go to station eighty-two, which was to the right, but the last thing they needed was more questions from anyone on duty there.

The exit to the street was only a few yards ahead, and John thought he felt the eyes of the ER staff on them. "Greg, which way am I going?" he said, louder than the first time. He saw Greg in the rearview mirror, struggling for the correct answer.

"I don't know. Just go anywhere. No wait! Turn left!"

John hit the indicator just as they reached the edge of the driveway and smoothly accelerated into the street. A patrol car was stopped at a traffic light a hundred yards ahead, and he pulled up beside it slowly, knowing that the cops were sure to be out looking for drunks. It was a little after 1:00 a.m., and the bars had just closed. True, they wouldn't be looking for a paramedic driving an ambulance under the influence; still, he didn't want to do anything to draw the attention of the university police.

As they sat at the light, Greg stuck his head through the narrow passageway between the driver's compartment and the back. The light changed, and John let the patrol car pull out ahead of them.

"Okay, Greg. Where to now?"

"Go straight. Just keep going."

As they drove away from the hospital, the spacing between the streetlights increased, and darkness closed in around them. Ahead, on their side of the street, was an illuminated bus shelter with a single occupant seated on the bench. As the ambulance approached, the figure stood and stepped out as though he were waiting for a bus. He raised his hand and turned to face the oncoming headlights.

"That's him. That's Matthew! Pick him up," Greg said, pointing at the elderly man who was slowly waving. John pulled over to the bus stop, and Nat opened her door to let the man climb in.

"Hello, Miss Doxiphus, Gregorio, Mr. Holden." He greeted them, smiling. "Congratulations. It seems our little bit of subterfuge was successful. I didn't see anyone following you out of the parking lot. Is Aida secure?"

"She's in the back, secured for transport," John said.

"I need to get in the back with your mother, if you'll excuse me, Miss Doxiphus."

"Who are you?" Nat asked him as he squeezed by.

"My apologies. My name is Matthew. My fellow monks and I are doing everything we can to help your mother. One of the reasons I came is that I'm a licensed doctor of traditional Eastern medicine."

John pulled away from the bus stop. "Okay, Matthew. Where to?" he asked, hopeful he'd have solid directions to follow.

"Head toward the interstate and get on I-80 west, if you would, Mr. Holden. We're going to New Mexico."

10 Confirmation

A steady rain fell with a soft *tak-tak-tak* on the office windows. Another in an endless train of Pacific storms was blowing through. The weather people called it "The Pineapple Express." Basically, warm tropical moisture streamed across the Pacific from Hawaii and then was dumped on the whole Puget Sound area. This summer was already on track to be the wettest on record. He hated it, but it did make certain aspects of their operation easier to accomplish.

At an angle, Jerome Gilden saw his reflection in the darkened floor-to-ceiling windows that wrapped around the exterior wall and wondered if he could be seen from the outside. He didn't like being publicly visible. He detested exposure; it was too much of a risk. For the umpteenth time, he wished there were curtains he could pull shut. He glanced at the controls for the adaptive windows and saw they were on the opaque setting. This damn high-tech building was going to drive him to distraction.

"Don't worry about it, muh boy," he reassured himself aloud, then continued silently. *There's nothing around here for twenty miles except mountains, hills, and trees. It's going on eleven p.m., and there's a heavy storm outside; no one's watching.*

He swiveled his high-backed executive chair away from the windows, back to the mahogany monstrosity that was his desk, blocking any chance anyone outside among the trees of Pacific County might have had of spying him.

Gilden's desk phone warbled, breaking the silence. He leaned over and hit the speaker icon on the touchscreen.

"Did he agree to the transfer? Is she on her way here?" he asked, leaning back in the chair.

"Well, hello to you too," came a woman's voice from the other end. "And no, he hasn't yet. He's pretty wrung out and couldn't decide right away. He asked for a little time. He'll tell us in the morning."

"And if he doesn't want to move her?"

"He will. He's very logical. This is the best thing for her, and he knows it. He just needs a few hours to work it through."

"What's plan B?" Gilden asked, allowing a little of his irritation to come through.

"Plan B is Kelley. He wants to minimize the attention this whole situation is drawing to the university. It's grant-renewal time, and NIH reviewers are here. He already said he'd authorize the transfer if Greg doesn't."

"Okay, that's good for now. How are you doing?" he said, switching to a more congenial tone.

"I'm in the doctors' residence at the hospital, going through Aida's records. It's fascinating. Her traces are nearly identical to those of our observers."

He checked the bottom right-hand corner of the touchscreen and saw the little padlock icon was on, indicating this call was encrypted and secure.

"Let's talk about that more when you all get here. I'm preparing a special welcome for you," Gilden said, trying to be charming. "How long until you arrive?"

"Well, it's a little before one a.m. here. Kelley will authorize the transfer in six or seven hours at the latest. Then there's an hour to prep and drive to the airport and transfer her, three hours for the flight, and then ground transport there. We should be back in time for lunch."

"Excellent," Gilden said with a genuine smile this time. "I'll make sure the hospitality suite is ready for them. We'll give the husband and daughter a warm welcome and provide them with all the support they need."

"And then?"

"Do you really want to have this conversation now, Beverly?" he replied. Gilden leaned across the desk, his voice dropping all pretense of pleasantry. The message was made all the more threatening for the velvet smoothness in which it was delivered. "This is business. The Project needs to understand what's going on here so it can be controlled and duplicated."

"They're colleagues of mine," she spat back, then caught herself. "The university will be watching."

"Like I said, we'll keep them happy here, learn everything we can from her, then kick them loose when we're done." He paused, allowing the opportunity for any other objections, but he expected silence, and he got it. "We need you all here as soon as possible. Be careful," he said, then hung up.

11 Aida's Day

Peace and comfort. Aida existed in nothing but peace and comfort. She was still asleep enough to be floating in her dreams and just awake enough to appreciate how wonderful it felt. Something beautiful wanted her attention; a gentle tug pulled her to the bank of the stream in which she was drifting. A gliding flute made a simple statement of four descending notes, which then reversed and repeated, climbing up, then going down again. *Wow, Morning Mood, I love this piece*, was her first thought of the day. She normally would hit the snooze button but decided to let Edvard Grieg's famous piece play on.

The sun was just rising, with beams of light revealing the lighter colors in the dark wood of their Mediterranean-style furniture. Out of habit, Aida's hand drifted over to Greg's side of the bed, but she only felt the pillows she had stacked up there to occupy his space. *He's still at Fermilab*, she remembered, now coming fully awake.

She pictured him there, in the middle of the work he loved, and was happy for him. *He'll be back in a few days*, she thought as she sat up and swung her legs over the side of the bed. She reached high in a stretch, inhaling the noticeably cooler and dryer morning air, and lightly rose from the bed. It was one of those rare mornings when she woke up just ahead of the alarm clock and was full of energy.

Aida's morning routine went faster than usual, and she got downstairs at ten after six, dressed in a simple tan skirt and white blouse. Breakfast was likewise simple: a cup of coffee and Greek yogurt with fruit and nuts. She gathered her things and, checking her watch, saw she was out the door at 6:25 a.m. In the front garden, the sun angled through the stargazer lilies, which were just blossoming, and their sweet, rich aroma made her smile. She loved this time of year, and today seemed to hold its own particular promise.

She arrived at building 87 a few minutes early, despite a detour that was being set up on University Drive South. She had caught all the lights on the way, which was weird, but God was smiling on her today, so she decided to just be grateful. She unlocked the door and went into her lab. The lab benches stood like low monoliths, gray in the shadows cast by the building across the street. As she walked around the benches to the left, her attention was drawn to the pale-blue sky subtly reflected off the linoleum floor. She flicked on the light in her office, put her purse in a desk drawer, and slipped on her well-worn lab coat. She had scheduled a calibration run of the TMS/TDS machine at seven fifteen, so she still had a few minutes to check her email. She knocked on the space bar twice as if to say, "Wake up" to the computer, then settled in to finish her morning ritual.

Right at seven, she heard Bill come into the lab. When he stopped at his desk, Aida heard the usual thud of a dropped backpack and the jingle of tossed keys. *He's on time today. That's unusual.*

"Hey, Dr. D. G'morning. I'm gonna grab some coffee. You want anything?"

Bill has his rituals too. "Good morning, Bill. No, thanks," she said, swiveling her chair to see him.

He was wearing his usual T-shirt, jeans, and sneakers. His wavy brown hair was disheveled and looked as though he had only run his hands through it. At thirty-five, he should've started dressing more age appropriate years ago, she thought, but he had no partner that she knew of, and he was more than a little socially awkward, even for a lab tech. In fact, offering to get her coffee was remarkably uncharacteristic of him. *Hmm, punctual and considerate today.*

"Calibration run at seven fifteen, right?" Bill asked.

"Yes, first run with the new detectors. Very exciting!"

"Cool!" he said, bobbing his head once to emphasize just how cool he thought this was.

Aida and Greg had finished building and installing the new detectors, called quantum evoked subatomic magnetometers, or QUESAMs, right before he had left for Chicago. The QUESAMs

91

were three generations ahead of the spin exchange relaxation-free (SERF) magnetometers that had come out of Princeton in the 2000s and perhaps a dozen ahead of the cryogenically cooled superconducting quantum interference devices (SQUIDs) that were initially developed at the Ford Research labs in the 1960s. These ultra-sensitive devices could sense the minute magnetic fields created by individual neurons in the brain and identify the exact location of any given neuron at the same time. What made them truly special, however, was their temporal resolution, which was down to the nanosecond, the same resolution as the NIST atomic clocks. If it worked as designed, the QUESAM device could show the electromagnetic state and exact location of every individual nerve cell in the brain at any one-billionth, or 10^{-9} second, window of time. It would be like filming all the activity in the brain, from the smallest level on up, with a super-high-speed camera. With this, they could start to produce a detailed map of human cognition. And that was only the beginning; this was the first stepping stone on the path to Aida's real goal.

If we get this to work, she thought, *no one will have to suffer like Mom ever again.*

Her mother's brain cancer, glioblastoma multiforme, hadn't just been the cause of her excruciating suffering and subsequent death; it had slowly, over the fourteen months from diagnosis to death, destroyed who her mother was. It had tortured the woman and, with insidious intent, murdered her identity and sense of self.

The first symptoms had been headaches and sensitivity to light. Then came the nausea and vomiting and double vision. The doctors discovered a very aggressive tumor growing in the back of her brain, in the occipital lobe, which explained the disturbance of the visual field. The chemo and radiation therapy barely slowed it down, and then in the course of the surgery, the parts of the visual center of the brain that hadn't been infiltrated, crushed, or corrupted by the cancer were removed in an effort to get "a clean border."

And then Mom went blind.

They thought they'd gotten it all, and Aida's mother had started to recover. That had been a hopeful month. But glioblastoma multiforme is particularly hardy. If only a handful of cells, perhaps only as few as ten, survive the therapies, they start dividing and growing again. Worse, they can infiltrate healthy cells, alter their DNA, and convert them to pluripotent stem cells, which then, under the influence of the cancer cells, become glioblastoma multiforme cells themselves.

And so it spread, a suicidal parasite bent on its own survival for as long as the host could support it. It nested in the midline of the brain, right in the hippocampus, and then her memory was gone.

Every bit of her that I knew ended then.

In her office, Aida's eyes stayed dry; she had exhausted that fountain many years ago. But it had been replaced with a single-minded determination to fight this thing and, through that struggle, to ease the suffering of others who would inevitably follow that same path.

"Ready to go, Dr. D? I'm gonna run the setup now if you're ready," said Bill, looking at her with concern. In her reverie she had missed him coming back in.

"Absolutely. Let's get going." *Let's kill this damn thing.*

***

"Ready for your login, Dr. D," Bill said as Aida stepped into the outer room of the double-shelled stim room complex. Bill had full administrator access to the computers and was already logged in at the operating-system level. But the control program for the machine required a second login. It was an annoying security feature that Greg had insisted on to keep their work secure, and after some debate, she admitted it was probably the right thing to do.

Aida had heard stories of work being sabotaged by peers, especially around grant-review time, but she was a trusting soul and couldn't bring herself to think of anyone she knew deliberately wrecking work that would save lives. Still, hackers were out there everywhere, and competition for funding was brutal. On top of that, there were potential defense applications to their work. Greg had won the security debate by reminding her of the Gang Lu incident during her medical residency at the University of Iowa on November 1, 1991. The papers said Lu was disgruntled over losing some prize. But he also was a foreign national studying particle physics who killed the four faculty members working on Ronald Reagan's

Strategic Defense Initiative, otherwise known as the Star Wars program. You could never know who was going to snap or what their motivations were.

"Sure. Let me drive," Aida said, motioning Bill out of the chair in front of the console.

He smiled at her and practically jumped out of the chair. "Right. Sorry. Here you go."

He's eager to please today, she thought as they squeezed past each other.

This second layer of security was little more than a simple username and password. A standard username and password verified your identity based on something you knew. You typed in those things you knew, and the system would let you in or not based on what it knew those things to be. A more secure login would require you to provide something you know and something you have and something you are. For example, your username and password (something you know), a smartcard with an embedded chip (something you have), and a fingerprint or retinal scan (something you are). The most secure systems required all three and from multiple people. But Greg hadn't insisted on going that far.

Sitting on the side of the control console was a USB smartcard reader, its blue LED glowing in the darkened room. Aida slid her university ID badge, which also was a smartcard with an embedded computer chip, into the reader. Immediately a prompt appeared on the screen, asking for her PIN.

She typed in "12241871." Greg didn't approve of her practice of using dates as passwords or PINs, but she had reasoned with him that if she was going to have to go through this added layer of security, she would use a PIN she would remember.

The QUESAM administration program splash screen came up with blinking text across the bottom that read "Initializing."

"There you go," she said, and got up to let Bill take her place.

"Do you want the default parameters?"

"No, not with the new QUESAMs. There are stimulation pulses in a default run that could interfere with the readings."

In addition to being detectors, the QUESAMs also could produce electromagnetic pulses at specific frequencies and for narrow slices of time. These pulses would run along all the cells in the brain, and based on how fast they were transmitted by each individual cell, you could tell what type of cell each one was. Like which ones were normal cells and which were cancer cells. And once you could locate exactly where they were, you'd place nanoparticles of heavy metals, like gold or platinum, in them and send another therapeutic pulse through. The second pulse would cause the metal atoms to kick loose an electron (radiation) that would fly out into the cancer cells and smash their DNA, killing them. But because their energy was so low, they wouldn't go much beyond the cancer cells themselves.

"Gotcha!" Bill said. "Can you check these settings, please?"

Aida leaned over to give the screen a quick glance. "Looks good."

She stepped onto the foil mat and grabbed the door handle to the inner room to release the latch. Bill's hands moved between the screen and keyboard, locking in the approved parameters for the run as she stepped in and closed the door behind her.

The silence of the inner room fell on Aida's ears, cutting her off from the outer world like Odyssean wax plugs. She swallowed to pop her ears and spoke to make sure she could still hear and to start the recording of the calibration run.

"Are we all sealed up?" she asked. "Good. This is a calibration run with QUESAM's version four point three. Readings only, no stimulation." She reached behind her neck to undo the clasp of her crucifix and took out her earrings as well. There could be no metal within thirty centimeters of the helmet, and the gold in her jewelry was an excellent electrical conductor.

"Turn down the lights a little, please, Bill. Don't want to overstimulate the visual cortex."

The lighting for the inner room was carried in by bundled fiber-optic cables from light boxes in the outer lab, which kept the electrical noise down. Bill lowered the lighting.

"There, that's good," Aida said.

She sat down in the chair, which reclined back when it sensed her weight. It slowly moved to the right position for the helmet to join it, then locked into place. Overhead, the ends of the fiber-optic cables looked like dim stars in an early-evening sky, except they didn't twinkle.

"Okay, ready here, Bill. Let's get going, and don't forget to log this in the notebook."

Aida couldn't hear Bill's response. They had elected not to put speakers in the inner room, and there was no room for nonmagnetic-style headsets used in MRI machines under the helmet. Instead they had suspended a mirror on the ceiling in which she could see the window between the inner and outer rooms. Glancing up, she saw that Bill held the notebook. He waved it a few times and gave a weak smile and a thumbs-up. In that moment she saw the color had drained from his face like water from a sponge. Then he sat down and was blocked by the monitors.

He looks ashen. "Bill, are you all right? We can postpone this if you're sick."

Another thumbs-up sign rose from behind the console, and the gentle hiss of hydraulics told her the helmet was moving into position. Bill had initiated the session sequence. *Well, okay. It's a short session, and he can always abort if he has to.*

The helmet was actually the open, hollow end of a four-foot-long telescoping cylinder and sat in a cradle suspended from the ceiling by a massive support arm. Thick cables, heavy with insulation and shielding, twined and twisted their way around the support arm as they ran to the helmet. In her mind's eye, the video of previous tests played, and Aida imagined she saw the cylinder approach the chair from above and behind her and then telescope out when it was level with the chair. She wouldn't be able to see the helmet until it was right on top of her, engulfing her head, with only a small cutout for the face. When the helmet was in position, she smirked; she thought it looked like an even larger version of that massive beehive hairdo that Elsa Lanchester wore as the Bride of Frankenstein.

Slowly, in the edge of Aida's sight, the darkness inside the helmet blocked out some of the putty-colored walls of the inner room, and pillows inflated by puffs of air gently stabilized her head and neck from either side. The overhead lighting dimmed for a moment, signaling to her that the detection cycle would begin in sixty seconds. She had to focus on her breathing now, calm her mind, and get her brain into neutral—not doing, just being. Aida rested her tongue on the roof of her mouth and half closed her eyes.

She noticed the edges of her nostrils being pulled gently inward by the cool rush of air, and then her attention shifted to her expanding ribs and abdomen.

In…

The release of breath came without effort as her diaphragm and chest-wall muscles relaxed.

Out. Twenty-one…

Relaxation spread downward from the top of her scalp and through her face, throat, neck, shoulders, and upper back.

In…

A slightly deeper breath in flowed to a deeper release as she breathed out the tension.

Out. Twenty…

In…

Out. Nineteen…

In…

Out. Eighteen…

With each cycle, the wave of release continued its journey downward, like a slowly falling line of dominos, ending at her toes and the soles of her feet.

In…

Thoughts and images flashed on the screen of Aida's mind, each vying for her attention. She let them slide away as they popped up, then guided her focus back to her breathing.

Out. Twelve…

In…

Her mind was starting to settle down now as she continued the cycle of breathing she had first learned in yoga class. But, like a child protesting bedtime, it wasn't quite ready to let go yet. It tried to latch on to the sense of pressure from the chair she felt at certain points along her back and legs. Aida acknowledged the sensation, then let it flow over the waterfall of the stream of perceptions.

Out. Eleven…

In the last ten breaths of the cycle, she visualized a warm, bright, nurturing light filling her body. Once it filled her, it would surround her like a cocoon.

In…

Out. Four…

Peace and comfort.

In…

The next step was to accept and send out wishes for love, kindness, and compassion to the entire world. Generally this was the hardest step of the meditation for every practitioner. It's human nature to show concern for strangers, for the unknown multitudes of the world, only after ensuring that your own needs are met. Aida was no exception, so she was more than surprised when a slight sense of that universal love came *to* her, not from her.

Out. Three…

In…

Peace and comfort and love.

Out. Two…

The last breath came and went without her noticing it at all. A slight hum built inside the helmet. *Why are the capacitors charging? I said no stim…*

***

Piece-of-shit computer! Hurry up. Bill mentally cursed as he sweated away the longest sixty seconds of his life. He sat with his arms crossed and his leg twitching. His eyes darted between the countdown timer, the "abort" button, and the settings he had just changed.

It's five grand, man, and it's just a machine. They'll fix it, the devil on his left shoulder said. Then a weak voice, screaming as loud as it could yet barely discernable to him, said, *What about Dr. D? What if she gets hurt?*

He felt as if he might puke as the timer passed through nine, eight, seven…

Bill watched her. When the timer showed five, the stimulation capacitors he had reconfigured to overload began to charge.

Three, two, one…

Her left hand tightened on the arm of the chair, and her legs lifted.

Zero.

A burst of stimulation pulses ran across the EEG window of the control screen as a sound like an old electric typewriter with a key held down, machine-gunning its way across the page, came through the speakers.

He stood up from the console, then looked down at an EEG that was all over the place. Through the window he saw Aida's arm, dangling over the side of the chair, her hand unmoving.

Oh, shit!

He jumped from the console and got both feet on the mat, then wrenched the door open.

"Dr. D? Are you all right?" he said, panicking.

He hit the "abort" button on the wall of the inner room, and the helmet started to retract. Aida's eyes were closed, her face blank. Bill grabbed her by the shoulders and shook, shouting, "Dr. D! I don't know happened. I'm sorry." Unsympathetic muteness was the only response he received.

A crushing weight fell on Bill's chest, and he struggled for his next breath. His vision narrowed, turning gray at the edges as his stomach collapsed on itself and his heart pounded in his ears. He staggered to the outer room and grabbed the trash can as his whole body convulsed, trying to vomit out the fear and self-condemnation. The taste of bile mixed with coffee filled his mouth and nose as a stream of stinging fluid erupted from him. Then the gray curtain in his field of vision closed off the world, and he passed out on the floor.

12 Waking Up

Peace and comfort. Aida felt she was being carried upward, like a leaf on a breeze. It was familiar yet different. She remembered the music from earlier and reached out for it, but there was only silence. She drifted outside of time and was content to do so. Weightless, she felt something wash over her and move her in one direction, then another in the same way. Silence and floating, and then the silence changed. She felt it change rather than hearing it. It was a physical sensation; she felt it vibrating her, and she resonated along with it in harmony. Her awareness grasped on to the sensation and began to focus. She tightened her grip on it and was surprised to discover it was coming from her and from outside of her. It was everywhere. And it was joyful and grateful, and Aida laughed in the pure delight of it. The sound of her laughter filled her and then everything else, and it too resonated in the vibrating silence.

She became aware of colors, lights, and movement...and darkness. There were things out there—she could see them but felt a slight sense of vertigo. They were out of focus, untouchable, and for a moment she felt she was falling—like in a dream, moving, and dropping, ungrounded and thrashing but motionless at the same time. Her entire field of vision was two-dimensional; everything was flat, with no depth.

A bright object moved toward her out of the shimmering light and the dark background. It took on a long, cigar-like shape, and Aida was able to focus on it. Then the one bright object transformed into many smaller bright objects that were close together, arranged in two triple columns of illuminated dots.

"What is that?" she asked and was startled to hear her voice aloud. Her hearing had cleared, and under her voice, the vibrating silence had turned into a low-pitched hum. It almost sounded like a voice, one immense voice of everything.

The lines were getting closer now. Each dot emitted a soft pearl-white glow and left a thin trail of the glow behind as it moved ahead in a straight line. Other objects grew out of the flatness, taking on depth and dimension, and her visual world resolved itself in one instant. Although the objects didn't change their color or shape or how they were moving, she was able to see them now.

This is all like a Magic Eye picture, and I'm seeing the 3-D image that was embedded in the 2-D image all the time. She understood now. All these things had always been there; you just needed to unfocus your vision and your eyes. Then your visual centers would reinterpret what they saw, and then—boom!—in an instant, your perspective would flip, and you'd see the 3-D objects. But this wasn't an eight-by-ten stereogram she could look away from and see the normal world again. This was everywhere she looked.

Filaments of light stood out against the dark background, and in them she saw the light-emitting pearls moving. The pearls and fine threads gathered in clusters here and there and into larger, brighter groups that moved with their own rhythms.

Tendrils of light connected most of the groups. Some groups sat isolated and out of contact with the rest of the formation. Although there was order in the pattern, nothing was straight and orderly in it. What Aida saw looked like the roots of a tree or the tangled runners of a strawberry plant, and it all moved in organic slowness. Between the strings of light, individual pearls sat in the darkness, glistening jewels set in velvety blackness. Some moved and left spider-thread trails behind them, while others were still and dim, or perhaps they were so far away that she was unable to see if they moved.

All was in constant motion around her, like the rising and falling of swells in the ocean. The rows of pearls were still moving toward her, or perhaps she was moving toward them. As Aida watched, their light blinked out for a moment and returned. She sensed the inky black background itself was moving. It had blocked out the pearls, like a nearby hill that blocks your view of distant trees as you drive along a highway. She watched the wave roll away into the distance and saw the ripples it left in its wake. The ripples didn't make themselves known on their own but by how they reflected and distorted the light from the pearls. One of the smallest ripples was coming toward her. When it reached her, it washed over her, and she felt it carry her, ever so slightly, along with it.

The two columns of lights were very close now, and Aida saw dozens of rows in the two columns. Each row had six lights in it, three on each side, separated by a small gap, like an aisle running down the center of a church. Voices came from the two columns—not the one voice of the background but multiple voices, like a room filled with people who were talking at the same time. She couldn't understand what they were saying, so she pulled back a little and tried to listen for just one voice. With some concentration, Aida could hear, out of the garble, one voice, a little girl's.

"Combien de temps pour qu'on arrive là-bas, maman?"

A woman's voice replied, *"Continue à chercher la mer Méditerranée, mon chéri. Si tu la vois, c'est qu'on est presque arrivés."* Keep looking for the Mediterranean Sea, dear. When you see that, it won't be long.

French? That's French! Aida understood the words, but they made no sense. *What is this?* She had to get closer to see. She closed the distance between herself and the columns of pearl-like lights. Other voices—she recognized them as adult voices now—filled in the background, but she concentrated on the little girl's voice. *It's a little girl and her mother on a trip*, she realized, and with the mention of the Mediterranean Sea and the sound of the roaring engine...*they're flying!* Then she knew what she was looking at and listening to. Each of the pearls of light was a person, and they were seated on a plane in flight. It explained the pattern she was seeing and the conversations she heard but not how she was seeing it.

Where am I? When Aida looked away from the columns of pearls at the vastness that expanded before her, the sense of vertigo returned. Panic was starting to rise in her, so she turned her focus back to the plane. She could focus on that and feel grounded.

Behind the two columns of pearls, a wave was approaching. It was something like the ripples that the other wave had left but more substantial. In what seemed like a moment, the wave overtook the lights and swept through them, scattering their order and throwing them out on random paths. And then she heard screams; everyone on the plane was screaming. As she watched, most of lights faded, then disappeared into the blackness. *Something happened to the plane!*

A few pearls, less than a dozen, stayed in their rows and columns, but they were silent now. They sat, barely moving, leaving thin trails of milky-white threads behind them in straight lines. Again, from behind the plane, a wave was approaching but moving much slower than the first one.

Aida knew something had happened on the plane, and she surmised what had happened to the pearls she could no longer see. She saw the wave continue to move toward the plane and the remaining pearls.

They're not moving. They need to get out of there. They need help!

"Wake up!" she shouted at them, but they didn't move, and she knew they couldn't hear her. *I have to get in there to help them*, she realized. As she had done so many times in her emergency room rotations and residency, she completely forgot about herself and focused exclusively on the people in front of her who needed her help. With hands she didn't have, she reached out to touch them, to feel and see where the wounds were. She listened to the sounds the wounded were making, smelled the aromas emanating from the wounds or other parts of the body. She processed each of these instinctively, using the information to order her next actions.

And then Aida was standing on the wing of the plane, looking through the cavernous hole at the interior of the cabin and at a boy and a little girl seated next to a woman. The plane was on the ground, and around her were broken trees and the torn brush of the jungle. Smoke was seeping out from the plane, and heat radiated off its metal skin. *It's going to explode soon.*

The little girl in the white dress started to move. She coughed, and the boy next to her, probably her brother, reached over to see if she was okay.

"You've got to get out of here! Now!"

The boy lifted the little girl and set her down on the wing, and Aida watched the little girl while the boy helped his mother.

"I've got her. Get the other children."

Without moving or walking, Aida was on the tip of the wing, urging them all to follow her. Then she was on the ground about ten meters away from the wing, right at the edge of the jungle undergrowth. She called to them, and they came down the wing toward her. *Still too close. I've got to get them farther away.*

In a blink she was standing in the thick undergrowth. "Follow me." She waited until she heard everyone force their way through the underbrush toward her. In another blink she was standing in a clearing on top of a hill about twenty meters from the group of survivors. On the opposite side of the clearing, a cut path ran down the hill and into the thick jungle foliage.

The group arrived at the hill, and Aida was at the bottom, at the beginning of the path. They came down the hill to the path, and she stayed twenty or thirty meters ahead of them. Once the entire group was on the path, the last of the fuel in the plane caught fire and exploded, but that was expected.

Aida had no idea how she was doing what she was doing or how she had gotten there. For now, for the right now, her whole world was just about rescuing these people and leading them to a safe place. The next thing she knew, the path broke out of the jungle and ended at the side of a gravel road. She heard the group behind her on the path; they would be here in a moment or two. They would be safe here. She wondered about any injuries they might have and how she could treat them; emergency field medicine hadn't been her specialty.

They're all ambulatory. They'll mostly be frightened, banged up, and bruised, but on the whole, they'll be fine.

She waited at the side of the road to greet them. With the immediate emergency over, the 3-D image of the pearls of light in their rows and columns flashed in her mind, and she felt a tug on her focus like an elastic band pulling itself back into shape after being stretched. She blinked, and the road and the jungle and the people were gone. She looked out at the 3-D stereogram world again, and the rows and columns of lights were gone too. A short distance from her, a half dozen or so pearls had grouped together. They spiraled slowly around one another, and the whole group grew brighter. The group moved en masse in the same direction, and the white spider threads that they left behind showed the path they had traveled. The threads ran back toward her, then turned at a hard-right angle and ran to Aida's right along a different path.

She looked at the group as it continued along a straight path away from her, and ahead of the group was, well, not much. There were no lines approaching it, no hills for them to go over, no waves to wash the pearls from their course. She looked out a little farther ahead of the group and saw another group, tightly clustered and moving together. The second group moved toward hers at an angle. She saw that the paths of the two groups would cross, but at the rate they were moving, that wouldn't be for a while.

"Most likely the second group will pick up your group from the side of the road. They're probably in a bus or truck on a cross-country trip," a calm baritone voice said. "As long as they each stay on their path."

"Who's that? Who's there?" Aida searched the lights and the dark rolling waves around her for an indication of where the voice came from, but nothing caught her eye. She turned around and saw different patterns and groupings of pearls. Like before, countless groups of clusters and clusters of clusters slowly orbited around one another and left their spidery traces of filaments behind them; together they all formed a vast interconnected and seemingly endless web. In one patch, though, the pearls had ceased their dance. They all moved away from one another off onto their own paths alone. It didn't seem natural, which disturbed her.

There still was no sign of who had spoken to her. "Please, I need help. I don't understand what this place is? What's happening?"

"Acknowledging that you don't understand is the starting place of wisdom." The man was silent for a moment, and then he asked, "Do you know who you are and how you got here?"

"I'm Aida Doxiphus. I'm a professor of neurology and a medical doctor. I'm a researcher in University City. I don't know how I got here. I don't even know where or what *here* is."

"What's the last thing you remember before being here?"

"I was in my lab, calibrating new sensors in my brain-scanning device. I heard the hum of the capacitors charging, and then I woke up here." *There must've been some malfunction in the helmet. I don't know what happened.* Her analytical mind couldn't explain what had happened or what she was seeing. Nor could it explain how she had helped those people on the plane. *Did I die? Am I dead? Is this some sort of near-death experience?* She reached to check for her pulse in her carotid artery. For the first time since she had woken up, she realized she had no hands, and there was no pulse to check. She looked down to where her body should be but only saw the endless web beneath her.

"Where's my body?" she cried out. Panic built in her as she thrashed about, trying to connect with anything solid and familiar.

"I'm over here," said the voice as a pearl appeared from behind the slow-moving curtain of the dark background. "Don't panic. You're alive, and you're safe. Clearly you've never seen the world in this fashion before."

The pearl that had just appeared was brighter than the ones Aida had seen in the plane. She drew nearer to it, and as she did, the background vibration—the one enormous voice of everything— became clearer and more distinct. She felt and saw the pearl vibrate in resonance with the voice of everything, and in doing so, it amplified it.

Aida locked her focus on him, on the pearl that was talking to her. The panic retreated as she held her focus. "Who are you? Where am I?" She was all business now.

"My name is Matthew. I'm a Buddhist lama in New Mexico. As to where you are, I can tell you that you still have a body and you're still in it. I expect you're still in University City. I know you're very disoriented by what you see, but you're looking at the exact same world you've seen every day of your entire life but in an entirely different way."

13 Understanding

The gravity of Matthew's last statement sank in as Aida looked around at the otherworldly world.

"I figured out that the pearls of light are people," she said.

"For the most part, yes," Matthew corrected her. "We certainly are the most plentiful around here. Each pearl is a living consciousness, moving through its day-to-day life." He anticipated her next question. "Humans aren't the only beings that have some type of consciousness. Many living things are aware of their inner experiences to varying degrees. The better they can distinguish between their inner experience and their outer experiences of the sensory world, the more self-aware they are. The more self-aware they are, the larger and brighter their pearl of consciousness is. Most life, though, isn't capable of being aware of the inner experience. This type of life has no pearl of consciousness."

"Please go on," Aida said.

"The world as you've always known it hasn't changed—it's your perception of the world that's changed."

"Yes, you said that," she said with some frustration, "but how did it change, and why?"

"I don't know how you came to view the world in this way," Matthew said. "I wish I did. Perhaps I can best help you by explaining how I came to view the world like this."

There aren't going to be any easy answers here, Aida admitted to herself. "Sure, that would be a good starting place," she said. *Any explanation would be good.*

"I first saw the world like this eight years ago, when I was meditating on the Buddhist theory of emptiness," Matthew began. "This theory holds that nothing has an objective existence; nothing is independent and whole in and of itself. Not material things, not events or thoughts or even abstract concepts such as time. Everything exists only in relation to everything else—everything is interdependent."

"Even us?"

"According to the theory, yes."

"Descartes would disagree with that—*Cogito ergo sum*. 'I think; therefore I am.'" *That was snarky*, Aida thought, regretting her statement. "I'm sorry. That wasn't helpful. Please go on."

She's a bit frightened and starting to become defensive. "It's okay. You're very disoriented and looking for way to get a handle on your situation. I'll help you." *She needs something concrete, quickly.*

He continued, more strongly than before. "I was very deep in my meditation, not holding on to any thoughts or images or sensations. I was just letting them pass me by and not even acknowledging them. I had moved into profound awareness of my internal experience and away from the experiences of the sensory world. My mind was very quiet, more so than I'd ever achieved before; I'd finally reached a state in which the relentless momentum of my thoughts was quiescent, and I just existed. At first I just let the experience occur without trying to interpret or judge it. Then something subtle but powerful shifted, I didn't know what it was, but out of the visual darkness of my inner experience, this world we see around us now emerged."

"So your first experience of this was seeing it? I felt the vibration first," said Aida.

"That happens sometimes when a person first makes the transition."

"What does that mean?"

"We're not sure if it means anything," Matthew said, "other than your first connection with this experience happened in a tactile way rather than visually."

"So how do you know we're not dead?"

"It's a little bit embarrassing, but the first time I saw things this way, I got so excited that I let go of the discipline of my meditation and tried to grab on to the experience of this place. As soon as I did that, I lost this experience and my world was back to normal. I was sitting on my meditation cushion in the Zen Center in Chama Valley, New Mexico. The sky was growing brighter in the east, so it was just before dawn. But the unusual thing—and I only found this out later—was that it was the day after I had started my meditation. Since then I've been practicing moving back and forth between experiencing the sensory world as solid objects and independent things and experiencing it as waves—and completely interdependent things and pearls of consciousness."

"Do you have a name for this place?"

"I call it the Wave World."

Aida was silent in disbelief. Something in Matthew's description was familiar to her. She knew what it sounded like, but the scientist in her knew it wasn't possible. Still, she couldn't deny the evidence of her senses. And the way Matthew described it, it just fit. *If this is what I think it is, and it can be reproduced...I've got to tell Greg about this!* She thought about her husband, pictured his face, heard his voice, remembered the feel of his hand in hers. *Wait a minute— this isn't right.*

"I wasn't meditating when all this happened to me," she said, "and I was just thinking about my husband. Why haven't I gone back?"

For the first time, Aida heard concern in Matthew's voice. "Those are the questions we need answered. I can help you with—"

Out of nowhere, a thick line carrying two pearls came toward Aida and struck her broadside. The world tumbled around her. When it finally settled, she was looking down a street at an ambulance rushing toward her, its lights flashing and sirens blaring. Jarred by the transition, she took a few seconds to get her bearings. She smelled freshly mown grass, and the tender golden light from earlier had strengthened since she had driven through here this morning. Now it warmed the world of trees, cars, buildings, and people. Gravel crunched beneath her feet, and with that she was able to set herself firmly in the world she was familiar with. *I'm at the intersection of University Drive North and University Drive South. I'm on campus; the lab's a little way over there*, she thought, looking to her left.

The ambulance slowed as it approached the intersection and moved to make a left turn. *That ambulance is probably for me.* Aida saw the woman who was driving. She had just hit her signal to turn onto University Drive South, which was already starting to back up.

No, not that way. There's construction. For a second, Aida saw the driver look at her; with both arms, Aida pointed to the right, trying to direct the ambulance around the construction. With a slight squeal of the tires on the pavement, the ambulance lurched and made the right-hand turn onto University Drive North. *They need to put up a detour sign here or traffic will be screwed up all day.*

Aida read "Medic 82" on the back of the ambulance as it sped away on University Drive North and started to go around the corner. *Now what should I do?* She was back in the normal world; she had feet and hands again, and people could see her. *Greg's still in Chicago, but Natalia should be in class. I can go to her.*

Aida went to take a step but felt the rubber band tug on her mind again. This time she tried to resist, planting her feet firmly in the gravel. She closed her eyes and tried to hold on to the world she knew, but the rubber band only pulled harder. When the tugging stopped, she opened her eyes and saw the endless tracery of fine light filaments against a deep black background.

"What are you doing?" Matthew sounded astonished.

"I was back on campus, and there was an ambulance. I think it was there for me—for the me that's in my lab, that is. It was going to turn the wrong way, so I showed the driver the right way to go."

"That's not what I mean. I mean, how did you get there?"

"I don't know. I was talking to you. Then suddenly it felt like something hit me and everything spun, and I was on campus."

"How did you come back here?"

Aida spoke rapidly, answering the question for herself as much as for Matthew. "I tried to stay there, but I felt a tug in my head that was pulling me out. I closed my eyes and tried to hold on. Then, when I opened my eyes again, I was back here." Now it was her turn for questions. "What did you see happen?"

"An event line carrying two pearls appeared from behind a wave. All three struck you. Then a flash of light jumped from your pearl of consciousness to the other two pearls. I saw you directing traffic, and the other two pearls made a slight turn off their previous path. The flash of light jumped back from them to your pearl of consciousness, and now you're back here. I've never seen anything like this."

"You mean you can't do that?" Aida asked. "I thought you could go back and forth anytime you wanted."

"I can move my perception of the world back and forth when I'm meditating. But I can't jump from here into other people's experiences—no one can. Remember, if we try to interact with what we see here, we lose it immediately. It's like a sieve; when you put it in a sink full of water, the sieve has water in it, but when you pick it up, the water runs out. The sieve can't hold water; water can only be in the sieve." Matthew paused. "Besides that, we have a rule. We don't interact with people we see here or use our knowledge in any way to influence their choices."

"Why not?"

"For several reasons, but primarily because we choose not to interfere with others' free will and to keep this view of the world secret. I'm afraid we haven't always been successful regarding that second effort."

"I'm not sure what you mean by that," Aida said, "but keeping this view of the world secret is wrong. Humankind only advances when knowledge is shared freely."

"I understand your concerns, and believe me when I say this is a point of intense debate among us," Matthew said empathetically. "I'll be glad to discuss the issue with you at length, but first we must get you back to yourself. I don't know how you got here, I don't know how you're able to do the things you do, and I don't know why you haven't gone back to yourself. But when I said we haven't been successful in keeping this view of the world secret, I wasn't referring to you. Other people are using artificial means to gain access to this view of the world, and they're using it to their own advantage—not to help others as you are. These people have noticed your presence and your activities here, and they're looking for you. I think you may be in danger."

"How can they hurt me here?" Aida asked.

"They can't hurt you here, but right now, even though you're still in your body, in the sensory world you'll appear to be in a catatonic, unresponsive state. You're vulnerable, and if they find you, they can do whatever they want with you."

"So what do we do now?" Fear crept into her voice.

"The first choice would be to get you flipped back, but since we don't know how to do that, we'll have to protect you in the sensory world. I'll have to leave you for a while, but other monks from my order will always be watching you. I'll need help in the sensory world."

"Call it the Particle World, not the sensory world," Aida said. "It makes more sense from a quantum physics perspective, and I'll be glad to discuss that with you at length when we can. You should contact my husband, Gregorio Doxiphus, and my daughter, Natalia, too."

"I'll need some way to convince your husband to trust me. He'll have no idea who I am, and I won't be able to explain the Wave World to him."

Aida thought for a moment, then asked, "Do you speak Greek?"

14 Death in the Wave World

Aida watched Matthew's pearl as he flipped back to the Particle World. She had just told him something he should have no business knowing, something that would immediately get Greg's attention and, she hoped, engender a feeling of trust for Matthew. If it didn't get Greg to trust Matthew, at least it would get Greg thinking, *which means he'll start asking questions.* After that, everything was up to Matthew.

Matthew's pearl dimmed and became opaque while the pale, glowing filaments that emanated from the front of it increased in intensity and luminosity.

His focus shifted. He was looking out the side of his pearl when we were talking, and now it has turned and faced frontward, looking down the direction he's going. Amazing.

The filaments flowed backward over the oblong body of the pearl and neatly wove into a tight thread behind it. Aida didn't know what those filaments were or why they persisted as a trail left behind by every pearl. She would ask Matthew when he returned.

Considering Matthew's pearl, Aida wondered about her own appearance. In her mind's eye, she still pictured herself with a body, arms, hands, legs, and feet all in the right place. With a bit of mental effort, she could resolve the contradiction of knowing she had a body, but she just couldn't see it. What bothered her, though, was thinking she had no face here in the Wave World. Much of a person's identity is tied up in the appearance of his or her face, and she knew major psychological problems occur in patients who've suffered serious damage to their faces. When the mental models of patients' faces no longer match what's in the mirror, they lose their identities, their self-images.

Aida pictured her face in the mirror as she'd seen it this morning when she was getting ready.

I'm not gonna give that up. I still look the same, she reassured herself.

Matthew hadn't mentioned anything unusual about her appearance, but then again, he hadn't mentioned anything about her appearance at all, so she really didn't know what she looked like, did she?

Well, that's not a comforting thought.

She tried to calm her mind. Looking out at the wonder around her helped.

This is truly amazing, she thought, then got annoyed that she couldn't find the right words to describe what she was seeing or what it meant to be able to see it. Her annoyance got in the way of calming herself.

Just be here now. This is where you are. Let everything else go by and disappear over the waterfall. She tried to take a mindful breath in and release it slowly, but that couldn't happen without a body. This realization and the realization that she couldn't do anything about it added to her mounting frustration. It occurred to her that this is how people who survive a stroke or who lose a limb might feel. They're accustomed to having control of their body and then suddenly don't. Acceptance of their condition is always the first step toward relearning and regaining control.

At least they can feel themselves breathing. I can't even close my eyes and shut this experience off! she fumed. With effort she pushed the frustration away again. *Okay, so I can't do any of the things I usually would do to calm down. I'll just have to try to keep focused on something.*

Aida allowed her eyes to be caught by a movement that was out of step with the rest of the intricate ballet. An opaque pearl had broken off from a group of others and glided silently in her direction, its vibration out of harmony with everything else. As the distance between them closed, she could tell that the person was upset and then, in a rush of intimate sensitivity, that they were very upset but were trying to hold it together on the outside.

This isn't some random stranger. I'm feeling her emotions! The connection was deep, and Aida realized, as the distraught pearl began to orbit hers, in part she, herself, felt complete and at home.

This was her daughter.

Natalia!

The joy of being reunited with her daughter blended with the immense relief of finding something familiar. She enfolded Natalia in her love and held tightly to the lifeline that had been tossed to her.

The rest of the Wave World fell away from Aida's notice as she saw only Natalia's pearl. The sensations of holding Natalia rose up from the deep wells of her memory. Her view of Nat's pearl and the memories of Nat's warm embrace clashed in a cognitive dissonance and gave Aida a sense of being unbalanced, like when she was first learning to ride a bike as a child. She loosened her hold on her memories in order to cling more tightly to the pearl, and then the two competing visions annealed into a balanced reality.

Aida saw Natalia sitting on a footstool with her back to a window. Her head was in her hands, and she was dozing off. She went to hug her daughter, but this time she had no hands, and a quick glance down confirmed the rest of her was missing as well.

I'm not fully here. This isn't like the airplane or when I was on campus. I must be like a ghost—I'm just seeing this.

Determined to make contact, she reached out to her daughter again, only this time she imagined placing her hand on Natalia's back. In her mind, she felt the indentation between her daughter's shoulder blades, as well as the slow movement of each breath. Her back was taut and rigid, filled with the tension of a terrible day.

She's all locked up; she always carries her stress in her upper back.

Aida let her mental hand linger there and was surprised when she felt the muscles in her daughter's back give a small release.

That's it, sweetie. Relax. Breathe.

She smiled inwardly and noticed in the intense sunlight Natalia's golden-brown hair showed its red highlights. She had it pulled back in a quick ponytail and had missed several strands, which were tucked behind her ears.

The footstool Natalia was sitting on was an institutional tan color and looked like it should have a matching chair. Her messenger bag

115

was at her feet. Schoolbooks and a laptop peeked out of it. The floor was eggshell white, with flecks of blue and gray; it too looked institutional.

She's in my hospital room, next to my bed.

Out of curiosity, she wanted to see how she looked. Maybe she could even see some of the monitors, which might help her decipher what was going on.

Aida pulled back a little bit to try to take in the rest of the room but found she could only see Natalia. The scene around her daughter devolved into an indistinct white blur, as if she were looking into the room at Natalia through a pinhole. As she watched Nat, she wondered when Greg would arrive and when Matthew would speak to him. Natalia's breathing slowed, and Aida could tell she was moving into a deeper sleep.

The scene, which before had been silent, now added a soundtrack: the slow, steady beeping of the heart monitor.

My heart monitor. Thank God! This proves I'm still alive and I still have a body. Despite the distress the current situation was causing Natalia, Aida was relieved to be in the hospital and receiving proper care.

Above the steady rhythm of the monitor, she heard a gentle tapping on the doorjamb, but Natalia didn't budge. Aida sensed that another pearl had approached at an oblique angle, one that would touch her path and then move off a short distance only to return later, like a stone skipping across the surface of a pond. She took a guess as to who it might be, and then she took a gamble.

"Natalia, get up. The doctor's here," Aida said in that commanding tone all mothers have. Natalia's head snapped up out of her hands, and Aida heard the beginning of what had to be her daughter saying "Mom," but the sound was cut off just as soon as it began as the pinhole winked closed.

The transition back to the Wave World wasn't as jarring this time; perhaps she was getting used to this. As she had thought, another pearl had approached the two of them at a flat angle, touched them, and glanced off. It was now slowly paralleling the two of them a short distance away. From what Aida could see, neither her own nor Natalia's path had been drastically changed by this gentle contact with the doctor.

Fascinating. This was very different than the hard, acute angles the paths of the people on the plane took after the accident or when I helped get the survivors away from the burning wreckage. Our interactions with people change the course of their lives and our own.

It was something she had always known, but to see it played out in front of her with real people experiencing real consequences drove the point home as it never had before.

How easily we get wrapped up in our own concerns and needs, and in doing so, we forget our actions affect others, she thought. *But it isn't just the actions of people—or the interactions of pearls as they appear here—that can change the course of a person's life. Events change them too, like the accident on the airplane, and that line that hit me and took me back to campus for a moment. The lines—they're events, moving through the world—and when they wash over the pearls, the pearls can be moved.*

"Did you see into your daughter's experiences?" said an unfamiliar voice. "My name is Max. Matthew asked me to keep you company. It looked like you did, and if you accomplished it so soon, you have an incredible gift."

A semitransparent pearl was playing peekaboo with her through the dark, undulating background. "He said I wouldn't be alone. Is that you over there?" she asked.

"I'm right here," replied Max as his pearl moved into full view. "Can you see me?"

"Yes, I can see your pearl. You're not as closed off; you're almost semitransparent."

"But can you see me as you just saw your daughter? Go ahead and give it a try. Focus just on me. You're right—I'm open to your seeing me."

Aida studied Max's pearl, starting from a broad view and then diving in to smaller and smaller details. Both ends of the elongated pearl were an off-white eggshell color and completely opaque. The milky threads that came out of the front end bent around at a hard angle to flow backward over the entire body of the pearl. They were easy to see against the blackness of the background but became the sheerest of white silk, almost invisible, when she looked at the body of Max's pearl through them. Then they wove into a tight, solid rope

117

as they came together off the back of the pearl like a snail's trail, telling the story of where the pearl had been.

The edges of the pearl vibrated and, in the speed of their motion, became indistinct to Aida's eyes. The closer she looked, the less certain she was of the edge's location at any moment. Max's pearl filled her entire view now. She moved her focus away from the edge and toward the brighter center, where the surface of the pearl was more like oiled paper, diffusing and spreading the light that came from within.

"There you go. You're getting warmer now." Max's voice was distinct and close; she heard the tip of his tongue slide off his top teeth when he said "There," as though he were only an inch away and whispering into her ear. "Bring your focus in a little tighter on the light."

Based on a lifetime of experience, Aida expected she'd squint, looking straight into a light source as she was. But the light expanded and caused her no discomfort. In the middle of the light she saw a figure, a man of color seated on a cushion and dressed in a simple loose-fitting robe. His head and face were clean-shaven, but the deep creases around his eyes and mouth told his age.

"I can see you!"

"Yes, it's me. Congratulations! What you did in your few short hours here took me four years to learn. Now back out and do it again."

"How do I do that? Back out, I mean?"

"Just let go a little bit. You might try looking away."

When Aida looked off to one side, the image of Max, in his robe, on his cushion, vanished.

"Oh! That was different. I just jumped right out. It wasn't like the long dive in when I was focusing on you the first time." Feeling empowered, she set herself to trying again, exhilarated at the sense of control.

"It always takes longer to find something when you don't know what you're looking for," Max said. "It'll be faster the more you practice."

This time Aida went straight to the center of Max's pearl and let the light block out everything else. She reached in, and there he was, sitting on the cushion, just as before. Without letting go, she tried to zoom out to see more of the room he was in, but again the edges of the pinhole got in the way and blocked her view.

"Why can't I see more of where you are? I can see you clearly, but only a little bit of your surroundings."

"In order to see the physical, me, as you are doing right now, your focus is so narrowed that you can see only me. There simply isn't room to see much of anything else." Max's explanation was gentle, as if to a novitiate. "Your reality is greatly influenced by what you choose to focus on, and the purpose of all types of meditation is to learn to control and direct your focus. You must be a long-time practitioner to have come so far so quickly."

"Actually"—the excitement drained from her voice as she spoke—"I'm not meditating, and I wasn't meditating when I came here. I practice mindful breathing when I do my yoga and while working on my research. What you taught me just now…it's the first time I've felt like I've had some control since I got here," she said, deciding to feel better about where she was.

"Matthew told me your situation was…different. I now see why he said that. You're having a remarkable experience, Dr. Doxiphus. You should consider that perhaps there's a reason for it."

Missing his point entirely, she replied, "There's always a reason; there's always a causal event."

Max was silent for a moment. "Aida," he suddenly said, "you need to let go. Someone's coming to you and your daughter."

Excited, Aida looked away from Max, exchanging her laser-focused view of him for a floodlight view of the Wave World, hoping the new arrival was Greg. Natalia was still orbiting and had been for some time; her filament trail had formed a spiral around Aida's perfectly straight line, both paths showing their immediate past. Another pearl was coming straight at her; it would hit her broadside when it got there. Aida focused on it, trying to peer inside, anticipating seeing Greg, but was disappointed when she was stopped cold; the eggshell exterior of the pearl was an impenetrable wall. She didn't feel any connection with this pearl. He or she was a stranger.

Hmm, not Greg. Well, I can't see who you are, but I can see where you came from.

Aida followed the approaching pearl's trail and saw that it continued straight back for short distance to where it had been entangled with a second trail. She followed the path of the second trail forward from the knot and caught a glimpse of the second pearl just before a black wave of the background obscured it.

The two of them talked or interacted somehow. The second one deflected this approaching pearl's path toward me, then hid itself.

The other pearl had reached her now and was slowly orbiting just like Nat had but on the opposite side, always keeping Aida between them. Now that it was closer, Aida tried to peer inside again. The rigid shell proved to be a thin veneer, but underneath she met a dense white fog that obscured her vision just as effectively as the outer shell had earlier. She pressed against it but couldn't make any further headway. After pulling back out, Aida realized the encounter had left her with the impression that this was a woman who was there to get something from her—she was in a hurry and was anxious. She definitely wasn't there to help Aida. Matthew's warning came back to her: in the Particle World she was in a catatonic state and vulnerable; people could do anything they wanted to her. She pictured herself in a hospital bed, powerless to defend herself against this person.

This isn't right. She shouldn't be here. What's she doing to me?

"Get away from me! Don't touch me!" Aida screamed in impotence at the stranger. "Nat, stop her!" she said, reaching out to her daughter. Nat's pearl sped up in its orbit, vibrating in anger, trying to catch up to the stranger, only to be outmaneuvered. In a move Aida had never seen before, Nat broke from her orbit and leapt directly between Aida and the stranger, her fury palpable. Aida loved her daughter for it, but seeing Nat endangered went against the core of Aida's being.

Oh, God! No! No! Nat's protecting me with her body!

"Nat, get out of here!" But Natalia's pearl didn't budge; it was glued to Aida and followed her straight along. After an eternal moment of panic later, the woman's pearl left the two of them with a hard ninety-degree turn and disappeared into the rolling black waves. Aida felt Natalia's adamant resolution soften as the woman moved away. It was replaced with the nauseated shakes of an adrenaline letdown.

She had been so focused on her daughter and the woman that she didn't notice another pearl that had been carried to them on the crest of an event wave; it moved along with them. Nat's steady spiral around Aida slowed and changed into more of a straight line that paralleled her own, the better to interact with this new pearl.

As Aida watched, Natalia's violent vibrations settled down. A quick check told Aida this wasn't Greg, though it was a male, and he was clearly having a calming effect on her daughter. She tightened her focus on him and, in a camera-shutter click of an instant, she caught the image of an anxious young man in a medic's uniform. *Why would a medic...* she stopped in midthought. *Ah, this is probably the man who worked on me and brought me in, but why did he come back?*

As the three of them moved along together, Aida found no answer to her question, but at least there was a certain peace and balance between Natalia and the medic that she found comforting.

I'll have to keep an eye on this one; he seems to be good for Natalia.

Aida turned her gaze back to the webs of consciousness. *The most distant ones are like stars*, she thought, except that in an hour's time, real stars would have moved against the dark background, and these had been fixed in place since she first had seen them. She noticed the larger groupings of pearlescent light had shifted their positions against those distant stars; the change in position was most likely from her own motion. From this, Aida reasoned that parallax still applied in this view of the world, and that was comforting too. *The laws of physics* are *universal!*

Almost imperceptibly, the stars in the distance sank below the triad of herself, Natalia, and the medic as she watched in surprise.

What in the world?

Her view of the distant stars pitched at hard angles up and down while Nat and the medic remained steady with her. A powerful event wave was passing through the three of them, making them bob like corks on an ocean breaker.

The source of the disturbance was a pearl rushing toward them, causing the lightless background to pile up in front of it like the bow wave off an enormous ship. The pearl stopped right on top of them, and the wave dissipated as it rolled away. Natalia moved straight toward the new pearl, coming so close that they almost touched. The two of them were so similar yet different, Aida observed; their identical vibration indicated the link.

Oh, thank God! Greg's here!

Both Greg and Natalia orbited her. As they did, she felt herself resonate in the common familial vibration they shared, and the sharing gave her strength.

"Aida," Max said, "there are some things I have to go do. You'll be safe with your family. I'll be back soon, and one of us will always be watching."

"Have you heard anything from Matthew yet? He left to go speak to my husband."

"That's one of the things I want to check on. I know he's on his way to you. It's more likely you'll see him before he contacts us."

"Thank you, Max. Thank you for being so helpful."

"It's all right. I'm glad to do it, and it was a pleasure to meet you. I'll be right back," he said as she watched his pearl turn hard opaque.

Aida gave an inward smile and looked at her husband and daughter as their two beautiful pearls orbited her, their trails extending and twisting out behind them in a graceful illustration of DNA's double helix. Her thoughts had slowed down from their agitated racing, and she was calm now. The medic had left—at least he wasn't visible to her anymore. In any case, she was grateful for the privacy she knew Greg and Natalia would need right now. Families need time to be alone together and to just be, especially when the times are trying. As the three of them paced out some measure of time together, their individual coronas grew brighter and larger until the intervening space seemed to glow itself.

This is new. But we've always drawn strength from being together. It makes sense.

The stabilizing and nurturing effects of loving relationships was something that everyone knew about on some level and could experience every day in their lives if they would just see them. The presence of larger clusters of pearls and how they came together and stayed together made sense now. It wasn't just that they interacted with one another; it was their personal relationships with one another that strengthened and supported them and bound them together.

It must be terrible when someone turns in on themselves and away from relationships, Aida thought.

Natalia's orbit expanded like a spring uncoiling, then straightened out.

She's going to go do something now that Greg's here.

Her daughter made soft, gentle turns and settled on the path that took her a short distance away from her and her husband. Aida looked ahead of Natalia's pearl to see where her daughter's path was heading; however, there was nothing but empty space in front of her. A little farther out from Natalia, but basically in the same neighborhood, someone was tracing out a twisted, misshapen path full of jagged angles and tight corkscrews. As crooked as the path was, the person was heading in Natalia's general direction. Then a third pearl appeared, its path relatively straight and heading in Natalia's direction.

The three of them are going to meet up pretty soon. This is getting to be a habit, she thought as she tried to see who was making the crooked path.

When her focus touched the pearl, a painful numbing sensation shot through her, like a shock from an electrical socket. Two separate sets of vibrations clashed against each other in shearing disharmony in the pearl. Aida recoiled from the shock, revolted by the man's inner experience.

That's Bill Fahy! How can he live with himself? As she felt the uneasiness from their contact fade, it was replaced with pity and apprehension. *Bill's truly unstable, and he was the last one I was with.*

It was Bill! He sent me here; he did something in the setup of the calibration run. I remember hearing the capacitors charge right before the run would have started, and he's heading right toward Natalia.

The third pearl, the one on the relatively straight path, met up with Natalia first. She couldn't tell what they were doing, nor could she reach her daughter, but Natalia wasn't alone. Bill joined up with the two of them, and he interacted with the third pearl.

Aida saw his vibrations shift. *He's getting angry, defensive.*

Natalia was quiet, intently focused on something, not really noticing the other two. Her pearl gave a deep shudder, and then Aida felt suspicion and anger rise in her daughter. Pulsating with anger, Natalia's pearl moved closer to the other two, and Bill responded in kind.

They're arguing. Nat found out something; she's confronting Bill.

The third pearl wedged the two of them apart, and they both separated like boxers at the end of a round. Natalia became preoccupied again but was still clearly agitated. Bill's pearl started to move off, having cut a hard angle away from Natalia and the third pearl, the distance increasing with every passing moment. Black waves lumbered across Aida's view of Bill, and soon he was lost into the background.

Meanwhile, Natalia practically had exploded. She was interacting with the third pearl, and Aida felt her daughter's desperation, then frustration. Natalia and the third pearl remained together, and the third pearl became agitated as well. Soon, three other pearls joined them. Aida reached out and saw one was University City police and the other two were university security. She focused on her daughter, hoping to hear something of what her daughter heard, but Natalia was too closed off, too focused on the Particle World. Aida could only guess what they were talking about.

Bill...that son of a bitch. What did he do? He put me in the hospital, my family through hell, and he used the new QUESAMs to do it—that's what he did. But why?

The small group broke up, and Natalia returned to the hospital room to resume her patient orbit around Aida with Greg. It was easy enough to picture what was going on in the room, and it made Aida's heart ache for her family.

Heaven help Bill Fahey if I ever see him again.

"It's never good to wish harm to another," Max called to her, announcing his presence. "It diminishes you." Control and caution laced his voice. Aida was so angry with Bill for putting her and her family in this situation that she missed Max's return.

"Turning the other cheek can be difficult," Aida said. "Look at what he's done. It's really hard to feel loving-kindness toward him."

"I know," Max replied. "I wrestle with my own issues too, but wishing someone else harm puts you out of tune with the background harmonies of the universe. When you do that, you're thinking about

124

yourself and the harm you've received. It's the opposite of compassion."

"I can't be compassionate toward Bill right now!" Aida's voice hardened.

"When someone thinks about themselves too much," Max said, "when they get wrapped up in their pain or ruminate on how they think they've been harmed by the world, they send themselves down a path like the one Mr. Fahy is on—crooked, jagged, and warped. It's one of the paths to misery," he added, then hesitated. "Look at what you know about him. Look at him now. I'm sorry to say he's going to come to an early end."

That caught Aida's attention.

Bill's pearl surfaced from the inky background; it was now moving in a tight spiral, like Natalia's and Greg's were around Aida. Bill, however, was orbiting no one. He was on a downward trajectory, turning faster and faster, like water circling the drain. Aida saw nothing ahead of him except a narrow furrow between two hills. At its bottom, the two sides of the furrow folded together in a curved line, as though they were two parts of a piece of cloth.

"Are you saying he's dying? I saw him just a little bit ago, and he looked perfectly healthy," Aida said.

"You're not perceiving the passage of time normally right now," Max replied. "The regular markers you use to judge the passing of time are missing. You've been here a day and a half. It's now evening, the day after you collapsed in the lab."

His statement stunned her. *How could so much time have passed? It would only have taken Greg a few hours to get back to University City, and he only just got here.*

"But Bill's still healthy; he's a young man," she insisted.

"The pattern he's in now, that downward spiral...that's the pattern of a person who's doing something destructive to themselves. It could be some sort of addiction or abusive relationship that they're in, or they're focusing only on themselves and they have no real relationships in their lives—no one to care for or to care for them. People can go on in those types of patterns for years and years, unhealthy as they are. I would guess Bill has been doing this for very long time. But yes, unless something drastic happens right now to

125

change his path, he's going to enter that fold that's straight ahead of him."

"I don't understand. I've seen people disappear behind these waves of blackness, and they come back out just fine," Aida protested. She didn't want Bill to die; she only wanted him to face justice, and Max was so complacent about what he had said. The subconscious emotions that remained from watching her mother die, the ones that never truly stopped weighing on Aida and had changed her as a person, stirred again.

"You're a medical doctor, Aida. You've seen people die; you've just never seen it from this point of view. When a pearl enters a fold, when it goes through it, that's what death looks like here. The light of the pearl disappears from our view, never to reappear."

"You can see everything else," she questioned. "Can't you see what happens beyond the fold?"

"No, I can't. No one can—at least that we know of. Sometimes I see people who approach a fold and run even with it, and then they dip in and come back out. I think those people are having near-death experiences. Remember, we're still alive and viewing the exact same world. Just as you can't see what happens after someone in the— what did you to call it?—the Particle World, the normal world, dies, you can't see it here."

Bill's pearl continued on and had passed the peaks on either side as he descended straight into the valley between them.

"You've got to do something! You can't just let him die like this," the doctor in her railed.

Unmoved, Max replied, "One of the ways we protect this view of the world is by never taking action on what we see and learn here. Besides, he's in Nebraska with you, more than a thousand miles away from me—there's nothing we can do. He chose his path, Aida. He made his own pattern of life."

Aida tried to reach out to Bill, to warn him, but he was beyond her grasp. Her mind raced, searching for some way to turn him away from the inevitable. He was close now, almost in the fold. All she could do was wait and watch. She was just as helpless here as she was lying in the hospital bed. She hated it; she would have cried if she could, but here in the Wave World, even that comfort was denied her.

"I know that, to your way of thinking, death is something to fight against," Max said. "I also know you believe in eternity and you have faith. Do you believe Bill's death is the end of his consciousness?"

Bill's pearl flared as it made a final turn, slipped between the edges of the fold, then vanished.

The practical, grounded, evidence-demanding scientist in Aida struggled against a faith that had been ingrained in her childhood. All she could choke out was a fragile and painful "I don't know."

15 Untangling the Knot

"It's practically impossible to rescue someone from themselves. There's nothing you could've done," Max said tenderly.

"I think I could've done something!" Aida protested. "I worked with him every day. I could've recognized the path he was on; I could've found out more about him. I should've talked to him more. If he was fighting some kind of addiction, I could've ordered drug tests through the university. I was his supervisor, you know."

Compassion for oneself is difficult to learn, Max thought.

"Maybe you could have, and maybe those things would've helped, but it's just as likely they would've driven him away and he would have died sooner." Max let those words hang in the silence before he continued. "I think you suspected he was a troubled soul, yet you kept him employed, handling things that are very sensitive and important to you. You did help him, Aida; you certainly gave him the opportunity to get on a different path."

That struck a chord in her, quieting her inner judge.

"How'd it happen? How'd he die?"

"I don't know for certain. I think it was an act of violence. It was fast…I can say that."

Aida watched the fold that Bill had disappeared into, hoping he would reappear. The distinctness of the dark crease that had swallowed him was starting to soften and would soon be lost as the furrow undulated and morphed into a shallow depression. Only Bill's trail remained. It stopped at the fold, a ghoulish pale finger pointing to his end. It would be the only reminder of the person and a poor tombstone here in the Wave World. The trail, which earlier had been bright and strong, was diminishing, fading until it was the finest strand, barely visible against the background. It didn't disappear, though, and Aida realized the evidence of where Bill had been was still there. The idea crowded out her reaction to his death.

"Max, what can you tell me about those lines, those trails everyone leaves behind them? They come off the front of a pearl, then flow back over it and weave into a thread."

"That's the path we've taken in life," he answered, stating the obvious, because he hadn't quite understood what she was asking.

"Yes, I know that, but what are they? They don't start off as a thread."

"Oh, I see. Look out just in front of a pearl. Is anything there?" The teacher was speaking again.

"No, there's nothing there." *Just answer the question.*

"There's a common misconception that people follow a predefined path in their lives," Max said, "and while they might emulate behaviors they've seen before or think they should emulate, in actuality there's no path in front of them. It's much more accurate to say that people imagine a path and then choose to follow it. At least that's true for anyone who isn't dependent on another for his or her care.

"Those white wispy things you see coming out of the front of the pearl, those are our decisions, our choices, our expression of free will. Matthew calls them decision fibers. They're the decisions we make, and they determine the way we go and create our path. They come out from the front of a pearl because decisions start as thoughts, and it takes a moment for us to turn them into actions. As we turn our decisions into actions, the decision fibers weave themselves together into the thread, the trail we leave behind."

"How far back can you follow one? I want to see what Bill was doing and who he was talking to. Maybe I can figure out why this happened," Aida reasoned.

"As far as you can see, really, but you'll only see the effects that his actions and passing events had on his path. You can't see what he was doing or hear what was said. It's not like rewinding a movie to watch a part you missed."

129

Aida focused tightly on the remains of Bill's life and traced backward. The pale, thin line was now indistinct against the background, and she had to take her time so as not to lose it.

This is like tracing a single vein in a leaf from the tip back to the branch, she thought.

From the spiral immediately above the fold, the trail meandered, sometimes straight, sometimes curving, up away from the dark background waves. "What's the time scale? I mean, how much distance of the thread equals a certain amount of time, like an hour or day?"

"It doesn't work like that here," Max said. "There's no way to tell how much time has passed."

Aida kept walking Bill's path backward. "Why not?"

"Like I said earlier, you don't have any of the standard markers that are used to judge the passing of time. I think it's cruel in a way. There are no clocks, no sunrise or sunset; your body doesn't tell you you're hungry or tired. You don't even have the most basic things to rely on—no breath, no heartbeat, no eyes to blink. When you think about it, you don't even have the urge to go to the bathroom."

"But that's for me—that's my own personal perception of time," Aida said. "I'm looking at how long his path is."

"That's the other half of it and exactly my point! Everyone's perception of time is relative to them. When you look at someone's thread, you see the effects of the decisions they've made and how other outside events have influenced them. You can't tell how much time might have passed between those things for someone else."

"I get your point." Aida heaved a mental sigh and wished she could feel it, needing the release it brought. *I never thought I would miss a simple thing like that.* "But I can see when Bill interacted with others. Maybe they're still around and I can learn something from them."

"We can do that," Max agreed. "I'll help you. I've got a different angle on his thread than you do."

Aida hadn't thought of that yet, and it made sense for them to work together. Two observers, each at different angles, would make better progress tracing the one thread. She followed the lab technician's thread back to the point where she and Max had started talking. Just ahead, it disappeared behind a hill.

"Okay, I lose his thread as it goes behind this lump here. Can you see it?" she asked.

"Yes, I have it. It keeps going; I have it about halfway behind that environment wave. It's still twisting and turning and...there it crosses and interacts with another line. Then he keeps going and comes out from behind the wave, right by that sharp corner. Do you see it?"

"Yes, I see him there. Before that is the tangle when he and Natalia and the security guard got into it. I have a good idea what happened at that point. Go behind the wave and follow the path that crossed his," Aida said, determined to find out who it was.

"Sure. That path is bright and strong. It comes out just at the top of the wave and curves off to your left. It's a smooth curve, no hairpin turns in it."

"I see it!" Aida concentrated on the bright, strong line, her focus racing forward, intent on finding this person and the next bit of data. Compared to the line that was the remnants of Bill's life, this line was remarkable in terms of its vividness and weight. It continued in plain view, not ducking behind any hills, slicing out languid curves like those a snake might leave in the sand. The vivid line intercepted another; the two lines then crossed and ran parallel to each other for a short distance before separating. Aida ignored this second line, which was paler and thinner than the one she was tracking, and continued on her hunt. The curving trail had flattened out into a straight line.

I must be getting close. This can't go on much farther. She picked up the pace, but the line eventually disappeared behind the oily black waves of the background.

"Max, I lost it just after it crossed over that other person's line and ran perfectly straight. Can you see it?"

He took a moment to respond. "No, I lost it as well. Wait...let me look again...no, I can't follow it. That's unusual."

"What's unusual? Lines go behind hills all over the place here," Aida said.

"The way it disappeared is unusual," he said, puzzled. "I'll worry about this line going forward. You should trace it back to where it ran parallel with that other line, then go forward on the second one."

131

Aida traced backward and found the segment where the two lines ran parallel to each other. She then went forward, tracking the pale, thin path. It went straight for a little bit, turned at a sharp angle and continued along straight and true, as if the person had a specific destination in mind. Aida's focus sprinted forward down the arrow-straight path and followed it behind a mound that would have blocked her view if she hadn't been moving herself and at a different angle now. The path pulled up hard, and then the line shifted into the erratic pattern of the EKG of a fibrillating heart, then went straight again. What she saw shocked her. Where the line had gone erratic, it had crossed over what was now a ghost thread in the background. A thread that, when it emerged from behind the hill, turned into a tight corkscrew and ended, pointing to an almost imperceptible fold. It was Bill's spiraling death thread.

"Max! This person might have been involved with Bill's death. They were definitely together right before he died." Aida followed the pale, thin line past the scene of the death and caught up to the person's pearl itself, interacting with others in a tight, tangled knot. Looking into the pearl, she glimpsed a man in a leather biker vest and jeans. "Max, I need you to come look at this," she called. "This one's a man in a biker vest, and he's still here."

"Hang on. I found this guy's thread again; he's either very lucky or he's getting help. I had a hard time finding him."

"How do know it's a man?"

"You're right—I don't know that it's a man. Sorry…just a force of habit," the monk responded, sounding slightly embarrassed. "I'm following the line, and it looks like the person headed toward where you're looking, near Bill's death…yep, there he is. I see him, and it's definitely a him; he's nearby."

"Where? Which one?" The single-minded scientist wasn't about to let up. The cluster of pearls in Aida's focus had become even more entangled, spinning and dancing around one another, their threads crisscrossing and crossing again until the entire thing looked like a densely packed cloud of fireflies, each trying to signal to one another at the same time.

"Where are you looking?" Max asked.

"At this tangle of people."

"No, he's not in the middle of that. He's on the periphery, observing the action but not getting too involved. Here, this is gonna feel a little funny. I'm going to help you focus your attention on him."

She felt, *actually felt*, her focus being physically moved, as if a hand were turning her head. The knot and the rest of the Wave World went slightly out of focus and left a single pearl in excruciating clarity.

The monk's voice was almost inside her head; that's how close his presence was. "That's your guy. He most likely is one of the major players in all these recent events. I mean, regarding what happened to you and your lab tech."

Aida had already reached this conclusion but wanted to hear Max's thoughts as well. "I agree, but why do you think so?"

"He and Bill interacted right after your daughter had her run-in with Bill. We know that set Bill on a course to die. Then he talked to the biker, and the biker interacted with Bill, wherever they were, right before Bill died. Then this guy showed up again. What disturbs me the most is the way he disappeared before." Now Max sounded troubled. "We use event lines and environmental waves to avoid being seen here in the Wave World by other observers. It takes an experienced practitioner to use all the waves and lines and hills and valleys to their advantage, and we know what it looks like when someone does it. This man disappeared at the conjunction of an event line and two background waves. It was very neatly done, so either he's here observing us, or someone told him exactly where to be and when to be there in order to disappear from view. No matter how you look at it, he's a danger to you and anyone who's near you."

God help me find a way to protect Natalia and Greg. "So who is he?" *I've got to see him.*

Anxiety made Aida cautious and warned her against diving in hard. *This man—whoever he is—set up Bill's death...murder...and he's probably behind what Bill did to me and what that woman was going to do to me in the hospital room.* With a feather-light touch, she narrowed in on his pearl. It grew larger until it was the only thing she could see.

Resistance.

She pushed a little harder and found the outer shell of his pearl was as hard as rock.

"He's been trained, Aida. He knows how to block someone who's trying to look at him. Plus, he's focused on the Particle World now; I doubt you could see him even if you knocked with a jackhammer."

That just infuriated her. *This bastard's behind everything that's going on—I will see his face!*

Although Aida pushed hard, the wall didn't yield. *Maybe I need a running start.* She backed off so the Wave World filled her view but kept his pearl as the bull's-eye. She then steeled herself and, with single-minded purpose, drove at the shell of his pearl as fast and hard as she could. The impact was like a battering ram against the side of a mountain—it stunned her, but it dented the mountain too, and for the instant of the impact, she saw him. He was a tall, hulking man with short-cut, military-style red hair and a pallid complexion. He had ice-blue eyes set in a solid, round head and wore a police officer's uniform. Beneath his feet, she saw blacktop and the white painted stripe of a parking lot.

As she rebounded, her view snapped back to the Wave World.

Gotcha, you son of a bitch!

She kept watching his pearl, now that she was able to pick it out. What surprised her was that he didn't seem that different from the others. His pearl vibrated like the others; his path didn't show any of the crookedness Bill's had, and she thought the pearl of someone who was a murderer, or who was at least behind all this, would be different.

"I see him, Max. He seems so normal. I expected something different from someone like him. He's done such horrible things," Aida said, bewildered.

Max replied without any judgment in his voice. "You'd think so, you know. But he doesn't see that what he's doing is wrong, and if someone doesn't believe they're doing harm, they don't act like it. I guess they don't really see themselves as being a bad person. He probably thinks he's serving some higher purpose or he's just doing his job. People justify their behavior in all sorts of ways."

"That's just not right. There should be something different," her insulted sense of fairness insisted.

134

"There is something that's different, but it's very subtle, and you might not be able to sense it yet. The background vibrations of the universe don't resonate through this man. His vibrations are a lot like those of most people you meet. They're so wrapped up in themselves and the day-to-day world that they don't have a sense of larger realities and ultimate truths. You've seen so many of them that you start to think it's normal and therefore right."

The cop's pearl lurked around the tight swarm, only interacting where it had to. Aida wondered if he knew she was watching him. She hoped so; she wanted him to feel her anger and didn't care that others were watching her.

Soon the swarm of pearls began to break up, and the cop drifted farther out—any farther and he would be disengaged from the group. Aida relaxed her focus, letting it broaden. She wanted to see where this guy went if he took off.

Another pearl was approaching him. Reaching out to touch it, Aida found it familiar. It was the medic. Resting her focus on him like a gentle hand on his shoulder, she listened. She got much more information from this encounter than from their prior one at the hospital. His name was John, and he was genuinely concerned about Bill and what Bill's death might mean for Aida and her family. John's pearl mingled with the cop's, and though John was focused on the Particle World, she caught snippets of their conversation.

"Turned out to be Dr. Aida Doxiphus, the director of the lab, and this guy's her lab tech," John said.

"Did he say what he was afraid of?' Another voice she assumed to be the cop's, with a slight New England accent, replied.

John again. "No, he didn't say…"—muffled noise—"…more going on, —more muffled noise—whole situation"

Though she was only catching snippets, Aida started to get concerned.

What's he telling the cop? She drew closer, and the next bit of the conversation came through clearly.

"It just didn't make sense," John said. "The way we found Dr. Doxiphus, with her arms and legs straight and at her sides, like she had just lain down. And the timing of his story didn't add up. He said he called 911 at 8:15, but we didn't get toned out till 8:25, and 911 never takes more than a minute to roll a medic unit."

Cop: "So you think he was involved somehow?"

John: "I don't see how."

Cop: "Have you told anyone else this?"

"John, no! Stop!" Aida cried out, scared at what the medic might give away. His revelations were putting both her family and him in greater danger.

John: "Yeah, I did, at the end of my shift yesterday. I was at University Hospital, and I needed to report this to the doctors and the family."

This was too much for Aida; John wasn't listening to her. She had to do something now to warn off the medic. Willing herself into the scene, she imagined standing there with them, feeling the solid ground beneath her feet, smelling the evening air, and hearing the summer cicadas' scratching chitter rise and fall, but it didn't work; there was no one there who was open to seeing her. She changed her focus, which had been resting lightly on John, to a sharp point, trying to bore a hole into the medic's shoulder to make him understand.

John: "What the…? Felt like someone pinched me. Must be some damn big mosquito."

The cop's pearl ceased vibrating for a moment, its eggshell color turning to slate gray. Aida touched it; at least she thought she did, because though it was visible, she felt nothing.

"He's on guard now, Aida. He definitely has received some training," Max said, "C'mon now. Let go. You're not helping matters."

"But we've got him now. We can watch him and see where he goes." She wasn't going to give him up.

"He's not gonna go anywhere, not while you're in contact with him, so we can't learn anything. Besides, you're showing yourself. They can see you!"

"What?"

"There are observers watching him. You're in contact with him, so they can see you too! And me as well!" Without warning, Max wrenched Aida's focus away from the cop's pearl.

She was livid. "Damn it, Max!"

"I'm sorry, but I have to protect us."

"Well, I have to protect my family and myself by getting this guy. Think about it, Max. If we can stop him, won't you and I be better protected too?"

***

Aida watched the cop's pearl. She had won that part of the argument after agreeing not to contact him any further. Max had flipped back to the Particle World; he said he had to discuss this turn of events with the other monks.

The cop was interacting with another pearl. He came back to John, and then the two broke off their conversation. The longer Aida focused on the medic, the better she could sense his emotional state. She knew John had been disturbed by his encounter with the cop and Bill, and he was concerned for her and her family, especially Nat.

I'll keep an eye on you, John, she promised as she watched him leave.

That left her with the cop. She kept her distance but never let him out of her sight. Within what felt like moments after John had left the scene, the cop departed as well. Tracing out a slightly different path than John had, the officer slid along the environment waves like a sailboat on a rolling sea. It looked to Aida like he was using the waves to help him move, allowing them to push him along. He paused in a trough between two waves, just sitting there while an event line in a wave came up behind him. He then accelerated and was pacing the wave; it rose up, lifting him along with it. He rode down the far side like an expert surfer, and then he was gone. Aida searched the spot where she thought he would emerge. Max had said the cop had disappeared before, like a slippery eel into its darkened hole. It appeared he had done so again.

John had performed no such vanishing act. He was plainly visible and moving toward Aida, Greg, and Nat.

He's a good man, Aida thought. *I'm glad he's with us. I wish he hadn't been pulled into this mess.*

After a quick check on Greg and Nat, she returned her attention to John. His pearl was perched on the crest of a wave, looking out over a trough. As the wave beneath him moved on, he began to drop into the valley that lay before the next wave.

Aida's gaze froze in shock. At the bottom of the hill John was sliding down was a deep fold, a death fold, and he was heading straight for it. Aida called, "Max! Someone help!" But no one answered. John was right on top of the death fold.

I'm not going to let this happen to him! She reached out to John and easily touched his mind, which allowed her to engage her senses in his reality and—

Blinding headlights clawed at her eyes from the darkness as she inhaled cool night air tinged with the smell of diesel exhaust. The buzzing drone of a streetlight came from above her to the right, its light bathing the vehicle and the intersection in an amber glow. John sat in the cab of the ambulance, not twelve feet in front of her. They saw each other. She had known what to expect. John, on the other hand, wore a stunned expression. On the driver's side of the ambulance, a figure casually walked to the window and raised its right arm; the gun it held was silhouetted black against the streetlight.

"John, get down!" When Aida motioned down and to the left with both arms, John got the message. He threw himself onto the passenger seat just as the figure fired a shot that shattered the driver's-side window.

"Go!" she shouted.

Two more staccato pops split the night air as the muzzle flash burst into the cabin. A fraction of a second later, John slammed his foot on the gas. Medic 82 jumped toward her as the engine roared. As it covered the distance between them, her mind did a quick calculation, and she knew she couldn't get clear in time. She spun and was leaning away as the ambulance struck her right hip and leg and passed cleanly through her. She stood there, on both legs, the brick cobblestones scraping underneath her feet, shocked that she was still in one piece. The last things she saw were the brake lights of the ambulance as it screeched to a halt.

Aida's focus snapped back to the Wave World. John's pearl had turned at a sharp angle and now was heading straight up, away from the fold.

Yes! He's safe!

She watched John for a little while longer. He had turned again and was heading straight for her. Aida was elated to have simultaneously saved his life and ruined what she thought was the cop's plan. Though she was unable to prove it, she was sure the cop had orchestrated this incident. And if she was able to stop this one, she could stop others as well. Her determination grew, feeding on this new realization.

Where is he now? she wondered, scanning the surrounding area for him, wishing Max were here to help.

Not finding the cop, she turned back to Greg and Natalia and found her relief short-lived. They were traveling in tight circles around her, their paths weaving a protective mesh. On the other side of the web, the slate-gray pearl of the cop maneuvered up to them. She easily touched her husband's mind; he already was half-asleep.

Alarmed, Aida called out, "Greg!" Her husband became fully alert, so she had to work harder to keep in contact with him. As before with John, she fine-tuned her contact with her husband and was able to hear what was going on. The cop was in the room, and Greg was on the phone talking to John.

John: "Good. Do it. Someone just tried to kill me, so it stands to reason that the three of you are in danger too."

Greg: "Yes, I see…I think you're right. Thank you. Hang on."

Greg hesitated, trying to process what the medic had just told him. He was a brilliant man who would do anything to protect his family, but he wasn't always the best in confrontational situations like this. Aida had to help him and Nat.

Cop: "What's going on here, Doctor?" His New England accent was laced with cold suspicion.

Aida touched Natalia as well and inserted her focus into the hospital room.

As she stood in semidarkness, her view of the room was framed by what had to be the open bathroom door. The cop's back was to her. Greg was working his poker face as best as he could when Nat drew in a sharp breath of surprise. Greg looked between the hospital bed and past the cop to her in the bathroom.

Locking eyes with Greg, she mouthed, *Greg! Grab Nat and get out! He's dangerous*, while pointing repeatedly at the cop. The cop's meaty hand slid away from what she assumed was a notepad, down toward his belt; everyone was silent. The silence, but not the tension, was broken by the loud squawk of the cop's radio.

"Unit 21 to KEA571. I'm at University Hospital ER in response to shots fired on an ambulance. Medic 82 is here. Only minor injuries, though the medic is a little shaken. Requesting additional units, CSI and shift commander on-site. Over."

Although the back of the cop's head didn't move as he stared at Greg, his hand keyed the radio microphone.

"Unit 54, KEA571. I'm at the hospital now. I'll meet unit 21 and the ambulance downstairs."

The startled sound in his voice was the best thing she had heard in a very long time.

Things not going according to plan, asshole?

The rubber band tugged on her, pulling her back to the Wave World. This time she didn't fight it.

***

The cop left. From the radio call, she knew John was at the emergency room entrance with other officers and would be safe. She spotted John's pearl close by and saw the cop hadn't gone anywhere near John, which gave her no small amount of satisfaction. Aida watched as he let the waves and event lines push him away, and then he slipped out of view.

Greg and Nat were agitated, and it was a little while before John was able to join them. Suspecting what they would be talking about, Aida reached out to Greg, but this time she was slow and lethargic. She couldn't contact him. So she settled back, content with what she had done. Max's pearl was close by and in view; it grew brighter as he flipped his focus from the Particle World to the Wave World.

"You'll need to rest before you can do anything like that again," Max said with a mix of admiration and exasperation. "That was incredible…and an incredible risk. You saved John's life, and then he saved you and your family."

"How'd you see that?"

"I didn't," Max said, "but another monk was watching. She told me. And before you ask, she's new to this. She heard you call for help, but she can't reach out to others yet or talk as we do."

"Well, I think I handled things pretty well on my own."

"Yes, you did. There's a lot I'd like to know, but now's not the time. I just spoke to Matthew; he's almost at the hospital, so we have to get ready to get you out of there."

"What do we need to do?" Aida asked.

"Hide you and your family from those who are watching. It'll be tricky, but there's an opportunity coming up."

"John too. He comes too," she said.

"He's already part of the plan. Don't worry. He'll come too. Now here's what's going to happen…"

16 Shell Game

"Ommmmmmmmmmmmm," Aida voiced, and as she did, the background vibration of the Wave World rose and fell in time with her breathing like swells on the ocean. She imagined herself lying still and quiet, reciting the mantra that Max had given her. She had heard of this one—everyone had—but had never tried it. The peaceful action settled her and allowed her to concentrate on the image of Greg and Nat she had pictured in her mind.

The monks were blocking her view of the Wave World. Several others had flipped over to join Max. They had taken up positions around her, Greg, Nat, and John. One monk had fallen behind the group and was following them.

"We're going to help you focus on your meditation by masking your view. There's nothing to be afraid of," Max told her.

She felt his gentle touch on her mind, and the mesh of light trails against the smooth darkness was partially veiled. In turn, each monk reached out to Aida, just brushing her pearl, dimming her view of the Wave World until she saw nothing but a formless, untouchable sparkling silver gray all around her.

"Ommmmmmmmmmmmm."

**

Max watched the partial cocoon form around Aida. They intentionally had left the front, the direction in which she was heading, open, hoping she'd look ahead into the Particle World where her family waited. If they could get her to do that, Matthew had reasoned, she would flip back, and this whole misadventure would end with everyone safe and sound.

From the outside, he could barely discern the effect of the cocoon on the appearance of Aida's pearl. That made sense, as its purpose was more to impede her perception of the Wave World than to mask the light of her consciousness. Her focus, which before had freely roamed like an errant lighthouse signal, had now settled and, to some minor degree, dimmed. Max attributed the stillness of her focus to the effectiveness of the meditation bolstered by the perceptual cocoon.

Now comes the tricky part, Max thought.

Both Matthew and he knew that the cop and the nurse were pawns acting on behalf of others—and it was those "others" who were observing Aida. They were the ones moving the chess pieces. He didn't know their actual names—no one did—and the monks of the Chama Valley Zen Center weren't going to try to find out. It was bad karma to associate with people who were so...

Unwholesome was the best word any of them could come up with.

Buddhism had a better term, *akusala*, for those people and their actions, and that was how the monks referred to them. The monks had been aware of the *akusala* for some years now. Their initial entry into the Wave World had been short-lived and, like most of their initial actions, also brutal and crude. The monks watched as more than a dozen people were forcibly flipped over to view the Wave World only to die a short time later. Recently, though, just in the past twelve months, the victims of the *akusala* hadn't died so quickly; they were living and observing longer. With this, the *akusala* were accumulating knowledge, and their observers and agents were becoming more skilled.

Let's hope they're not as skilled as we are yet, Max thought. *It doesn't seem that they are.*

The *akusala*'s first actions against the Doxiphuses had been direct, confrontational, and violent. At least one person was dead, and more would be if their plan failed. But if the monks had read the movements of the Wave World correctly, it looked like the *akusala* were about to switch tactics and try a softer, more manipulative approach to ensnaring Aida and her family. The *akusala* were

143

withdrawing the stick and offering the carrot, as it were. They probably would present the opportunity to solve the puzzle of Aida's condition in a location Greg believed to be safe.

I imagine the fox telling the gingerbread man to avoid the rising water by hopping onto the tip of his nose, Max thought.

If the monks' plan worked, Greg would take the bait, doing exactly what the *akusala* expected him to do, but with one minor change. Then, if Aida stayed quiet, and if Greg listened to Matthew and put the pieces together himself and no one else noticed, and if everyone did what the monks believed and hoped they would do, then...

The Doxiphuses will disappear from the view of the akusala, *and we'll have a group of people hunting us who are undoubtedly well financed and who won't hesitate to kill us to get what they want.*

The thought of death didn't bother Max and Matthew; it was part of the endless cycle of samsara they both were trying to escape.

Perhaps this act will count as one of the ten wholesome acts we need in order for our next rebirth to occur on one of the higher planes.

***

Beverly Michelson stepped out of the private jet and into the waiting car. She wasn't surprised to be here in University City, though she was annoyed that Gilden and his trained attack dogs had wasted almost two days. They had failed to get what The Project needed from the subject and risked exposing everything.

Men who hold power are such arrogant, egotistic assholes, she thought.

Finally, after one murder, one attempted murder, and a direct confrontation with one of the most brilliant men Michelson knew, Gilden admitted his way wasn't working, so he turned to plan B, which was always Michelson and the Predictive Sciences Section (PSS).

Greg has been through a terrible ordeal these past two days. He'll be looking for a way out. He'll want to take care of his wife. I just need to provide them with the easy way to go. It was simple, really.

144

With a touch of anticipation, she realized, *I need to get ready for Greg.*

She raised the partition between her and the driver before turning on the vanity lights and dropping down the mirror. The bright lights overpowered any view she had of the outside and would have made her visible to anyone watching her but for the heavily tinted windows. She freshened her makeup and brushed out her shoulder-length blond hair and added a touch of her custom-made perfume—just a little, no need to overpower the man. She only wanted to get Greg to notice her.

That shouldn't be hard, she thought as she admired her legs and figure. He was only a man, and she wanted something from him.

***

Max watched Greg as he spoke with these two new people. He didn't dare touch any of their minds and risk exposing himself. One—if not both—of the interlocutors was certain to be *akusala*. The brief, as far as he could tell, encounter ended, and Greg returned his attention to Natalia and John. Greg's pearl separated from their small group, advancing haltingly, weighed down by the decision to take the unavoidable opportunity he'd just been offered and didn't want. Greg then slid down in between two waves, disappearing from view. On the crest of the far wave, Matthew was waiting for Max to let him know the opportunity had arrived.

"Now, Matthew!" he called out.

The monk's pearl dropped between the opposing waves to take advantage of the limited amount of privacy they would have.

Good luck, my friend.

Matthew emerged, maneuvering along the background waves to minimize his exposure. This grouping of waves was more than a little unusual. Their size, orientation, and the timing of their arrival coincided so neatly with their needs, and he was grateful for it. Every once in a while, the universe conspired with you to bring you what you needed when you needed it. Laypeople referred to this as the "everything is going my way" experience.

The two waves rolled away, revealing Greg alone.

Now we'll see which decision he made.

The answer was immediately apparent in the way the man moved. Gone was the weight he had carried before. Max pictured Greg striding decisively ahead, toward his prior destination, which was unchanged, and the words he would say were also unchanged; it was only the outcome that the man expected that had changed. With a gentle stroke, Max let his attention fall on Greg. Keeping his distance, he opened himself to feeling Greg's emotional state. *Hope. Relief. Empowerment.* He checked them off in his mind.

"Let Matthew know Dr. Doxiphus has accepted our offer of assistance," said Max to a novitiate who would flip back and call Matthew.

***

Dr. Qian Yan, a tall, spare man, circled the projection stage, eyeing the 3-D holographic projections of quantum space in the darkened observation room. The hologram was a composited view of quantum space, an assembly of the live feeds from the observers. In the center were the quantum representations of mind (QRMs) of the Doxiphuses. Their past and projected paths were overlaid on the composite view in brightly colored lines.

Being one of the designers of this system, Qian knew that roiling background of quantum space, called quantum foam, was portrayed using the same imaging code used to model fluid dynamics in 3-D. Whenever he looked at the holographic projection, he thought of the time he had spent at the ocean in his childhood. Waves rode over other waves and collapsed into one another, not on the surface of a plane but from all directions, agnostic of concepts like up or down. Infinite ocean breakers piling up on one another and then shrinking to the tiniest ripples, which looked like lines crossing, only to dissipate as they lapped over one's feet.

The QRMs were represented as points of light embedded in the background. They bore more than a slight resemblance to galaxies and stars in the 3-D models of the universe Qian had seen. It took the eye some time to get used to seeing the world this way.

In the far field, toward the edges of the projection, computers tracked the motion of trillions of points in order to predict the future state of quantum space. With this, he could know with almost perfect accuracy when and where waves or events would converge on a subject to produce actual effects in normal space.

The primary subject, Aida Doxiphus, was quiescent. Right now, he was mostly interested in one of the secondary subjects, Gregorio Doxiphus. Dr. Michelson, represented by a green dot labeled "actor A," had just finished offering subject B, Gregorio, the opportunity to come here to The Project. If he took the option, his blue dot would turn and start following the desired path, projected as a gold line in 3-D space. The gold line molded itself to the contours of the background and represented the path of least resistance; it was the easiest way to go. This was a sign that there was more than a 99 percent chance that subject B would take the offer and follow the path, a fact that was reflected by the prediction-accuracy counter projected in the corner of the hologram as part of the heads-up display.

PredAcc
99.999%

Subject B started in motion, heading right down the entrance of the gold path. Though it wasn't a surprise, Qian nodded in approval; confirmation was always gratifying. It was just a matter of time now.

The subject then entered a valley between two crests and was lost from sight. He was still on the gold path, so the momentary interruption didn't worry Qian. This sort of thing happened from time to time, and it never influenced the calculus of the prediction. It always amazed him how people stuck to a course of action once they had decided on it, even if it wasn't beneficial for them.

He walked ninety degrees around the circular platform to get a different angle on subject B. The crests rose, still blocking his line of sight.

Wait it out. Doxiphus is already on the path.

Qian checked the time on his mobile device; these things usually lasted only two to three minutes. He could use the break to update the observation log. He sat down at his station and keyed in his notes, which would accompany the video recording of the important activities in quantum space.

Gilden preferred to watch the replay with colorful arrows and callouts already inserted; it made it easier for him to follow.

Personally, Qian thought this was demeaning to the science they did here.

Americans…everything has to look like an instant replay of one of their brutish football games. At least Michelson understood the art of observing.

The shrill screech of the integrity alarm, followed by a recorded voice, broke the quiet of the observation room.

"Warning. Warning. Observational integrity failure. Loss of reference point."

"Gǒu shǐ!" he cursed, spinning in his chair to face the hologram. The safeties built into the capture and rendering system had frozen the image at the moment in time just before the reference point was lost. It took Qian a moment to reorient himself and regain his composure. Doxiphus's blue dot had emerged from between the crests that had hidden it and was still squarely on the path. He glanced down to the clocks at the base of the observing platform. One showed actual local time; the other showed elapsed time since the occurrence of a major event, which in this case was the loss of the reference point.

Days	Hours	Minutes	Seconds	.1 Seconds
00	00	00	12	50

Twelve and a half seconds and counting.

This was critical, because for every fraction of a second that they didn't have a live feed from the observers and were blind to the state of the quantum world, their predictions became less accurate. The prediction accuracy percentage already was dropping.

PredAcc
99.995%

PredAcc decay was linear for the first few hours. It would decline at a constant rate until it reached about 95 percent in about eight hours. At that point, the predictive models would break down due to too many unknown data points, and the decline would be exponential, doubling every tenth of a second.

148

Chaos theory in action, Qian mused, not that knowing why the system behaved as it did would help them out here. He knew what was coming next.

Days	Hours	Minutes	Seconds	.1 Seconds
00	00	00	31	23

The phone in his pocket vibrated.

"What's happening, Qian?"

"We just lost the reference point, Mr. Gilden. The last known good projection showed subject B had decided to take Dr. Michelson's offer; he was firmly on the desired path, and PredAcc was at 99.999 percent. The prediction is good for about eight more hours."

Qian heard Gilden's sigh of exasperation. "How long until we're back up?"

"It takes about six hours to get another reference point online…but there's a snag, sir. We need Dr. Michelson here to perform the procedure."

This time there was no sigh on the other end of the line, just silence. Qian knew to keep quiet and wait until he was spoken to.

"I'll handle that. You start the prep."

"Yes, Mr. Gilden," he said, the muscles around his torso clenching at the thought of the task.

After hanging up, Qian moved to his console to ensure the raw feeds from the three remaining observers were being recorded. Although the data they captured wouldn't be as useful now that they lacked a reference point to anchor them together in time and 3-D space, the recordings would be accurate within the scope of each observer's view frame. The constant movement, the expansion and contraction of quantum space that the observers were embedded in, would cause a drift they would be unable to account for.

***

Like a traffic webcam, Observer 113 watched, and through him, Qian and The Project saw the quantum world. Observer 113 had no idea what he was looking at; in fact, he had no idea that he had no

149

idea, as his conscious ability to comprehend, to be aware of the information his senses were feeding him, was gone. He didn't even know his name was Charlie anymore.

The overpowering beauty of his perceptions had no meaning; the profoundness of the subtle, complex interconnections of all life and events was lost on him. Thus, he had no reaction when the tightly packed group of lights that had been placed in the center of his view slipped behind a rolling mound and disappeared.

17 Volunteer 119

The sweltering day after their high school graduation in June 1989, Ray Stevens and his buddy Tom Shelley were picked up in a police gang sweep in East St. Louis, Illinois. True, they were in the gang, but joining was what they had to do to survive. Their real goal, ever since they were boyhood friends, was to finish high school and get out of what the FBI's Unified Crime Report called the most dangerous city in the country.

It was a testament to the strength of that promise that they did graduate, and it was miraculous that they did so without ever having committed a violent crime. The judge, a former naval officer with a reputation for being unsparing with gang members, recognized these accomplishments and uncharacteristically offered them the option of enlistment in the military now or the certainty of the penitentiary when they reached their third strike. Ray and Tom saw their way out and took it.

They ended up in the Naval Construction Battalion, or Seabees, and considered themselves lucky. The judge had kept the matter in juvenile court, where their records would be sealed upon their eighteenth birthdays and their promised enlistment. By the end of that summer, they shipped out to the Naval Construction training center in Port Hueneme (pronounced "why-nee-mee"), California. They were out of East St. Louis, and with the construction skills they'd get, they saw union jobs for themselves with steady paychecks after they finished their tour. Life was looking up.

Tom died in a helicopter crash early in their deployment to the Persian Gulf. His death, which seemed as cruel and meaningless as any death they had witnessed in East St Louis, broke Ray's spirit. Defeated, he finished his deployment driving a bulldozer, sweating, drinking, and getting high.

The Seabees' motto, "We Build, We Fight," turned out to be true for Ray. He lost his right arm and the hearing in his right ear during a mortar attack on a special forces camp his unit was building. On some level, the loss made sense to Ray; he told the doctors that he and his body were now right with each other. The injuries were his ticket home, and eight months later, he was released from the VA hospital with an honorable discharge, a Purple Heart, a few bucks, and a diagnosis of PTSD.

Ray went back to the St. Louis, Missouri, area and found a foreman at a road-paving company who was sympathetic to his situation. The foreman, who was also a vet, hired Ray to do quality assurance reviews on a nice long contract the company held with the Missouri State Department of Roads.

The consistency of work and the location allowed Ray to settle down, during which time he met Rosie. She was from a small farming town outside of Jefferson City, and for a year or so they made a go of it. When Rosie told him she was expecting, his hope for the future blossomed along with the new life she was carrying.

Renewed, Ray took the news of the end of the state road contract with calm confidence and directed his energy into looking for steady work. Like migrant farm workers, he and Rosie moved from place to place, following seasonal paving and home construction jobs. Eventually the work dried up and the stress of constantly moving and little money made Ray's PTSD worse, driving him back to the bottle and drugs.

His erratic behavior and withdrawal became too much for Rosie. She took their beautiful daughter, Jenny, and went back to her hometown. In the letter she left for Ray, she said it would be better if he never came around her or Jenny again, and she would tell Jenny her daddy had died in a construction accident.

Ray took to drifting and joined the ranks of other homeless vets, living on the street and picking up the odd job where he could. Over the years, he made his way west across the country, moving until he came to Seattle and couldn't go any farther. He found some peace in the long months of rain and gray, which were so different than the blazing heat and dryness of the Gulf, and in that peace, he started to heal. It was a good city for him; there were many other vets he could relate to. He still had to move around, though. Sometimes he stayed in the Nickelsville homeless camps, sometimes under the Alaska Way Viaduct or in The Jungle. After being assaulted once in Pioneer Square, he avoided that place from then on.

In the cool of November, as the relentless winter rains were starting, a college kid from Seattle University, just up the hill from Ray's tent on Cherry Street under the I-5 overpass, came to talk to him. He said his name was Derrick, and he was a volunteer for PUSHH, the Puget Sound Homeless Haven. PUSHH was offering thirty-day vouchers for motels and meals, new clothing, plus access to a full medical clinic at a place called The Project, down in Pacific County, in the hills by the coast. With appointments backed up for months at the VA, Ray took the offer and the bus with about eighteen others to a small but sophisticated private clinic about two hours south of Seattle.

The doctors and nurses were great there. He got better medicine for his arthritis and pain, all his dental work done, and a new hearing aid. He also talked to a therapist who specialized in PTSD. She referred Ray for some brain scans and psychological tests there at the clinic. Based on his results, they asked Ray to come back for more therapy and neuropsychological exercises on the computer, which he was happy to do. This went on through the holidays, and after years on the street, Ray became accustomed to sleeping safely in a warm bed again.

Early in the New Year, during one of his therapy visits to the clinic, they told him they were so impressed with his progress that they wanted him to stay on there and take a position as a resident counselor. Because Ray didn't have a degree, however, they said he couldn't be paid, but they would give him his own room at the clinic and continue to meet all his needs. What clinched it for Ray was when he realized he would be helping people like himself. He would have purpose in his life again.

He skimmed the acceptance paperwork they gave him and was pleasantly surprised to find an additional benefit: a ten-thousand-dollar life insurance policy the clinic paid for as long as he stayed on, and he could name whomever he wanted as the beneficiary. He

153

signed his name right below the beneficiary's name, Jennifer Lynn Stevens in Sage Bend, Missouri, and left the life of a homeless vet forever.

The Project took a new picture of him for his volunteer ID badge. Ray smiled as he looked at it. Next to his photo, the caption read: "Ray Lee Stevens, resident counselor, volunteer 119."

***

Three days later, in the benefits department of a shell company twenty-one levels removed from The Project, a brand-new benefits associate got a file on Ray Lee Stevens in his inbox. He didn't know the sender had mistakenly chosen "Benefits: West Coast" instead of "Benefits: West Coast Special" from the automatically populated names in the "To:" line of the email. Wanting to make a good impression, he filled out form FRD-395 to open a ten-thousand-dollar five-year term life insurance policy with the North Plains Life Insurance Company in Minneapolis.

18 The Production Floor

Feeling drained at what should have been the end of a long day, Jerome Gilden faced a very long night. The security measures that controlled access to the most sensitive section of The Project were taking longer than he thought they should, adding to his irritation. Chafing at the perceived delay, he waited in a sealed cubicle and closed his eyes, thinking through his next steps.

Oversee the disposal. Then call Michelson.

After a loud thunk announced the release of the magnetic locks on the inner doors, he pushed his way through to the operations area of the Predictive Sciences Section—or the production floor, as he called it—annoyed he even had to be there.

Gilden didn't like involving himself directly. Michelson or Qian usually were the ones to handle this, but Qian was occupied with a more distasteful task, and Michelson wasn't here.

Well, when you're the boss, you're the boss.

The technicians had screwed up the disposal of an observer before, leaving evidence that could have been traced back to The Project. Fortunately, the mistake had been caught by the redheaded man, who was now the head of field operations. So now each disposal had to be supervised by a member of the senior leadership team.

With a hiss of pneumatic cylinders, the last set of double doors swung open. The production floor was brightly lit and cool, and though it resembled a hospital floor, it lacked the antiseptic aromas one would expect. Instead there was only a trace of the thin, sharp smell of off-gassing new computer cases.

Conversations died on the lips of the thirteen staff members in the room at the sight of Gilden. His visits to the production floor were rare, to say the least. He ignored their "What the hell is he doing here?" reactions. In Gilden's mind they all were as disposable as the observers and just as leveraged.

He strode through the ring of four nurses' stations around the centrally placed control dais. A nurse and two technicians worked at each station, remotely monitoring and maintaining the observers' operational conditions. Once an observer was operational, no one was allowed into the sealed production suites that lined four of the outer walls of the pentagon-shaped room. The data from each of the stations was consolidated and fed to the shift production manager, who was at the dais. Gilden went to talk to her; she waited for him to speak first.

"Show me the failure," he said, indicating she should bring up the video from the dying observer's room on the main screen, which occupied most of the fifth wall.

She knew to give him only what he asked for when he asked for it. "On the screen, sir."

In the center of the screen was a large featureless white pod, the size of the outer shell of an Egyptian sarcophagus, with multiple sets of cables and tubes connecting it to the outside world. A large steel pipe exited from the lowest point of the pod, and a series of smaller video windows lined the perimeter of the main screen, showing the dwindling vitals of the occupant. Ignoring the EKG, pulse ox, temperature, and respiration rate, Gilden focused on the EEG, which was almost completely disorganized; some of the lines had already gone flat.

He scowled at the data before him. He was no doctor, but it didn't look good. "How much longer?"

"Five, maybe ten minutes," she said.

Why did this have to happen now? And why wasn't it predicted? A printer can tell you when a new toner cartridge is needed; we should be able to do the same with the observers.

"Show me the activity monitor."

In the silence of the room, her mouse clicks were nearly deafening. The camera view of the production suite was replaced with a semitransparent 2-D view of a 3-D model of a human brain.

Overlaid on the image were coordinate lines with labels at specific points. Waves of colorful activity washed through the projection, running over the outer surface of the brain, called the cortex, while flashes of light echoed around the interior of the structure. The cortical waves slowed, then stopped.

"There's no longer any organized activity," she said, narrating the swift decay into death. "Observer 113 is insentient." After another moment, the flashes of light, which represented activity along the major tracts of nerve bundles that connect various areas of the brain, ceased as well, leaving only the scattered random sparks of individual neurons that continued until the last of their chemical energy was spent.

For the record, she said, "Brain death, 02:10 a.m.."

"Pull the plug." It was ridiculous that he had to say that; this should've been automated years ago.

"Removing operational support," she replied. They used to call it life support, but the term "operational support" was more palatable.

The pulse and blood oxygenation monitor—pulse ox— plummeted, as expected, with mechanical respiration cut off. The EKG slowed, became erratic, and then stopped.

"Open it up. Pull the marker," Gilden ordered with a sigh of exasperation.

Time for a new toner cartridge.

The magnetic locks to production suite one released, allowing the outer door of the airlock to swing open. A technician from station one went into the airlock. Another few keystrokes and the door sealed behind him. A security glass window allowed Gilden to see jets of high-pressure air from the ceiling bathe the man while powerful fans under the floor pulled the air down and out. The man donned a white clean-room suit and sat on a bench to wait out the next part of the disposal procedure.

After the shift manager typed a few commands on her keyboard, the end of the pod pulled away, revealing two feet.

"It's the left one this time, sir," she said.

"Go."

Her mouse clicked again, and the faint hum of an electric motor vibrated through the walls, followed by the ripping and snapping of the observer's left foot as it was disarticulated at the ankle, a

157

notoriously weak joint. A surgical cut would have been neater, but a necessary part of the deception involved forceful trauma associated with the removal of the foot. The foot was dropped into a thick plastic bag with an airtight seal before the inner door of the clean-room airlock opened and the technician went in to retrieve it.

In the next week or two, there would be another story on the Internet of a human foot in a running shoe washed up on a beach somewhere, only this one would be identifiable. The knot in Gilden's stomach released a little bit now that the gruesome part was over.

"Okay, retrieval complete. Close it up. Soak it and flush it," he said.

"Closing it up, sir."

The pod had been sealed again, and fluid rushed into it. The liquid contained genetically modified versions of the naturally occurring bacteria in the human gut that break down all animal tissue after death. These hungry little microbes were further nourished and made hyperactive by the nutrients and chemicals in which they floated.

Gilden smirked. *People think dissolving a body is hard, but after death, the body dissolves itself.*

Depending on the environmental conditions, this could take anywhere from weeks to years. Postmortem, the chemical processes of life no longer inhibit the activity of the anaerobic (not needing oxygen) bacteria in the gut and uninhibited they start to break down the surrounding tissue; this is called putrefaction. It stank like hell, and Gilden was grateful for the sealed pod and airlock.

It's a beautiful thing actually, thought Gilden. Nature was taking care of the problem for him; they just had to speed it up a little.

Their genetically modified version of the bugs would accomplish the decomposition in about an hour, leaving only the skeleton. From there it literally was a child's science fair project to remove the calcium carbonate from the bone, leaving it rubbery.

A basic garbage disposal took care of the last step. That left the biomedical waste and electronics to be burned in the facility's small incinerator, for which they were fully licensed.

The shift manager worked on her computer, closing out Observer 113's file. Once she finished, she sent the file to the PSS senior leadership team. Gilden sat down in a computer workstation chair and crossed his arms, waiting for her to finish. He still had one task to perform.

"I'm all done, sir. The file is ready for you."

"Fine. Thank you. Go get a cup of coffee." Gilden rolled his chair to her workstation as she exited the dais. He stared at the camera and waited for the facial recognition to identify him and unlock the last section of the file for editing. Before coming down here, he had looked up Observer 113's recruitment records to see the general area of the country he had come from; turned out it was from along the Gulf Coast.

In an innocuous field labeled "plant," he typed in the value "Florida." He authorized the operation with his PIN and certified the disposal. Observer 113's left foot would be placed in a beat-up running shoe and dropped in the waters off Florida in a few weeks. The tides would eventually wash it up onto a beach, where it would be found and collected. In the meantime, someone who looked very much like Observer 113 and who had his ID would have a minor jaywalking encounter with some local Florida law enforcement or go into a social services office for a food voucher. It wouldn't be enough to book him, which entailed fingerprinting, but it would be just enough to establish his presence there. He would be released back to the streets and then disappear.

Later, local law enforcement would come into possession of the foot, and if they bothered with forensics testing and managed to identify the owner of the appendage, their own records would show he had been alive and in the area recently.

The evidence would support the death of the individual; the disarticulated foot could be from a boat accident, or a feeding shark. Scavenging crabs would further mutilate it. Since he was homeless, there was a greater than 99 percent chance that the investigation would stop with the notification of the next of kin, if they could be found.

Neat and clean. No trail leads back to The Project. Now to Michelson.

She picked up after one ring.

Well, she's not asleep.

"Hi, Bev. How are things on your end?" he opened, letting a little of his irritation come across.

159

"We're doing well here. What's wrong, Jerome?" She was surprised he was up; he rarely slept less than eight to nine hours on the nights they spent together.

"You're needed back here now." Even over a secure line, which this most certainly was, Michelson wouldn't ask for more details. She knew what this meant; there were few activities at The Project that required her personal attention.

"I'm still waiting on a response to the offer of help I made," she said.

"Don't worry about that. It was already committed and on track," he replied.

"Are you positive? Things aren't so clear here."

"You can watch the instant replay when you get back. It's the best we've got. A car and driver are waiting for you out front."

It was useless to protest further, and if Greg was already en route, she'd rather be there anyway.

"I'll be down in ten minutes," she replied, and ended the call.

19 Through the Night

Westbound I-80 droned away under the wheels of the ambulance as the headlights pushed a hole in the slick darkness. In her anxiety, Nat willed the night to close completely behind them, erasing all traces of their passage. She was taking her turn driving, fresh from a three-and-a-half-hour nap in the back of the rig. They rotated the driving between John, Greg, and Nat. Matthew excused himself from that duty, still tired from his solo sixteen-hour drive from the Chama Valley Zen Center to University City. Instead, he spent his time meditating, tending to Aida with John, and trying to educate them on the basics of transperceptual meditation.

University City was four uneventful hours behind them. They were halfway across Nebraska now, somewhere between Lexington and Cozad, according to the road signs. Overhead, layers of dense clouds blocked the moonlight that earlier had painted the surrounding landscape pale and spectral. For the most part, Nat's perspective of the world was restricted to the meager distance of illuminated roadway in front of her. When she did look up, she could see semitrucks by the outlines of their running lights. Every ten or fifteen miles, clusters of quick marts, fast food restaurants, truck stops, and gas stations interrupted the night like illuminated islands in some strange archipelago.

Her father sat sideways in the passenger seat, craning his neck so he could look at Matthew as they talked. In a different situation, Nat would have found the exchange fascinating. As it was, though, both of them were exhausted, slowing their work on this Gordian knot.

161

Frustration weighed her father down, and several times, she expected him to dismiss what Matthew was saying offhand because there was no supporting empirical evidence and no scientifically sound method to frame the experiences Matthew was explaining. She also recognized her father's struggle was the same as hers, one of understanding, not belief.

With almost inhuman patience, Matthew continued. "Gregorio, your wife insists on referring to what we see around us now as the Particle World. I understand why we call the unfocused view the Wave World—it just makes sense, as everything in it but individual consciousness generally appears as waves. But why call this the Particle World?"

Greg grinned. Aida was trying to describe her experience in a way that she knew he would understand. "Particles and waves are a quantum mechanics reference. You were almost right when you said, 'We see what we choose to see.' It would have been more accurate to say that reality becomes what we choose to measure it as."

"I'm afraid I don't understand," said Matthew.

Now it was her father's turn to tug at the knot. "You say—and all the current evidence supports your claim—that the physical reality we encounter around us, including our bodies, can be seen or understood in two different ways. One way is through our five senses. We can feel the air against our skin; we taste, hear, smell, and, most important, see. The other, which can only be attained through a very high degree of training and mental discipline, is through a different type of functioning of our perception of our interior experience. In this other view, the physical reality we've all taken for granted since birth exists but isn't perceivable through four of the five senses. It is only through visualization that physical reality is perceived as wave structures, and the only substantial object in the Wave World is consciousness, which cannot be seen or quantified in the particle view of the world."

"That's a very good summation," the monk encouraged him. "Go on." *Maybe he's finally getting this*, Matthew thought.

"And while you're viewing the world one way, you can't view it the other way. The two ways of perceiving are mutually exclusive, yet they're one thing?" Greg's chin was tucked down into his chest, and his eyes were closed.

162

"Correct."

"Okay, then let me give you some context before I continue. I think I know what Aida's getting at. Until the late nineteenth century, the accepted scientific thinking held that light was a wave. Just like waves on the ocean or ripples on a pond, or sound waves, for that matter. This had been scientifically proven."

"Right. There are the visible wavelengths of light and others that are invisible to our eyes, the ultraviolet and infrared," Matthew interjected.

"Exactly, good. Now, in 1905, Einstein published a paper on the photoelectric effect that postulated that light wasn't a wave. He proposed that it was made of tiny particles or packets, called photons. This was considered heresy in the scientific community, but given Einstein's standing, he was permitted some latitude. Never mind why he thought this, and that he wasn't the first to do so, but it turned out to be true. It forced others to investigate, to try to resolve the particle or wave paradox of the nature of light. Subsequently it was scientifically proven that light was composed of particles.

"To make a long story short, the only answer they found is that light is both. I can do a simple demonstration that proves light is a wave. I also can do a different demonstration and prove that light is a particle."

"So you're saying that two different demonstrations that look into the nature of light give contradictory, mutually exclusive results?" Matthew asked.

"Precisely! And not only light—in 1923, De Broglie expanded the wave-particle duality model to include all particles, including matter."

"So what's different between the two methodologies?"

"Plenty, but the only important thing is that they're both scientifically sound," Greg said. "The results of these demonstrations brought modern physics to the edge of what it can understand, and it implied something else." He paused. Not only was modern physics at the edge of its comfortable envelope of authority, but so was he.

"What? What did it mean?" John asked. Nat couldn't see him in the back and didn't realize he was paying attention.

"It implies that light or potentially any type of energy becomes what the observer chooses to demonstrate it to be the first time it is measured. That somehow the conscious choice the observer makes in selecting which demonstration to do determines the physical reality of a particle or wave. Stated another way, nothing has an independent, objective reality that is separate from perception." He finished, then fell silent, grappling with something else.

Matthew smiled. "Why, Dr. Doxiphus, are you a student of Buddhism? This makes perfect sense to me. The Dalai Lama has written about the similarities between Buddhist world views and quantum mechanics."

Greg ignored Matthew's comment, finishing his train of thought. "What my wife is saying is that you've revealed a view of reality where everything appears in its wave form." *She must also be curious why your group hasn't made all this public*, he thought.

"So what's it mean? I mean, what does it matter?" Natalia asked. "How's any of this going to help us get Mom back?" This was all amazing and had to be studied more, but the prospect of being chased by people who would kill them and do God knows what to her mother was more pressing than the academic possibilities of this discovery.

"Every piece of the puzzle helps, and Matthew has a plan for getting your mother back," Greg replied, looking at the monk. The physicist shifted in his seat; something had been digging into his right thigh for the past sixty miles, and the discomfort it was causing had finally percolated its way up into his conscious mind. He fished in his pocket and pulled out his dead cell phone. He hadn't thought about charging it since they had left University Hospital.

Not much good like this. Dangling from the power outlet on the dashboard was a charger with a micro-USB adapter. He took it in hand and was pleasantly surprised when it fit his phone.

"Natalia," Matthew said, "I think if we can get your mother to calm her mind and focus on the Particle World, the two of you in particular, she'll come back. We've just started obscuring her view of the Wave World to help, and we'll be able to do more when we get to New Mexico."

Unsatisfied, Nat hammered at Matthew, unintentionally unloading on him. "But how did she get like this in the first place, and why is she trapped there?"

Unperturbed, he answered, "Well, we know Mr. Fahy had something to do with her transition. I don't know what's keeping her there, though. I think the best person to figure this out is your mother."

Greg's head popped up. "There are other implications too, I think. Matthew, tell me more about how you see future events in the Wave World."

Matthew shook his head. "No, that's not right. We don't see events before they happen. There's no precognitive aspect to the experience. Anyone viewing the Wave World can see the causes of many events before those causes come together to make something happen. The view is just broader, more encompassing. When you can see all the causes and you understand how they move and flow, you can more easily predict how they will come together to produce an outcome. It's kind of like a forensic investigation but run in reverse. Instead of looking for the causes of an event after that event has happened, you can see what look to be unrelated causes coalescing into an event."

"Are there other peop—" Greg started to ask, but his daughter interjected.

"How is that different?" Nat said.

"Imagine you see a drinking glass fall from a high shelf, and below it is a brick floor. Once that glass leaves the shelf, can you tell me what's going to happen to it?" asked Matthew.

"Sure, it falls to the floor and breaks."

"But have you seen it shatter yet?"

"Well, no, but…oh, okay, I get what you're saying, but that seems very mechanical and deterministic. I thought we were talking quantum mechanics—'Things don't happen until someone decides to see them that way.' Dad?" she finished, asking her father for help.

Matthew answered before Greg could. "Please don't misunderstand me. The Wave World is much more complex than that. I was only trying to explain the difference between seeing a future event and being very certain what a future event is and that it will occur and when it will occur."

Nat could see they were heading into some showers; already drops were accumulating on the windshield along with the summer insects that had splattered there. She switched on the wipers. With a

165

rhythmic *thump-thump* they mixed the water and bugs together, leaving wide gelatinous smears arcing across the windshield.

"Heading into some rain," she announced. "I can't see very well. These are old wipers. I'm gonna have to slow down." No one seemed to notice or mind.

"I understand what you're pointing out, Matthew. However, there are also greater implications. Let me ask you a different question," Greg went on. "You talk about waves, events, and consciousness; I need to understand the interaction between the three. Can you tell me how it appears to work, from a viewer's perspective, without any interpretation?"

Matthew rubbed his hand across his head. "I'll try, but it's very difficult to do it justice." Closing his eyes, he pictured the Wave World in his mind, then spoke. "The background is all dark, but it's constantly moving, like the surface of the ocean, perpetually rising and falling with smaller waves sitting on top of larger and larger ones. These waves can wash across you from every direction. This sea has no surface, and you're embedded in the background. When a wave washes over you, you can feel it tug on you and move you. Set in the background and moving on it are pearls of light; these are conscious minds. As they move, they leave a thin trail of light that traces out where they've been. Most have gathered into clusters, some of which are very, very large."

"What about events?" Greg asked.

"Events are sometimes the consequence of some previous action by a pearl of consciousness, or sometimes they simply appear— perhaps randomly, perhaps not. They move through the background and leave one with the impression that they are lines. When they hit a pearl of consciousness, sometimes they influence it, and the pearl moves in a different direction. It's possible to watch an event line move through the background, and based on the background waves it will move through—and everything else it will encounter, including other event lines—you can predict fairly accurately when and where something is going to happen." He breathed deeply. "There's so much more to it than that. Forgive me."

Greg fixed the monk with eyes that were clear and alert. "You've mentioned others who are viewing the Wave World; I assume they're the ones behind all this?"

166

Matthew nodded.

"Then why haven't we been caught yet? They obviously can make the same predictions you can."

"They can't see us right now. The minds they use to view the Wave World don't have an objective viewpoint. No one does for that matter. They're embedded in the background too, and when the background moves, so do they. Sometimes background waves rise up and block a person's view, and then we take advantage of such conjunctions to slip into other areas where we can hide. After years of practice, we're quite adept at it. We also saw...something that was about to occur, something that would blind them for a period. It was coming, and we chose to take advantage of it to get all of you out of the hospital." Matthew's hesitation hung in the air, and the steady road noise and the *thump-thump* of the wipers were the only sounds in the stuffy cabin.

"What's the issue?" said Nat, glancing over her right shoulder.

"We have a rule not to use anything that's learned in the Wave World for personal gain. We are only to watch, never act. Violating that rule hasn't been easy."

Greg sighed. "I don't think anyone else would share your sense of restraint, Matthew."

"So what do they want with Mom?" Nat asked everyone and no one in particular.

"We know it has something to do with the stim device," her father offered, leaning his head against the high seat back.

Matthew cleared his throat. "I think their interest started with your device—they were trying to sabotage it. In the process of doing that, something unexpected happened, something they can use. Now they want both your mother and the machine. Given what we've all seen her do, that's understandable."

John chimed in. "Whatever we're going to do, we'd better hurry up." His voice dropped after delivering the warning. There was no sense in trying to hide this information from the family, but his being alarmed wouldn't help either. "Aida's showing signs of exhaustion, which will make it harder for her to concentrate. Her blood pressure has been slowly dropping since we left the hospital, and her pulse is going up. She's having more PVCs. Uh...those are extra heartbeats.

But those are benign. Her temperature is up too. I don't have a reason for it. It just is."

Matthew supplied the answer. "She's wide awake. She's been wide awake, and her mind has been running at full speed since she flipped over to the Wave World. Her body is working to keep up with it. It'll keep doing so until it can't."

"What can you do? Can't you give her a sedative?" Greg asked John and Matthew, looking for a way to hold off the inevitable.

"No, we can't do that; it'll interfere with her ability to concentrate. Besides, I don't think we have any," said Matthew.

John reached up to change out the IV bag of D10W. "I can give her supportive care, fluid, electrolytes, and glucose, and monitor her vitals, keep her cool, be ready for…" he said, stopping himself before he could say, "Be ready for kidney failure and to resuscitate her when she goes into cardiac arrest." That was more than they needed to know now. "Just be ready."

20 Back to Square One

everly Michelson looked out the window of the private jet. Last night's storm had moved over the Cascades, leaving the tarmac glistening fresh and bright in the sunrise as they landed at the Astoria Regional Airport. She had managed only a few hours' sleep on the way in before the bumpy descent through said storm and was decidedly not feeling fresh and bright. It was a six-hour procedure to insert a new reference observer, and she knew she wouldn't be at her best.

Just like surgical residency, except I was a lot younger then, she admitted to herself in a rare moment of honesty that was spurred by the lined face reflected in the window. That train of thought led to a distasteful place, so she stopped her self-examination. *No benefit in second-guessing life choices that can't be changed. Just move on*, she rationalized.

A car was waiting for her, and a few minutes later, from the high rise of the Astoria-Megler Bridge, she watched the plane take off and head east. *Probably back to University City.* Kelley should have authorized the transfer by now, and the Doxiphus family needed a way to get here. He hadn't answered when she had called him a few minutes ago to check on them. She'd try again before she scrubbed in.

***

The bright sunrise at 5:30 in the Pacific Time Zone found Alvin Kelley at 7:30 in the Central Time Zone scrambling around his office, preparing for the grant auditors. The Doxiphus situation had gone quiet, thanks to Beverly. He hadn't heard anything from her overnight, so he assumed Greg had taken her up on her offer and they were all on their way to her facility.

Glad that's out of my hair.

In any case, as he saw it, his role in the situation had changed. No longer the manager of the crisis, all he had to do now was show appropriate concern for the Doxiphus family and protect the university's income. Since they were on their way to Washington state and beyond his help, he could focus entirely on the latter. Intent on the task ahead, he had forwarded all incoming calls and texts to Randy and turned off his phone. The hospital and university could survive without him for a few hours.

***

In a way, Michelson felt envious of the man who lay on the surgical table before her, his brain lying underneath a flap of tissue called the dura mater. True, his life as volunteer 119 was now over, but she was giving him an exceedingly precious gift in exchange.

In a few hours, you'll see reality in its truest form. The best view I've ever had of the quantum world is a third-hand, digitally processed representation.

The limitation gnawed at her. That she hadn't found a noninvasive way there first galled her. That it was Aida who'd found it, and then only through a stupid accident that The Project, and by extension herself, had fomented, was almost beyond her comprehension.

It was more than unfair. Aida didn't deserve it. The woman hadn't even been looking for it!

She shut down her roiling indignation; such agitation wouldn't do before starting the procedure in earnest. Michelson did take comfort in several things. All the data in Qian's imaging system told her Aida should be on her way here, as was Greg. They would be under her control. That was excellent. But she took deeper satisfaction in knowing she was much more familiar than the Doxiphuses were at navigating quantum space, and after spending a few hours studying Aida's EEG traces, she wondered if she could reproduce the conditions that had sent Aida over in the first place. If so, it represented an entirely new way to get observers engaged in viewing quantum space. Getting them back safely was another matter.

The expertise of The Project was in insertion; they'd never even considered bringing an observer back. If Michelson could get into Aida's lab and to the machine, she and The Project would be done with this messy business of inserting observers.

I need to finish this and get back to University City. I need to get to that machine.

Before entering the surgical suite, she had called Kelley to find out where things stood with the Doxiphuses, but he had forwarded his calls to his assistant, and she was forced to leave a message. Any news of the family would have to wait; she didn't allow interruptions in the surgical suite once she entered. Except from Gilden.

Her surgical team had performed the initial craniotomy while she was flying in. The observer's head was held stationary in a halo clamp, a stainless-steel ring that encircled the skull like, well, a halo. Screws extended from the inside edge of the ring directly into the skull itself, anchoring it in three dimensions. The vast majority of the cranium had already been removed above the ears in a single, long circumferential cut made with an electric bone saw. The bowl-shaped pieces of the occipital, parietal, and most of the frontal bones rested on a tray to her left. The tough, fibrous dura mater had been sliced circumferentially around the brain in a similar manner as the upper cranium, with the exception of a small piece in front, which remained connected. This allowed Michelson to lift the dura like the flap of a tent to expose the beauty of the most complex structure she knew of in the universe.

After the craniotomy prep, her team had effectively removed all sources of sensory stimulation to the brain from the torso and limbs. This was necessary, as any stimuli coming from the body into the brain could distract it from what they needed this magnificent structure to focus on. All the sensory and motor neurons in the spinal cord had been transected, leaving the subject completely paralyzed and on a respirator, which was rhythmically pushing air into the observer's lungs. The necessary cranial nerves had been cut as well. The nerves that carried the electrical signals that regulated the heart were the only exception.

The senses of smell, taste, and hearing had to be dealt with too, which was more difficult. You couldn't just cut those nerves; they played too large a role in the sensory information stream the brain used to build the perception of reality. They actually arose from the same tissue as the brain did during embryological development and were extensions of the brain itself. If you severed the auditory and olfactory nerves, it would result in neurochemical imbalances and hallucinations caused by the brain trying to replace the flow of information it had always received. People self-induced these types of hallucinations by spending too much time floating in the hypersalinized fluid inside sensory deprivation chambers. No, those senses had to be fooled. The Project, under the guise of a perfume company, had awarded a contract to a biochemical engineering team in China to develop a molecule that the chemical receptors in the nose and tongue would latch on to and thus produce sensory input but was chemically neutral. They had no taste or smell. Tubes, now permanently implanted during the prep, delivered a steady stream of the white-noise molecule into the observer's mouth and nasal cavities.

Hearing was likewise hoodwinked through the bilateral implantation of modified cochlear implants. A similar white-noise signal was permanently fed into the cochlea, the snail-shell-shaped organ of hearing embedded in the bone of the skull, by a microelectrode array.

The brain was now cut off from all sensory input except for the crucial sense of sight. A precarious, unbalanced position to be in, but a necessary one. The Project had lost many subjects early on by such drastic alteration of the relationship between the brain and body. The minds of subjects in the initial trials, deprived of sensory input, went through massive bouts of hallucinations as the brain desperately tried to build a world for itself. It was amazing to watch the tenacious efforts on the EEG traces and fMRI, but eventually, the psyche collapsed, and the EEG shifted to the pattern of a persistent vegetative state and then to brain death.

The key to achieving their goal was to compel the brain into attending to a view of the world that it had at best glimpsed in a fleeting moment during infancy when the neuronal controls for attention and consciousness still were developing. Once those controlling neural systems became active, the brain would spend the rest of its life purposely ignoring quantum space.

So how do you get someone to see a thing that can't be seen by looking at it? The first part of the answer lay in taking advantage of the two different types of attention in humans, overt and covert, as identified by Hermann von Helmholtz in 1894.

Overt attention, so intimately linked to our visual system, is when you elect to attend to what you are looking at, leaving the other visual stimuli present in the visual field to be filtered out. The brain, under the direction of the consciousness, recognizes they aren't important and so can be safely discounted. The example Michelson always thought of was that of an audience watching a movie in a darkened theater. The audience's entire focus is directed toward what's on the screen. They can still see the seat or person in front of them, and the walls of the auditorium, but they ignore these. Literally, the audience turns a blind eye to them.

Covert attention proved to be Michelson's ally. It's a peculiarity of the human consciousness that every individual can lock their gaze on any given part of their visual field yet choose to attend to something in another part. An aspect of the internal experience that defines human consciousness as a distinct mental state from animal consciousness is the ability to disconnect our focus from what we're looking at and place it on another set of stimuli, either endogenous or exogenous.

She discovered that if you could permanently sever the link between attention and the visual system, the human brain could perceive another world. To do that was simply a matter of turning off the spotlight of overt attention and amplifying the activity of the parts of the brain that controlled covert attention. A set of nano sensors embedded into the visual centers in the occipital lobe sensed the activity and fed the data to Qian's imaging system.

Time to get to work.

Turning off "the spotlight" consisted of systematically destroying both the visual systems of the brain and the portions of the brain involved with overt attention. Michelson listed them off in her head as she started the procedure. First, she used a laser to burn the neurons in the fovea, the area of the retina where the neurons are most densely packed and thus the area with the highest spatial resolution. Then she severed the extraocular eye muscles, which moved the eyeballs around, and inserted screws through the eyeballs and anchored them into the bones behind the eye socket fixing them in place.

Now into the brain itself.

Her team had mapped out and marked the particular regions that controlled vision and overt attention. Michelson verified these and proceeded with the ablation of the frontal eye field, an area in the frontal lobes that functioned to establish gaze as directed by conscious effort and the intraparietal sulcus.

With patient, deliberate movements, she removed—scooped, really—portions of the brain while the assistant surgeon, a brilliant Filipino woman by the last name of Santos, cauterized the severed blood vessels. Brain tissue is amazingly sticky, so flicking the wet scraps of the observer's brain tissue off her instruments was almost like trying to flick peanut butter off a knife, and it was a motion she now casually performed.

In a fluke of evolution, one of the brain structures, the temporoparietal junction (TPJ), which regulates covert attention, sits only on the right side of the brain, behind and slightly above the right ear. This lateralization of function is unusual in an organ that so exquisitely distributes functions between the two hemispheres.

The TPJ serves to help shift focus to new stimuli as they come into the brain. Being a cortical area, it is on the surface of the brain, so inserting the cannulas (thin needlelike tubes) that would introduce the excitatory neurotransmitters to it for the rest of Observer 119's life was relatively easy.

A glance at the clock showed an elapsed time of four hours; the most sensitive part of procedure lay ahead. She had to set cannulas into the pulvinar, the posterior area of the thalamus, deep in the center of brain. The pulvinar, when excited, enhances covert shifting of attention. The area she had to hit was only about the size of a sugar cube, and it was entirely encased in the pineapple-size organ. A mistake at this point meant a waste of a brain and her time. The subject wouldn't die for several days, as long as it was on support, but that was immaterial to The Project's goal. It was only with painstaking slowness and multiple measurements, calculations, and recalculations that she was able to locate the area she needed in three dimensions of space.

Michelson placed the cannulas and started the feed of the gamma aminobutyric acid (GABA), itself an inhibitory neurotransmitter, into the pulvinar. In essence, she was inhibiting the inhibitor to produce greater activation of the pulvinar as discovered by Buchsbaum et al. in 2006.

There, the hard part's done. She glanced again at the clock; it was a little after 2:00 p.m. *Six hours and seventeen minutes.*

Aida and Greg should be here by now.

Why didn't Jerome let me know?

She left the insertion of the nano sensors into the occipital lobe to her assistant while she sat on a couch in the surgical suite to call Gilden. She wouldn't actually leave the suite until Qian confirmed they had a good feed. Gilden picked up on the first ring.

"Are they here yet?" she asked.

"No, the plane is waiting for them at the airport now," he said in a low tone. "The last prediction shows him taking the offer. What's Kelley saying?" She sensed the barb of an accusation in what he'd said; working this through Kelley had been her idea.

"He hasn't returned my calls."

"Are you done in there? We don't have a signal yet." The barb had grown a very sharp point.

"The team is making the connections for the feed now. We should have a signal within the hour."

"Let the team finish that up. Find out what's going on with Greg and Aida." The line clicked dead before she could reply.

Stiff and sore from her hours of labor, Michelson stood up and went to check on the team's progress. Satisfied, she left the surgical suite, changed into some fresh scrubs, and got an apple juice before calling Kelley. This time he too answered on the first ring.

"Hello, Beverly," he started. "I've been with the auditors all morning. I'm sorry I haven't had a chance to return your calls...university business and all."

"That's okay," she lied. "Did Greg accept the offer? The air ambulance is waiting for them at the airport."

"What do you mean? I saw the discharge report myself. It said Aida was prepped for transport and the whole family left for the airport sometime after midnight."

Disturbed, she repeated the obvious to him. "They're not here, Alvin." *You idiot!* "Are you sure they actually left?"

"Let me double-check. Paperwork errors happen. I'll call you back in five minutes."

She laid down on the bench in the surgical locker room, closed her eyes, and waited for the call. Four minutes later, she answered her chirping phone. Without interrupting, she listened and sat straight up, swinging her feet to the floor.

"We need to find out where they are, Alvin! Yes, you can reach me at this number."

Thanks to the multiple walls between the locker room and the surgical suite, all the team heard was a muffled scream from Michelson as they confirmed with Qian that Observer 119 was online.

21 Hunting

"Where are they now?" Gilden asked in a low voice, starting the meeting with the obvious question. "How did they do it?" He tapped his pencil on the desk. "And are they a threat?"

Michelson, occupying the seat facing him, was fuming. Qian paced and didn't take the seat next to Michelson. The room's fourth occupant, Angus Baka, stood silently next to the sealed door. Michelson detested the hulking red-haired brute. He was Gilden's handpicked attack dog and chief of security and operations. His bungling of the initial contact with Aida and her daughter had put the Doxiphuses on their guard, priming their suspicion and making them receptive to the assistance they so obviously had received.

Baka spoke first. "They're driving, and they've had a little more than a ten-hour head start. They didn't switch to a plane, so that puts them in a circle with Chicago on the east, the Missouri-Arkansas border on the south, the Nebraska-Colorado border on the west, and about halfway into Minnesota to the north."

"Why should we assume they didn't get on a plane?" Qian asked.

"All flight plans have to be registered with the FAA, and they'd have to get a medical charter," Baka replied. "That was the first thing we checked. We also grabbed a partial image of the ambulance from the ER security video. It shows the Doxiphus family getting in with the medic; he's driving. They're in an older vehicle, white with striping, as best we can tell—it was a black-and-white camera. We weren't able to get the plates from the image either...wrong angle."

177

"So they could be anywhere in the Midwest. That's not much help," Michelson said with disdain.

"If I'd been told about this as soon as your system went offline, I could have put eyes on them round the clock," Baka countered. "Is Kelley going to be of any help?" The question was to Michelson.

"Kelley refuses to involve the state police. He's afraid to drag the university into this and says no crime has been committed."

"Probably just as well." Turning to Gilden, Baka continued. "We're monitoring traffic cameras in all the states they could be in. There won't be that many vehicles of this type, and we have traces on their cell phones and credit and debit cards. I'll find them." He said this with absolute certainty as he leveled an accusatory glare at Michelson.

"Fine. Find them and report back. Take no action," Gilden commanded. Baka turned and left the room. "We're one hundred percent back online. What can we do in quantum space?" he asked Michelson and Qian.

"I've been working on that," Qian answered, then motioned to the screen on the wall. "This is a recording of the feed from Observer 113 as we were monitoring the subject and her family yesterday evening. Mr. Baka was present as well." He made no mention of the hospital room or any other context. "In the center of this view, the subject's QRM—that's quantum representation of mind—is surrounded by the QRMs of actors A and B. Mr. Baka is outside the circle that A and B describe."

Gilden watched the glowing spots of light in the computer-generated background. The whole thing resembled a Jell-O fruit mold to him.

"Now watch carefully," Qian went on "At time counter three, you see a burst of light emanate from the subject's QRM and move to touch the QRMs of A and B." The recording continued to play. "Now at time counter fifty-nine, you see the burst of light again move from A and B back to the subject."

Although Gilden hadn't spent the thousands of hours watching and interpreting the information from quantum space that Qian had, even he knew this was something The Project had never encountered before.

"What is it?" he asked.

"This event is unique in nature. Based on Mr. Baka's description and the data, I believe Dr. Doxiphus is somehow able to extend her consciousness into the perceptions of other people, and when she does that, she can see and hear what they are. She sort of piggybacks onto what their senses perceive. Furthermore, Dr. Michelson and I believe she can communicate with those whose minds she touches. It's a most fascinating phenomenon."

"That's tremendous, Qian, really," Gilden said with only a little bit of sarcasm, "but how does this help us find her?"

"We believe this ability is unique to Dr. Doxiphus. So we'll monitor and wait for her to do it again. It should lead us right to her."

Gilden nodded and dismissed him. "Thank you, Doctor." As Qian walked toward the door, Gilden added, "Qian, I want updates every six hours on the status of the other observers. There will be no more observational blackouts. I'm accelerating the pilot, and we can't afford to go dark again."

"That'll make it harder for us to find them," Michelson protested. "We'll have better coverage if all four observers are tasked for searching, and we haven't discussed accelerating the pilot!"

"They're running from us; they're hidden and probably want to stay that way. I don't think they're an immediate threat. We'll find them before they can do any harm," Gilden said in response. "Right now the pilot is more important."

"No, Jerome! Finding the Doxiphuses and figuring out how Aida got over has to be our first priority. She's the key to all this. If we lose her—"

Gilden cut her off. "It'll be no different than if she had died in the first place. I understand your concerns. That's why you need to get back to University City and get to Doxiphus's scanner. The grant application is waiting for you on the plane."

***

Now they want to see the Doxiphus lab! Alvin Kelley cursed silently. It was 6:04 p.m., and he had just finished with the auditors for the day. Thankfully they had turned down his requisite invitation to dinner. A full day's university business was stacked up in his inbox; he'd at least have to look through that before calling it a night.

179

He walked through the quiet outer office into his own. Randy had left a stack of papers for him to sign, along with a turkey sandwich, a bag of chips, and a bottle of water.

Kelley removed his phone from his suit jacket and laid it on his desk. Ever fastidious, he hung his jacket neatly in his office closet before sitting down.

Greg and Aida…where are they?

***

They had gotten through Denver, Colorado Springs, and Pueblo during the morning and early afternoon. They were on I-25, near Walsenburg, about three and a half hours from their destination. Stops were limited to restroom breaks; they hadn't purchased anything for fear of being tracked. Aida had spiked a fever, and her breaths were coming faster.

"Could be a systemic infection," John offered.

"Perhaps, Mr. Holden," Matthew replied. "The sooner we get home—my home, that is—the better. Aida's prolonged engagement in the Wave World seems to be taking a toll on her body."

Greg was drowsing in the passenger seat when his phone buzzed, indicating it was fully charged. Intent on driving, John didn't hear the buzz or see him pluck his phone out of the console and power it on. After a minute, the device sang its startup music on radio and sound frequencies to let the world know where it was and that it was ready.

"*Dad!*" Natalia shrieked from the back.

Greg's eyes snapped wide open as he came fully awake. Last night, John had warned them about being tracked through their cell phones.

"Greg! Kill it!" John shouted from the driver's seat.

Greg stabbed at his phone. Mortified, he looked at John and Nat. "Sorry. I didn't mean to…"

***

Angus Baka was pacing behind a row of seated technicians, each intent on his or her bank of screens. The room was dark and overly

180

cooled, the only light coming from the screens. A popup flashed on one of the screens.

"Got a hit on Greg Doxiphus's mobile," the tech reported. "A cell tower near the I-25 and Colorado state 160 interchange by Walsenburg."

"Cameras," Baka barked, and another technician set to the task.

"Got 'em! Ambulance, New Mexico plates—older ones, yellow and red, BCF-1122." His fingers danced on the keyboard for a moment as he ran the plates. "Registered to local government...Abiquiú."

Baka was already reporting in. "They're in Colorado, heading to New Mexico, probably to Abiquiú." He nodded once and hung up. "Let's go," he said to one of the techs, and both left the room.

***

On the live video feed, the ambulance pulled to the shoulder, and the driver got out. He dropped several items under the front wheels, got back in, and drove back and forth over them several times, grinding them into the Colorado dust.

22 Abomination

The ambulance turned off the last of the paved highways onto a gravel-and-dirt driveway overgrown with tumbleweeds. The stones ground against one another under the weight of the vehicle, and some were sent skittering out from behind the rear wheels as Greg tapped on the gas to get it up the steep slope. Whereas it seemed slightly out of place on the interstates of Nebraska and Colorado, the dust-covered, careworn vehicle fit right in here in New Mexico. As the roadbed curved around, it leveled off and opened into a dirt parking lot in front of the high walls of the Chama Valley Zen Center. The compound sat on hill in a bend in the Chama River, thick with cottonwoods, piñons, and junipers. Greg pulled up to a broad, solid wooden gate where several monks waited. They surrounded Aida as John and Greg wheeled her into one of the buildings.

"We'll tend to your wife while the final preparations are made. In the meantime, would you follow me, please?" a monk in a burgundy-and-saffron robe said.

He led Natalia, John, and Greg to a private room where they could rest and freshen up. A platter of warm frijoles, arroz, fresh corn and flour tortillas, and tamales greeted them. After the long trip, nothing had ever smelled so good.

"Thank you for this," John told the monk.

"Mollie prepared this for you. She'll be back soon. You can thank her then. For now, please eat. There are cots if you wish to lie down. The restroom and shower are through the other door. We're almost finished with the mandala. I expect we'll be starting in about ninety minutes."

***

Aida had ceased her mental repetition of "Ommmmmmmm" some time ago as she tried to rest. The gray-silver cocoon the monks had woven around her was gone now that the monks were resting too, leaving her with an unobstructed view of the Wave World. Max checked on her periodically and kept her informed regarding the progress of the ambulance to their compound.

He told her they would start the cocooning process again after they arrived. She looked forward to being cocooned; there was something peaceful and restorative about it. Now that it was gone, she noticed something else about herself.

I'm slow, foggy. I must be tired.

Max wasn't around, but both he and Matthew had promised someone always would be watching her, even if they were unable to talk to her.

I'll have to ask him how long I've been here when he comes back.

"Hello. Anybody out there?"

No response.

Aida had become more comfortable with the Wave World and no longer needed to anchor herself by focusing in tightly on something. The feeling of falling, as in a dream, had been replaced with the acceptance of being untethered, ungrounded. Now she found it easier to broaden her view and take everything in. Innumerable pearls, gathered in brocades of incandescence, dominated her view and gave structure to everything she saw. Vast stretches of open black ocean separated great islands of light, with only a few groups of travelers riding the unseen waves.

In some groupings, though, she saw the dance of the pearls had broken down. The paths they traced, once intertwined and healthy, had gotten out of step with one another, and then the dance ended, each pearl going off on its own and shining less brightly in its isolation. Aida was unsure whether this dissociation was happening more frequently or whether she was better able to notice it. It bothered her; whichever it was, it was happening on a grand scale.

183

People are pulling away from each other. Relationships are breaking down...

"Aida?" It was Matthew. "I've arrived with your husband and daughter at the Chama Valley Zen Center in New Mexico. After some rest, we'll try again to get you flipped back. Everyone is okay, just tired. How are you doing?"

"Okay, I guess. I'm feeling slow, like I'm tired. What day is it? How long have I been here?" she asked.

"You are tired. You've been here for about a hundred hours. It's time to get you out. We'll get started as soon as we can."

As the light of his focus started to turn forward, she called to him. "Matthew, wait!"

"Yes?"

"I've noticed that in some areas, people aren't relating to each other like they used to. The clusters of pearls are breaking apart, and they're going their own ways. It doesn't feel right. Is this normal?"

Matthew was silent for a moment before answering. "That's a penetrating observation. It's not right, and it's not normal. Society is breaking down. It's only gotten worse over the past fifty years. You see, the more people focus on themselves, the more humanity marginalizes the weak and the most vulnerable, the faster the fabric of our global society breaks apart. We believe the actions of the people who are pursuing you and people like them are making matters worse. But we can't worry about that right now. We can talk about this more over a good cup of coffee later. You'll be back home with your family soon."

His focus turned away from the Wave World, and Aida was alone again.

Matthew's suggestion turned her thoughts to Greg and Nat, to seeing them again and the tenderness of holding them and being held by them.

I'll see them soon!

Her anticipation was palpable but mixed with reluctance to let go of the wonders before her.

Will I ever see all this again?

She tried to relax and open up her perceptions so she could drink in everything she saw and permanently imprint it in her memory.

I don't want to forget this. I have to remember it so I can describe it to Greg and Nat.

A small event wave rocked her. These were fairly frequent, and she was accustomed to them now. It was followed by another, and then another, each one increasing in size and force.

That's different, she thought.

Turning her focus toward the origin of the waves, Aida saw the darkness of a massive event wave looming in the distance. The wave grew as it bore down on her, blocking all the remaining light. The hand of fear touched her.

The wave hit her, rolling her over and over like a pebble in a flood. Finally, the spinning world settled.

What was that?

Aida searched for the source of the titanic wave while she was in a trough. Following the path backward, she spotted four dim lights with perfectly straight trails behind them.

There!

She turned to where she had last seen Matthew and called, "Matthew! Anyone!"

Another wave struck her from behind. More powerful than the previous one, it left her stunned and disoriented. Waves continued to pound her. Helpless and out of control, Aida endured the onslaught. Immeasurable time passed until the waves abated and she drifted. Eventually her mind cleared, and the Wave World calmed.

That was horrible!

She searched about for the four dim pearls.

Where are they?

Despite the distortions that the event tsunamis had left in their passing, Aida found the four dim lights she thought to be their source and homed in on them.

"Aida! Aida!" It was Max.

"Here. I'm over here."

"Are you okay? Stay still. I'll be right there." Like a powerful searchlight, Max's mind shone brightly against the shaded, storm-tossed background. He found Aida and touched her mind.

"What were those?" he asked.

"Enormous event waves. Have you ever seen anything like that before?"

185

"No, something terrible has happened. We need to get you out of here now!"

"Listen, I saw where they came from. We have to take a look. We have to understand them in order to deal with them."

"All right, but let's make it fast." He knew arguing the point would only prolong their time here.

"Those waves came from the direction of four very dim pearls, off on their own. Their decision lines—threads, whatever you call them—are completely straight."

"Yes, I see them," Max said. "They're sick, barely alive…"

Aida narrowed her focus on one of them. It wasn't moving on its own; it was locked into the background. The light the pearl emitted was murky and weak.

What's wrong with you? she wondered.

Bewildered that there were no troughs around for a death fold to hide in, Aida reached out to touch the pearl. Its outer boundary gave way like the rotted flesh of a corpse.

"I have to find out more," she told Max.

"Aida, *no!*"

Her need to understand this illness and heal it drove her to engage her senses. Agony and revulsion ripped through her. This wasn't a person, not anymore. It was alive, but only in the same way that a bacterium can be said to be alive. This was a butchered and twisted remnant of a human.

I have to know…

Dr. Doxiphus fought against the revulsion and eased deeper into the experience, mind, and memories of this person. In the center was a flicker of light, the flame of human consciousness. She tenderly palpated it.

His name was Ray Lee Stevens.

"Help me," he said weakly. "Please help me."

Feeble and wan though his being was, he shared his memories with her. Images flashed in her mind's eye. She saw trees and hills and a low, modern two-story building hidden among them. He showed her Seattle, and she saw the inside of a tent and a young man with a baseball cap with "PUSHH" embroidered on it. A bus was leaving Seattle, heading into the hills to the south, and there were

186

other men and women on board. A medical facility, the faces of people dressed in lab coats. One face shocked her.

Beverly Michelson!

The images continued in rapid succession. A photo ID badge read "Volunteer 119." The progression of images froze on one face, an Asian man who was injecting Ray with something.

The memories ended there, leaving only the agony. This patient was beyond her help. Unable to bear his torment, she pulled herself out.

"He's somewhere south of Seattle. His name is Ray, Ray Lee Stevens. Something appalling has been done to him," she cried out to Max.

***

Qian saw the flash of light jump from a QRM right into the view of Observer 119. The holographic stage flared brilliant white, obscuring everything. Alarms blared, and for a few seconds, Qian thought the entire system had collapsed. He snatched up the phone line to the production floor.

"What's going on down there!" he shouted. Alarms went off in the background.

Over the din, a panicked voice replied, "Observer 119's feed just went haywire. There's a massive power surge through the nano probes. We're trying to compensate."

"Do it fast or you'll lose him!" Qian pulled up the diagnostics from Observer 119 and gasped. A system that had been designed to detect and process the faintest of electrical signals was being flooded with energy that was millions of times more powerful than it could handle.

"Trying to attenuate the signal!" he said into the phone, but no one was listening.

Qian heard techs yelling at each other on the production floor. "Terminate the connection before we lose the whole system!" "Kill it. Cut it off. Cut it off."

Suddenly the alarms stopped.

"What's happening? What's going on?" Qian raged into the phone, but on his screen, the readings were normal again. He spun in his chair to see a last spark jump from the view of 119 back to the originating QRM.

It's her! Qian thought.

It took a second or two for him to lock the imaging system onto the QRM of Aida Doxiphus. He snatched up his secure mobile device.

"Mr. Gilden, we have located her."

***

Matthew and Max were under a large cottonwood tree that stood at the center of the courtyard, speaking in hushed whispers.

"How is she?" Matthew asked.

"Traumatized, horrified, in shock. She touched the mind of one of the *akusala*'s victims," said Max. "They've butchered his body and mind. She told us where they are. We've got to stop them, at least from doing to others what they've done to that poor man."

"I agree, though I don't know how. The others will need to be persuaded. Will you attend to that, please?" Max nodded, and Matthew continued. "Talk to John. Perhaps he'll have an idea."

"She's weakening, Matthew. I don't think she'll last another day."

"I know."

"Those massive disturbances…if they hit her again…"

"There's no doubt the massive disturbances were created by the *akusala*," said Matthew. "But how are they doing it, and why?"

"This is extremely dangerous—for the world and for us. Up until now, they've been content with using what they learn from the Wave World to benefit themselves financially and politically. The only thing that makes sense to me is that they're trying to move beyond reading the causes of events to generating causes in the Wave World in order to effect outcomes here in the Particle World."

23 The Choice

Gilden had made it a practice to monitor local news feeds from key cities around the world. Each of them reported outbreaks of interpersonal violence. Stabbings, shootings, and gang violence were the most frequently reported. Incidents of road rage made a few headlines, along with an uptick in the number of petty robberies and carjackings. The local authorities were dealing with each case individually. Lately there had been more than the usual number of reports of excessive use of force by police, particularly against people of color, but that didn't matter to him.

All the events were local, spontaneous, and unrelated as far as anyone else knew. Fortunately there was nothing major, no mass rioting or looting, and no nation had acted against another. Without a doubt, the desensitized world would dismiss the reports as just more bad news to be forgotten as soon as the next commercial ran. They might be left feeling a little more defensive, a little less trusting of their fellow inhabitants of this planet, and therefore they'd be willing to pay more for security, which was just fine by him, thank you. The pilot had been fantastically successful. The Project remained an unseen mover of events, invisible in the shadows, and would continue to profit from its position.

Qian had complained that the induced waves were too strong, and in addition to risking damage to the observers, there might be unexpected consequences. Gilden might have heeded the warnings until Qian also told him how the induced waves had affected Aida Doxiphus. After reviewing the data multiple times, it was clear that

189

her QRM felt the effects of the induced waves an order of magnitude more than other QRMs.

"Keep tracking her," he told Qian. "Let me know of any changes. Baka will be there shortly to take custody of her. If we can use the induced waves to keep her off balance, we can stop her from warning anyone. When can you induce waves again?"

"Not for at least eight hours. We have to finish analyzing the data and allow time for the previously induced waves to dissipate. If new waves meet and join with the older ones, they would add to one another."

"Make it four hours. We have a tool. I want to use it."

***

It was still several hours before sunset in the Chama Valley. Greg, Natalia, and John were escorted into the main hall of the Buddhist temple and seated on low cushions that had been placed for them on the Saltillo tile floor. They sat around a six-foot-by-six-foot colorful geometric sand painting that occupied the center of the hall. The thick adobe walls kept the room surprisingly comfortable considering the cloudless New Mexico summer day outside. To one side, a small golden statue of the Buddha, adorned with garlands of fresh flowers, rested on a raised dais.

Matthew came over to them. "I'm sorry for the delay. The mandala was finished just minutes ago. Your presence and participation are crucial to returning Dr. Doxiphus to this world. We will again mask her view of the Wave World," he said, gesturing to the other monks, "while leaving her view of this world open."

"Where she'll see us, right?" Nat was anxious to get started. "So she'll see us and be drawn back."

Matthew nodded. "As we proceed, try not to pay attention to any negative thoughts or feelings that enter your mind. Keep your focus on your love for her. Visualize her waking up, and imagine your reunion."

"Of course," Greg said.

"Then let's begin." Matthew clapped his hands together once. A chime sounded somewhere in the shadows of the room and resonated with the monks' deep-throated chant. Four monks carried Aida into the room on a pallet. The extra blankets were gone, replaced by a burgundy drape. A fifth monk carried the IV bag. They placed her over the mandala and hung the IV bag from a small camera tripod set up nearby.

"This is a healing mandala," Matthew explained. "My fellow monks started constructing it when I left for University City the day before yesterday. They placed each grain of sand by hand using a *chak-pur*, a small metal funnel. The mandala helps concentrate our energies."

Matthew stepped over to take his place by Aida's head. He seated himself on a cushion, rested his hands on his knees, and closed his eyes. "Start your visualizations now," he instructed.

***

Typically, a missing person report on a homeless vet never would garner the attention of the FBI. It would remain with the local police, in this case the Seattle Police Department. There it would sit at the bottom of a stack, along with thousands of other reports, cases, and incidents they were too understaffed to work on. It took FBI Special Agent Dan Kozlowski more than a moment of reading to understand why he was even looking at this file on Ray Lee Stevens.

As it turned out, a woman claiming to be his daughter, one Jennifer Lynn Stevens of Sage Bend, Missouri, received a letter from the North Plains Life Insurance Company in Minneapolis telling her she had been named the beneficiary a ten-thousand-dollar policy, on the aforementioned Ray Lee Stevens. The letter indicated his residence as simply "Seattle, Washington."

Her mother had said her father had died before she was born. Jennifer never knew her father, so this news was an understandable shock to her.

Boring

Kozlowski read on.

The same day, an anonymous tip came in naming Mr. Ray Lee Stevens. This time the report said he and a group of others, all homeless, were "being held against their will somewhere south of Seattle in the hills by the ocean."

Time to call Seattle PD and Washington State Patrol.

Layer after layer of silver gray enveloped Aida, supported her, and gave her strength. Unhindered by exhaustion, she felt like herself again.

"How are you?" Matthew asked from outside the cocoon.

"Fresh, energized, sharp. Like I just woke up after a great night's sleep. I didn't realize I was so tired."

"Good. Let's make use of that. You need to engage your senses, just like you do when you jump into someone else's mind. Reach out. Feel yourself breathing. Your husband and daughter are just inches from you. They've been through a terrible ordeal, and they need you back. You can touch them; you can be home right now. All you have to do is reach."

In her inner experience, Aida placed herself in Greg's arms and felt his touch. She held his hand, strong and warm. She stroked his unshaven cheek.

"Reach, Aida. They're right here waiting for you. Your daughter needs you. She's been so brave these past few days, but she needs her mother to come back to her now."

"I'm trying!" If Aida could cry tears, she would have.

My daughter and husband need me!

"I can't see them. Help me see them!"

"You can see them. Just look out the front of the cocoon. Look away from the Wave World."

She reached out with the will people find deep in themselves when their life is threatened, committing her entire being to the attempt, giving everything she had. She would succeed or die. Out of the silver gray, sliding in from her left, she saw something she didn't recognize. It was white with dark bands across it.

"That's it!" Matthew encouraged her. "You're nearly there!"

Elated, she realized that while she didn't know what she was seeing, she did know it wasn't the Wave World.

***

"Aida!" Greg called.

"Mom!" Natalia begged. Her mother's eyelids fluttered, and her head turned toward Nat's voice.

***

Against the white background, Aida felt the back of her head shift against some cloth. There was Natalia's face, streaked with tears and worn with fatigue.

"Nat…"

***

The strain on the dozens of monks was excruciating. Matthew had positioned himself toward the open end of the cocoon while their pearls clustered tightly around her, almost forming another outer layer of cocoon. They could keep this up only for a few more moments.

"Matthew!" It was Max. "Something's wrong! The cocoon is opening up."

"Where?" he said, trying to split his focus between Aida and Max.

Alarmed, Max said, "At the other end!"

***

A vision entered Aida's mind and grew into a reality. She saw people on a tropical beach somewhere, hundreds of them. Most of them were standing, looking toward where the water should have been. A few dozen people, including curious children, were running out away from the beach onto the wet sand, where a few moments before they'd been playing and splashing in the surf.

Behind Aida, inland, were streets, houses, hotels, and restaurants filled with people—thousands, tens of thousands. Locals, workers, and vacationers all going about another day in their life.

Aida became aware of an event wave moving toward them all. Not as big as the ones that had battered her senseless before, but broader…much broader.

Oh, my God. No!

From this new reality came a certainty. Thousands of them were about to die unless they moved away from the beach now. A natural tsunami was coming. A disaster of unprecedented proportions, with monstrous cost in human life, was heading straight for them. In horror, she watched as they just stood there. All were curious; only a few sensed something was wrong.

"Aida."

She heard Greg say her name and felt him touch her face.

Everyone stood there, not believing anything would happen to them.

Don't make me choose. Oh, God, please don't make me choose.

The wave was still a little way off. There was still time to warn them, to rescue them.

So she released her hold on Greg and Nat. The shimmering silver-gray cloud fell away from her view. She tumbled and was pulled from every side. A moment later, she landed on the beach, looking out at the brown line on the horizon.

"Run! Tidal wave! Tsunami!" she screamed. A few sunbathers turned toward her. "It's a tsunami! Run!"

Desperate to get them to move, she shouted and ran along the beach. Some local children heard her, and they took up the alarm. Still, the crowds remained transfixed, unmoving. The heat of the sun on Aida's shoulders and head was almost painful, and the thick, humid air made it hard to breathe as she ran and screamed.

The brown line had expanded as it drew closer. Those farthest out from the beach now saw it for what it was. Death. Relentless death in the form of a wall of water forty or fifty feet high, miles across and miles deep, rushed at them across the shallows. They started to run, but it was useless.

Aida stopped running on the beach. She couldn't look away, and she couldn't help. "No!"

The tsunami engulfed all of them and surged up the slight incline of the beach, not slowing at all.

Before it hit her, she felt the rubber band tug.

The event wave moved through pearls too numerous to count. Lights rolled, and some persisted after the event wave passed before they joined those that were snuffed out by the wave's first touch.

They're all dying. I can't save them.

194

Never had Aida felt so powerless, so impotent.

I couldn't save them. Why didn't they listen!

An all-consuming feeling of frustration, fury, and despondency welled up within her, and she broke.

"Damn it all!"

She had no legs to run with, no fists to hit with, no lungs to heave out burning sobs with, no eyes to cry with or even to shut out the world with. All she had was the realization that she hadn't been able to save these people.

"Matthew…Matthew?" Her voice rang in the darkness, unanswered. She pulled her focus in to look around herself. The cocoon was gone. Greg's face was gone. Pearls spun their webs around her, but no one was talking.

"Nat? Greg?" she pleaded.

Mental numbness greeted her when she reached out to them. Her focus wasn't working the way it should; it wouldn't latch on to them. She looked around.

Pearls, decision threads, dark background, clusters, grouping, swirling clouds, distant spirals of light. All was just as it had been before.

Something had changed in her, though. She felt it. An ugly, painful realization clawed at her, but she had so far refused to let it in to her conscious mind.

No! No. No. No. No. No.

It was there; it wouldn't go away. Eventually she weakened, and in it came. The window back to Greg and Nat was gone. She couldn't return. She had sacrificed her family in her attempt to save others, and she had failed at that too.

No!

24 New Mexicans at the Gate

In the warm evening sun, Mollie Garcia mudded up a crack in the one-hundred-year-old adobe wall near the front gate of the Chama Valley Zen Center. Adobe mud, the same color as her skin, was caked under her nails and in the deep creases of her calloused hands. She had done physical work like this for most of her sixty-five years and still looked young for it, her salt-and-pepper hair notwithstanding. While she worked, she hummed a tune her mother had sung to her when she was a child on the family ranch in Las Vegas, New Mexico.

She didn't turn right away to look when a big, shiny black SUV came up the gravel drive and parked on the other side of the vacant lot from her pickup truck. She did stop working when two imposing men in black suits stepped out. The big pale one with the close-cropped red hair started to come toward her. The other stayed back, standing behind the passenger door.

"Hi. We'd like to go in and see the center. Can you open the gate and let us in?" he growled in a barely civilized voice.

Leaning back on her knees, Mollie wiped her hands on her jeans and heaved a satisfied sigh as she admired her work and ignored the man. Pricked at being ignored, he took a few steps closer to her and drew himself up to his full height.

"Look, lady. Maybe you didn't hear me. But we're going into that compound, and it'll go a lot easier for you if you help us."

Mollie stood up to her full height, not quite five feet tall, and faced him. She squinted one eye at him. "To hell with you," she said. "Go on and get yourself outta here."

He advanced on her, clenching and unclenching his fists.

She didn't move from where she stood except to hold out both hands and shout, "That's close enough, *pendejo!*" when he was twenty feet out. The man didn't break his stride, a malevolent grin stretched across his face.

A subtle zinging sound parted the air, followed by a loud pop and hissing as the driver's-side front tire of the SUV expelled its contents. Less than a second later, the sharp crack of the shot followed. The man froze in his tracks while the vehicle slumped to one side. His partner pulled out a handgun and drew down on Mollie.

Another zing and the passenger side mirror exploded, raining plastic and glass shrapnel on the man. The message was punctuated by four more shots—two through the windshield, one into the passenger rear tire, and the last into a headlight just for good measure.

"*Las lomas tienen ojos, y rifles de caza tambien,*" Mollie said, then translated: "The hills have eyes, hunting rifles too. Sounds like they're loaded for big game. Lots of bears around here. You have to be careful."

The big man flinched as she took a step toward him and his partner, knowing he was standing in the middle of a kill zone.

In the cold, rock-hard voice of the person in charge, Mollie said, "Now that we're clear on things, you'd better drop that little toy *pistola* of yours before you get hurt." The man's partner dropped it as commanded. "Keep your hands out where we can see them. Go back in your truck, leave, and don't come back. We'll be watching."

Humiliated, the two men slowly worked their way back into what was left of their vehicle, started it, and backed out. Seething, the redheaded man glared at Mollie.

She permitted herself a short chuckle as the SUV lurched, creaked, and hissed around the lot to exit the way it had come.

"I'd like to see how they're going to explain that at the car rental agency," Mollie muttered.

A few minutes later, as the sun set in the west, and its rich yellows, golds, and reds gradually gave way to pale and then the deeper blues of twilight, her two nephews, Miguel and Francisco, strolled into the lot, hunting rifles with scopes on their shoulders.

197

She wiped her hands with a wet towel to get the mud off, then picked up her cell phone from a rock near her workspace and made a call.

"You were right. Two big guys came by...no, no one got hurt. My nephews had to scare off some coyotes, that's all...no, I don't think they'll be back," she said, not believing the words as they came off her tongue, but she didn't want to scare the monks.

Mollie's nephews loaded the rifles back into the rack in her pickup and pulled it inside the compound. "You boys better get ready, just in case they do show up again," she called after them.

***

"Thank you for making yourself available, Dr. Michelson. I understand you just flew in," said the grant auditor as he proffered a polite handshake. "Herb Redwood, NIH."

"Of course," she said, smiling back. "Happy to help. I did examine Aida—that is, Dr. Doxiphus. I have a passing familiarity with her work. Given the terrible situation, it's the least I could do."

They were in Aida's lab which had been sealed off after she was found unconscious. Kelley was speaking with the other auditor in Aida's office, so Michelson was only able to catch portions of their conversation.

"Well, no crime was committed, so there's no reason to involve the police," she overheard Kelley explaining.

"Still, you have to admit that Dr. Doxiphus's collapse, her lab tech's sudden death, and her and her family's disappearance from the hospital could rouse more than a little suspicion," the other auditor said.

"They didn't disappear—that was just a paperwork mix-up," Kelley replied. "The Doxiphuses have every right to seek medical treatment wherever they choose, and they have my complete confidence. We've been completely transparent in this matter."

Kelley will be busy for a while, no doubt, she thought.

"Dr. Michelson, Dr. Kelley was hoping you could help us with the QUESAM device," Redwood said.

Qian said this is how it would be.

Redwood gestured for her to enter the stim room first and left the outer door open. "The console was locked," he said. "Dr. Kelley was kind enough to have a technician come and open it. We found this screen still up. What can you make of it?"

"Well, I don't know. I'm more familiar with the generalities of Dr. Doxiphus's work, not the actual software," she lied as she seated herself at the QUESAM console, "but let's take a look."

The grant proposal, its revisions, and quarterly reports Gilden had provided her contained more than enough information to decipher what she saw, and she knew the NIH had access to the same information. She was personally acquainted with all the leading experts in the field, but Redwood wasn't one of them. Still, it always paid to be cautious.

"They were working on developing a next generation cortical monitoring and stimulation system. You can see here in these windows the readings for the commonly monitored EEG wave rhythms." She gestured to the screen. "Alpha, beta, theta, delta, mu, and lambda. Here's some information from the last experimental run."

Michelson clicked on a multicolored image of Aida's brain that was frozen in the center of the screen. Immediately below the image was a timeline bar.

"I think we can replay the last run," she said.

When she clicked the "play" button in the lower left-hand corner of the window, the image jumped to the beginning of the run. Even though the 2-D rendering was crude compared to the imaging system Qian had developed, it sufficed. Waves of color played across the surface of the brain image, and by dragging on the image, Michelson was able to rotate it in a simulation of 3-D.

"What's remarkable about this is the temporal and spatial resolution," she continued lecturing to Redwood. "A normal EEG would have at most a few dozen leads taking readings across the skull. This device"—she waved her arm to the long open-ended tube suspended from the ceiling of the inner room—"has thousands, maybe tens of thousands."

Redwood watched silently from behind.

"These waves, the patterns you're seeing here, are all completely normal for an adult brain at rest with the eyes closed."

There was a subtle flicker in the rhythms, shorter than a heartbeat, and then image on the screen flared, and glowed for a moment. Then the light dimmed and contracted into flat gray nothingness. The playback stopped there.

That's when it happened! All the settings are here, captured in the system. I can fix it and do it again!

"What was that?" Redwood asked.

Michelson shrugged. "I don't know. Looks like some sort of power surge burned out the sensors, like a light bulb burning out. With more time, I'm sure I could get a clearer outline of the events."

"Thank you, Doctor. We're not doing an official investigation; we're just confirming the reports."

"Excuse me, Dr. Michelson, Mr. Redwood, could you join us, please?" asked Kelley, who had stuck his head through the open door.

Redwood swung around. "Sure, we're all wrapped up here."

In that moment, Michelson deftly reached up and turned off the screen.

"Dr. Michelson?"

"Coming. Just locking the console."

Out in the lab proper, Redwood spoke to Kelley while the other auditor packed up a briefcase.

"Thank you both for your time," Redwood said. "Our official report will be released at the end of the month."

"Can you give me some indication...?" Kelley trailed off. He hoped the auditors were in a merciful mood.

"Well, you can depend on our report to reflect the accidental nature of the events here. We'll just consider the Doxiphuses' disappearance as—"

Kelley interrupted. "They haven't disappeared. I'm sure they just went somewhere private. It's only been two days. They'll be in contact at any time."

"—a short-term medical emergency," Redwood finished. "I'm sure your office will track them down."

Kelley breathed a mental sigh of relief.

Later that night, over a large brandy, he would congratulate himself on a job well done and be grateful the research and scientific establishment in this country made frequent allowances for its members who sometimes went off on a wild bend. *Brilliant minds, after all*, he thought. *We must make accommodations.*

25 Despair

The keening of her soul went on. Unable to bear the agony that was her existence, a fragment of her mind pulled away from the tortured whole and retreated into itself until it came to know that it existed separately from the pain. Its arm's-length distance gave it perspective on the pain, and for a while it watched the pain happen and waited, but it didn't feel. The pain was happening to someone else.

It stirred when the experience of the pain began to recede, and it expanded to fill the empty space left by the diminishing sensation. Tentatively it grew, making sure it didn't touch the agony. Slowly other things presented themselves for its consideration. Shapes—squares with jagged edges in brilliant orange, violet, blacks, and grays—slid over one another, folded, hid, and blossomed forth again. Indistinct amoebic blobs swam across her vision and joined with one another, trying to create something more, only to lose their grip and slip away.

A new stimulus, a sound, came to it. Hesitant to touch, it examined the novelty from a distance. The sound evoked a dim, foreign memory of a whisper of self-identity.

"Aida."

The strange sound repeated.

"Aida."

"Aida, come back. Don't be afraid."

Compassion illuminated her and coaxed it out into the full light.

"Aida, it's me, Max. You're safe now. You've been hallucinating."

I'm Aida...he's talking to me. She came around, slowly and dully, to detached reality. *That's Max.*

The Wave World oozed into flat, colorless focus. Aida recognized it now and remembered Max.

"Max," the alien voice that was hers said. "Max."

"I'm here, Aida. Can you see me? I'm right in front of you." His strength, warmth, and compassion cradled her. She drew from that, and the world lost some of its unreality. She clung tighter to him. Memories came back.

"My family?"

"They're all okay. You were almost back. You opened your eyes," he said.

That registered somewhere within her, and then the memory of the beach flooded forth.

"I couldn't save them, Max. No one listened. I tried. I screamed and yelled, but no one listened." She started to relive her abject failure.

"It's okay now, you did try to..."

"They all died, Max! Children! People with families! Everyone gone...just gone."

"I know. We saw; the whole world saw. Aida, you couldn't stop it, but you did try to change it."

She collapsed back, mute, destitute of the willpower to act.

"Aida, we were so close before. It would have worked, but then something happened and...and you went to try to help those people," he stammered out.

Another emotional spasm erupted in her, and she vomited out her next words. "I abandoned them. I abandoned my husband and my child...I'll never get back." Her guilt and sense of impotence crushed her.

"Yes, yes, you will," Max encouraged her. "We were so close. Everyone's okay, and we can still do this."

His pearl was right in front of her. She tried to reach out to touch him but couldn't; she didn't have the strength.

"I'm not going to leave you here, Aida. I'm not leaving, no matter what happens. Everyone needs to rest. We'll try again in a little while. You just rest too."

Max's pearl shone brightly in the darkness of the Wave World, bathing Aida in blissful relief. His warm energy trickled into her, and in a timeless moment, she rested and let go of the pain, the self-recrimination, and guilt.

"You have to see how beautiful you are, Aida. You have to see the good in yourself. There will never be anyone like you, ever, in all time. Forgive yourself."

Her mind cleared, and she saw Max, seated, radiant, composed, giving freely of his own life-force.

"Max..."

"Shh, I'm okay. Just giving you a little help here. Honor the gift by accepting it graciously."

"Max, no. Look, he's coming."

Behind Max, a blank momentum moved in the background, carrying a dozen or more pearls straight toward them. She knew one in particular as the cop. Reckless in his approach, his pearl was completely unguarded, and it throbbed with deep hatred and a need for vengeance. Clear, above all, was his murderous intent. Angus Baka would be there soon.

***

"We're gonna do what? *Esta loca, tía?* They'll catch us in a minute! Then what do we do?" Miguel Sanchez thought this was the stupidest idea he'd ever heard in his life. He stood gaping at his aunt while he wiped gun oil from his hands. Their three hunting rifles and three semiautomatic pistols, all freshly cleaned, shone like new on the table under the workshop light.

"Don't you talk to me that way!" Mollie snapped back at him. "There's more of them coming this time. Maybe a half dozen or more. There's only one road in and out of here. They'll block that off easy. No trucks!" Mollie's steel, never far from the surface anyway, came through loud and clear. That was that.

"Okay, so how are we gonna move her?" Miguel asked as he plopped the oilcloth on the table.

"That poor lady is on a stretcher already. We'll tie it between two of the horses and head into the hills to wait them out. If they decide to follow us, we'll have the advantage there."

"Is it just her, or are they all coming?" he asked, already knowing the answer but hoping for a different one.

"All three of them. The medic was in the navy, so he should be able to handle himself."

Miguel grimaced. "What about the others?"

"Matthew and the others are staying here, though I don't know what the hell they think they can do."

"How long do we have?"

"Twenty, maybe thirty minutes. Find your brother, and get the horses ready. I'll grab the packs."

He made a last appeal. "This is gonna be a bitch to do at night, *tía, que no*?"

"What? You think they're gonna be friendly to us when they come back? Hell no, Miguel. We need to get out of here too."

That, at last, made sense to him. Twenty-five minutes later, a line of shadows slipped through the back gate of the Chama Valley Zen Center. A last-quarter moon hung low in the crystalline eastern sky and provided just enough light for them to pick out the faint trail that wound between the junipers and brush. Although the path steepened, the footing was sure, and soon they were looking down on the small square of buildings three hundred feet below. From this height, they saw a sweeping expanse of the Rio Chama glistening faintly in the moonlight as it ran through the valley. Around them the air was perfumed with the smoky-sweet smell of piñon fires.

Soon the path leveled out and disappeared around the side of the hill, which towered another four hundred feet above them. They were well around the bulk of it and fully hidden from view when the headlights of the first Humvee came to rest on Mollie's mudded-up wall.

***

It had taken a joint effort of the FBI's Operational Technology Division (OTD) and Criminal Justice Information Services Division (CJIS) fifteen years and hundreds of millions of dollars to realize this vision. It could have been done sooner if it hadn't been for the politics involved in choosing the location. Both the OTD in Quantico and the CJIS in Clarksburg were in the running. Quantico won out in the end by virtue of its more convenient travel time from FBI headquarters and Capitol Hill. The FBI was rightfully proud of its state-of-the-art Crime Visualization Center (CVC), and there was no shortage of VIP tours in its first year and a half of operation.

The CVC was the result of a massive upgrade in the 911 and crime-reporting systems of all the first- and second-tier cities across the United States. Considered the next step in the evolution of the Unified Crime Reports and the National Incident Based Reporting System, it was funded by a shining example of cooperation between the DOJ, DHS, NSA, and the 2R Corporation, a privately held technology and investment firm.

It started with a simple software upgrade to the 911 call systems, provided at no cost by 2R, which labeled every 911 call that came in with a simple metadata tag. Once the call was classified as a robbery, assault, homicide, theft, domestic disturbance, or what have you, the system then sent data to a central database in a private cloud housed at the OTD. It was a routine big-data visualization exercise to compile and project it all on a massive screen here at the CVC.

In a few months, with phase one a huge success, the Free America Bill passed, due in part to the strong support of a political action group called Main Street for a Peaceful America. If anyone had bothered to examine the financial statements of the Main Street group, they wouldn't have been surprised to find it was generously funded by another offshore shell company that was in turn owned by 2R. The Free America Bill contained a deeply buried provision allowing the national law enforcement apparatus to legally collect recorded audio, video, and GPS data from mobile devices. Phase two of the CVC then took this data, analyzed it in near real time for violent criminal activity, applied filters, and correlated it in time and location. This citizen feed, as it was called, was then used to supplement the 911 feed. The result was the single most accurate projection of criminal activity in the world.

***

Tejinder Johar glanced at the OTD's motto, "Vigilance through Technology," emblazoned above the big screen for the hundredth time this shift. He did it so frequently that it didn't even register anymore. Color-coded symbols, each representing a different class of crime, continually bubbled up on the map. Vivid to start with, each would fade with time. The point of the visualization system was to see what was going on right now. As the data aged off the big screen, it was preserved for further analysis later if needed.

Fascinated by the patterns in which certain crimes occurred, he could now predict where there might be outbreaks. For example, a heat dome over the New York City metropolitan area would spike assaults and burglaries, while nighttime in Los Angeles during the summer meant increased gang activity. Johar had a bet with his shift supervisor that during the next Super Bowl, everything would quiet down during the first half.

He didn't notice the red dot, indicating some type of personal assault, which had materialized in Olympia, Washington, nor the others that followed thirty seconds later in Seattle. The CVC system dutifully logged the activity, and when other incidents simultaneously rolled in from Portland and Spokane, some bit of logic flagged the activity for scrutiny by a higher-level process. The higher-level process started to get interested when Helena, Boise, and Eugene popped up within seconds of one another. The temporal-activity filter function got involved and crunched the pattern for a microsecond when Sacramento, San Francisco, Salt Lake City, Denver, and Cheyenne were added. It then calculated the correlation of events in time and location and posted a "significant event" alert on the big screen.

"What's this?" Johar watched the wave of red dots popping up in major cities and state capitals as they progressed from the northwest to the southeast across the continent. Assaults occurred across the country all the time in the expected locations, but these were all linked in time and by locations. He paused the live feed on his local monitor, allowing the incoming data to buffer while he slid the timer control back to the left. With this he could play events backward and forward in time while he watched. The epicenter seemed to be somewhere in Washington state.

"This is very unusual," he muttered.

The shift supervisor's voice came over the headset. "Johar, what do you make of this?"

207

"It certainly looks real, but I can't rule out anomalous behavior in the system."

All eyes in the CVC locked on the big screen as wave followed wave, about five minutes apart, rolling across the continent.

"Zoom in on the origin," said the shift supervisor

Johar centered and magnified his map on the forested hills by the coast in southwestern Washington.

Another analyst came on the loop. "The local authorities are all responding. They're a little overtaxed. No one at a local level is reporting any connections between these events."

"They wouldn't. They're too close to it," Johar offered.

And then the events stopped.

"Notifying response coordination," the shift supervisor said. "They'll get this to the Seattle field office."

***

For the third time in a day, the attention of Special Agent Dan Kozlowski was turned toward the lumber forests along Washington State 101.

His first response of "What the hell?" was followed by a call to the Washington State Patrol. Something was going on down there, and they needed to find out what it was. His next call was to the US Attorney's office to modify his warrant request to add suspected terrorism. The last step in the chain was to activate the incident response team. Nothing was obviously on fire, no bombs, active shooters, or crashing planes, which would have complicated the situation, but once WSP had a list of probable locations, they would need to act quickly.

Another agent popped his head over Kozlowski's cubicle wall.

"PUSHH, the Puget Sound Homeless Haven, was handing out vouchers to the homeless for food, shelter, and medical."

"Where's the medical facility?"

"They don't have an exact location, but some of the homeless who came back from there say it's in your hotspot by the coast."

"Let's go. We'll meet up with the response team on the way."

208

26 Max's Gift

"Qian's lost sight of her again. I want her here, in one piece, Baka, okay? We clear on that?" Gilden snarled into the secure phone. "I've approved everything you asked for. I expect this to be clean and quiet."

"Yessir, we're ready. It'll be a fast operation, in and out. Time on-site less than ten minutes."

"Just get it done."

Gilden did expect Baka to get the job done. Clean and quiet, well, that was another story.

The man's lost his head. This is a personal thing for him now. Baka's use to Gilden–and, by extension, his life– was limited to the next few hours.

Gilden summoned his personal assistant into his office. "Get ready to dump Baka."

"Even if he's successful?"

"Wait until after he hands the package off. Then dump him. No traces. I think one of the cartels is looking for the person who intercepted a shipment of theirs and got the money too. That'll wrap things up nicely."

Nothing worse than a broken tool, Gilden thought.

***

"Yessir, we're ready. It'll be a fast operation, in and out. Time on-site less than ten minutes."

You're goddamn right I'll get the job done.

209

It was a matter of pride and professional reputation for Angus Baka now.

"There. Set down between the headlights," he told the helicopter pilot. The Humvees had taken up positions at the corners of the parking lot of the Chama Valley Zen Center with their headlights pointing inward, illuminating the landing zone.

"I want the lights out and that gate open as soon as we set down unit one. These are a bunch of monks, so there won't be any resistance. We go in, secure the package, get her on the chopper, and fly her out," he ordered into the open comms channel.

Unit two broke in. "Sir, what about the hostile contacts?"

"Deal with any hostile contacts immediately and directly."

Kill them.

Its running lights off, the chopper swung in low, doing a pass over the center before settling into the illuminated patch, kicking up sand and debris in an intentionally noisy display. Two armed men in tactical gear went over the wall to open the gate from the inside.

"Cutting power," unit three reported, and the center went dark.

Good, they're in the dark and disoriented.

"Put your eyes on," Baka said, lowering his night vision goggles into place. The world turned spectral shades of green as he climbed out of the chopper and raced into the open courtyard.

"We have them all, sir, in the building on your left as you come in through the gate," unit one squawked over the comms. "They were all in a large room, praying."

"Any issues?"

"No, sir. Just like sheep."

"Unit two, stay with the vehicles. Unit three, sweep the compound. I don't want any surprises."

Baka marched into the temple. The monks were seated on the floor around a square geometric design, their fingers interlocked behind their heads, their robes only appearing as brighter and darker shades of green to his eyes. But there was no Aida. The husband, daughter, and medic were missing too. The two men in unit one stood at either door to the room, blocking the exits and staying out of each other's line of fire.

"Where's the woman and her family?" Baka barked.

No answer.

210

"Just cooperate. No one needs to get hurt." Baka's voice floated menacingly on the night air. No one answered. Worse yet, not a single one of them seemed frightened. They all sat like stone statues—no anxiety-filled glances, no quaking or cowering, no fast breathing or sweating.

Out of the darkness, a voice tinged with concern offered, "What you are doing is unwholesome for you. Put down your guns, and sit with us."

Baka stood there, dumbstruck. Unconsciously his gloved fingers tightened on his weapon. His men were looking at him. He had to act, not stand here flatfooted, taken off guard.

I'm in control here, he reminded himself. *More pressure.*

He was done playing. He raised his weapon and closed his eyes against the muzzle flash as he squeezed off two rounds over their heads. The shots embedded themselves harmlessly into the thick adobe wall. He waited a few seconds for the shock of the shots to sink in and for their hearing to return.

"Where are the woman and her family?" Baka demanded between gritted teeth. A bead of sweat trickled down his cheek.

"You are only harming yourself, Angus. This path is destructive." The disembodied voice was now paternal in its concern. Fear brushed up against his mind. How did they know his name?

Unit three broke the spell. "Sir, we're in the barn. We've found the pickup and a jeep here. No sign of the subjects, but there are two empty horse stalls with fresh manure, and the tack is missing. My guess is they headed into the surrounding area on foot some time ago."

Baka's face clenched into a grimace as he finally came to understand his blind spot.

They can see too. They knew we were coming.

He had let his mental guard slip as well. Someone was helping the woman and hindering them right now. He cursed himself for the mistakes. Fear wasn't the lever to use against this opponent; it was time to switch tactics.

"All units, take off your eyes. Unit three, gimme light." A few seconds later, the room burst into brilliance.

Baka slowly paced around the kneeling monks, looking at them for something.

One of them is over there, watching, right now.

"Got another one. Black guy here in the corner of the courtyard. He's hidden behind some plants," unit three called out.

"What's he doing?"

"Nothing. He's just sitting there cross-legged with his hands on his knees."

Got you!

"You two stay here." Baka strode into the courtyard.

Enough of this shit.

A lone man sat in the shadows, his eyes half-closed, breathing slowly.

Baka took out his phone and made a call. "Qian, can you see me?...Yeah, with two men. No one else?...Good."

With a single smooth movement, like pushing a button in an elevator, Baka drew his sidearm and fired a single shot into the monk's head, the sound reverberating off the walls of the compound.

"Can you see her now?" he asked Qian. "Great. I need interference to blind her and anyone else who might be watching. At least one of these monks was able to watch us." He hung up and opened up his comms. "Unit two, stay with the group. Make sure they keep their eyes open and stay awake. Shoot anyone who does different."

Baka reached down and grabbed the blood-soaked collar of the monk's robe. He dragged him across the courtyard through the dirt and into the temple. He then kicked over the Buddha statue and replaced it with the corpse; blood flowed from the gaping crater in the man's head, staining the flowers and white linen of the altar. The monks looked at the grisly spectacle in front of them and cast their eyes down. One's eyes moistened; others appeared shocked and revolted.

There, that's better now.

Baka left the room, heading for the front gate. "Units one and three, regroup to the LZ. We're heading into the hills."

***

"Ignore him, Aida. Try to be calm," said Max. "The more you focus on him, the easier it will be for the *akusala* to see you."

212

Max had guided her into a broad, shallow, platter-like depression. Undulating waves, dark as charcoal, surrounded her. Occasionally the troughs aligned, creating a gap through which she could see the cop's pearl. He kept an irregular distance from her. He'd come closer and then move off, leaving her with the impression of a circling shark. He was hunting for her, getting warmer, then colder, then warmer again, but relentlessly drawing the trap tighter.

Nat, Greg, and John remained in their tight orbit around her. They'd been joined by three others, Max explained. The newcomers were the caretaker of the Chama Valley Zen Center and her nephews. Two light-brown spherical objects, distinct against the background, attended as well. From her current vantage point, she couldn't see Max at all. He had hidden himself like a hunter in a blind. Even so, she could feel his presence, as they were talking to each other.

"What's going on, Max? What time is it?"

"It's night. This might sound a little weird. Mollie and her nephews are taking you and your family up into the hills for a little while. Everyone is safe. They'll wait it out, then bring you back to the center."

"How are they moving me?"

"New Mexican ingenuity," he said, chuckling. "You're on a litter, a stretcher, tied between two horses, one in front and one behind."

She imagined herself bouncing along between the horses on a mountain trail. It struck her funny bone, and she laughed. There was just something hilarious about it. The music of *On the Trail* from the *Grand Canyon* suite with its clip-clopping train of braying donkeys played in her mind like an earworm. *Doop-da-doop-da-doop-da-do-daa-daa-doop-da-doop-da-doop...heee-hawww.*

"Aida, shhh."

"Sorry it's jus…" She tittered again, then broke out into a full laugh. Trying to stifle the urge only made it worse. The image played on, and the pearls around her stretched and warped. They started bouncing in time with the music.

Follow the bouncing ball, a cartoon voice said, so she sang along with the music.

"Doop-da-doop-da-doop-da-do-daa-daa…" A pearl became Bill Fahy's face; another appeared as the boy from the plane crash whom she had helped rescue. Multiple faces from the beach floated before

213

her, wearing expressions of shock and horror. The music stopped as the Wave World spun around her like her dorm room had that one time she had flopped onto her bed after drinking too much, and she became frightened.

"Maaaaax, make it stop."

The drunken spinning stopped, and the Wave World snapped back to solidity. She could see Max clearly. The tendril of his life-force that fed her was larger now.

"Aida, you must be quiet now. The cop—his name's Baka—he and his men are here in the temple, and they're searching the compound."

"Okay, I get it, shhhhhhh," she said.

Baka's pearl had become stationary around a cluster of vivid, vibrant pearls.

"I have to help them. Hold on, Aida. Keep it together," said Max.

His lifeline to her diminished to the barest filament. Max had turned his focus directly to Baka. Over their connection, she heard Max speak to Baka.

"What you are doing is unwholesome for you. Put down your guns, and sit with us."

Baka's pearl froze. Max's unexpected comment had rattled him. "You are only harming yourself, Angus. This path is destructive," said Max.

Baka shuddered. He was losing control; he was afraid.

"Max, be careful. You're backing him into a corner," Aida said.

Baka's pearl hardened, changing to an impenetrable wall of concrete. He looped around the cluster once, then made straight for Max.

"Max, he's coming for you!" she yelled.

Out of nowhere, a yawing, fathomless fold appeared right in front of Max. Through their link, she knew Max saw it too. Panicked, she thrust her consciousness at Baka and Max, trying to interpose herself between the two.

"No, Aida. I can't let you do that. I'm sorry I can't keep my promise...here, you're going to need this." Light surged down the link and into her. Baka was right on top of him.

"Max...*no!*"

His pearl fell soundlessly into the death fold. Baka's pearl arced around the cluster of monks, then headed on a path she could see would soon cross hers.

"Help! Anyone! Damn it, he killed Max," she cried out desperately.

"Matthew!" her voice shot into the void, but no one answered.

The monster was coming for her and...

Oh, my God.

Her family.

They have to leave me. They have to get away.

Energized by the infusion from Max, she reached out to touch Greg, only to be slammed by the vanguard of Qian's second massive set of induced event waves.

***

"We have a hit on the FLIR," unit three reported over the comms.

"Call it out!"

"Looks like a set of footprints or hoofprints leading away on a path out the back of the compound."

The summer sun had heated the soil throughout the day, and it was cooling evenly at night, making the ground appear a uniform orangish yellow through their infrared scopes. But where the horses' hooves had dug into the dirt and dust, they exposed a cooler layer of soil that showed up dark blue, with the very center of the hoofprint brighter. Unit three followed the path. Every few yards, the outer ring darkened and took on a distinct horseshoe shape around a brighter and brighter center. The trail couldn't have been easier to follow if it had been breadcrumbs.

"One and three, continue on foot. I'll be in the air." Baka made a circular motion with his hand to the chopper pilot, telling him to spool up. The ending was clear in his mind now. They would run them down, secure the woman, kill the rest, then disappear off the face of the planet. The balance of power made the outcome inevitable. It made him feel good.

27 *Cabras de la Montaña*

It had only taken the Washington State Patrol about twenty minutes to identify the target as a cluster of modern buildings called The Project. Tucked away in the lumber forests that covered Grays Harbor and Pacific counties, it sat low between the outstretched arms of two long ridges and was conspicuous for its attempt to look inconspicuous. State and federal records listed it as a nonprofit medical treatment facility for homeless veterans. A quick review of the Washington state auditors' records revealed that an extraordinary amount of money had been spent to create it, with payouts to the state and the lumber corporation that managed the land. Political capital had been spent too. The environmental impact studies had been rushed through the EPA, and all the necessary state and federal permits had been approved so quickly that the ink from the rubber stamps hadn't had time to dry.

Kozlowski had instructed the WSP to set up a perimeter five miles out along the logging roads that led from SR101 to The Project. The FBI response teams were in place and ready to serve the no-knock warrants. The satellite imagery showed everything was quiet, which was just as it should be at 4:34 in the morning.

What's holding up the warrant approval? Kozlowski fumed. His phone buzzed; it was Virgil Williams, the US district attorney for the state of Washington.

"What do you have for me, Virgil? Can we go?"

"Not yet, Danny. You'll have to wait. There's some serious political sponsorships behind this place that I'm working through. I've had to bump this up to the AG's office. I expect she'll have to sign off on this one herself, along with the Intelligence Surveillance Court."

That confirmed The Project as the target for Kozlowski. There was no reason the AG and ISC should have been involved in reviewing this.

"Whatever this place is," Kozlowski said, "it isn't just a treatment facility. You've gotta push this through fast."

"I'll get back to you before the top of the hour."

***

"I'll notify you of any changes at once, Mr. Gilden," Qian said as his boss stalked around the holographic stage, where the clock at the bottom changed to 4:36 a.m. Gilden had come down when he had learned that the monks had the ability to see the quantum world. For a man who prized anonymity and control above all else, the feeling of exposure that came with this revelation was torturous. He hadn't stopped stalking around the projection stage for more than an hour now.

"I'm not leaving, Doctor. Just do your job," Gilden shot back.

For his part, Qian was equally ill at ease with Gilden's looming presence and badgering.

"We're safe, Mr. Gilden. The observers are inducing disturbances into the quantum foam. We can barely see what's going on ourselves."

What they did know was that Baka and his team were chasing Aida Doxiphus and a group of others through the canyons, arroyos, hills, and slopes of New Mexico at night. Baka was airborne, and two teams of two men each were on foot. Their IR and night vision equipment made the tracking easy. It should be just a matter of time now.

***

"We've got one bad situation here, *hermano*," Francisco said as he joined his brother, who was crouching behind a boulder. They had stopped again.

"No shit. How's the old man doin'?" asked Miguel.

217

"Puking his guts out. It's altitude sickness. How far behind us are they?"

The group had been on the move throughout the night, scrambling over the rocks, ducking random fire from behind, and hiding from the chopper as best they could. Miguel and Francisco had been in these hills since they were small boys and knew the terrain well. That was probably the only reason they were all still alive. They had purposely chosen passages through narrow slots so the chopper couldn't come too low in the darkness for fear of crashing into the convoluted, rapidly changing terrain. But their hunters were tenacious, and given the accuracy of their shots, they probably had night vision and IR gear.

"About three-fourths of a mile now. I wish I had my nightscope. I'd wax these motherfuckers real quick," Miguel coldly commented.

"That air cover is killing us. We'd be out of here if we could get rid of that," said Francisco.

"Don't believe what you see in the movies. We can't take it down with what we've got here."

John skidded in beside them. "Greg's not going to make it much farther. Then we'll have two people to carry. We need a defensible position, somewhere we can draw them in, make them come to us. I hope you guys have something in mind."

"Hold that thought," Miguel requested as he rested his 30.08 on the rock and sighted down and to the right. John recognized the pattern, a slow and steady release of breath, the finger steadily increasing pressure on the trigger.

Crack!

"Winged his leg!" Miguel said as he cycled another round into the chamber. Then he yelled, "Hey, c'mon, *cabron*. Got some more here for you!"

In response, the fast *thump-thump-thump* of the heavy rotors came closer.

"Shit, we gotta move."

Multiple shots peppered wildly around them as they ran back up the trail to the waiting litter and the rest of the group.

"So can I ask where we're going now?" John yelled over the thunderous clamor of the passing chopper.

"Oro Y Azul. What do you think, Francisco?"

218

"Anything beats being out here!"

The sound of the chopper steadied, and there was a single shot. One of the horses screamed in the fading night.

"Son of a bitch! I was afraid of that!" John gasped. Their path led through some large boulders, and on the other side they saw one of the horses was down, dropping Aida off the litter. Nat and Mollie were gathering her and the IV.

"Damn it," John said. "We're on foot now. What's Oro y Azul?"

"An old turquoise mine," Miguel said. "The entrance isn't too far. At least it'll give us cover from that *pinche* chopper."

"*Tía*," Francisco said. "Oro y Azul. It's about five hundred yards over that ridge ahead of us. You and Natalia take these." He and Miguel handed over their rifles. "Us four men will carry Aida on the stretcher."

"No, you're the better shot. Francisco, you know the way. You, Greg, Natalia, and I will carry Aida. John, can you handle a rifle?"

"Yes, ma'am." If there were ever a better example of someone who should've been in command school, he couldn't think of one.

They turned the other horse loose; it wouldn't do them any good now anyway. John strapped Aida into the stretcher and wedged the IV bag down by her legs, where it would be held but not compressed. Mollie and Francisco picked up the front two handles, Greg and Nat the back, and off they went. Mollie set a brutal pace over the rocks and up the slope, never slipping, surefooted as a mountain goat. Soon, Greg was panting again. John and Miguel followed thirty yards behind, trading shots with the men in pursuit. The chopper orbited high overhead, like a hawk waiting for its prey to show itself.

Thirty yards from the top of the ridge, the boulders and brush they'd been using for cover vanished, and the path continued into the open.

"Francisco, how far after the top of the ridge?" Mollie grunted through gulping breaths.

"The treeline is just over the side, and the path picks up again off to the left. After that, maybe two hundred yards or so to the ravine with the entrance."

"Okay. Hold up here. Everyone catch your breath." She looked back at Greg and Nat, both of whom were winded and tired but on their feet.

Miguel and John caught up to them a few seconds later. Miguel traded a look with his brother when he saw the open space that was between them and the safety of the mine.

"*Tía*, you all make a run for it. We'll wait behind here and try to slow them down. Maybe we'll even take a few shots at the chopper."

"Okay, *mijo*. You guys ready?"

Nat and Greg nodded.

"Let's go."

The four of them took off, their rapid footfalls kicking up clouds of dust in the purple-blue light of early dawn. Shots, popping off like firecrackers on the Fourth of July, sounded off behind them. Straining, heaving the stretcher, they crested the ridge and almost lost their balance as they descended on the other side. In a few panicked breaths, they made it to the treeline and cover. The path descended, with walls of rock rising on either side, and they slowed their pace. Straight ahead was a dark rectangular shape in the rock wall. As they got closer, Nat read ORO Y AZUL carved into the wooden beam that served as the lintel over the entrance to the mine.

The six steps they took into the mine robbed them of what little light they had. Spent from their dash, they put Aida down and collapsed onto the tunnel floor. Francisco dug a flashlight out of his pack and flicked it on. No one spoke; they just all lay there, panting and looking behind them out the entrance, waiting for Miguel and John.

***

Miguel popped off a few shots to discourage anyone from following too closely. The chopper circled overhead; no one returned fire. John watched the group of four—plus Aida—haul ass over the ridge and disappear.

Oh, God, keep them safe.

Still no one fired, and it dawned on him. "They want Aida— they're not going to fire on them."

"Yeah," Miguel said, "sorry to tell you, amigo. I don't think they're gonna do that for us." He grinned in the gathering light. "What branch were you in?"

"Navy, I was a rescue diver, medic, and did underwater demolitions."

"So you were a SEAL?" he asked, the admiration obvious in his voice.

"No, we'd go in ahead of the SEAL teams, set things up. We were the brains; they were the brawn. You?"

"Semper Fi, brother! I was a grunt chewing dirt in Iraq." And as men under fire do, they shook hands and clasped arms. An *abrazo*, as it was called in Spanish.

"Let's go, Navy!" Miguel said as he headed out, wearing a wicked grin.

Their sprint to the top of the ridge drew immediate fire, from the chopper and from behind. They had waited too long under the cover at the end of the path, and unit one was almost on top of them. Unit three had moved off the path to get a flanking angle. Miguel and John were in a crossfire from behind, from the side, and from above.

Between the two of them, John was in better shape, and with legs and lungs pumping, he made it to the top of the ridge first. He was a perfectly dark figure silhouetted against the eastern sky.

"Drop!" Miguel screamed at him as he heard the report from a shot off to his right. He saw the spraying burst of blood and tissue from John's right thigh. John collapsed and rolled out of sight on the other side of the ridge.

Instinct and training drove Miguel. In an odd crouching run, he zigzagged his way to the top and over the ridge. He saw John dragging himself along the ground halfway to the treeline.

"Shit, Navy. What the hell are you doing?"

"Waiting for the dirt-slow marine to come save my ass. What took you so long?"

Miguel grabbed John and slung him over his shoulder, just as he had been trained to do, and stumbled into the path through the treeline. Hot, wet stickiness ran down his back from the wound in John's leg. A few yards in, Miguel put him down and propped him up against a rock.

"We've got to bind that up. Good thing you're a medic so you can tell me how to do it right."

"Just take any piece of cloth, rip it into lengths, and wrap it around the wound and just above it. Make it tight. I'm lucky it didn't hit the femoral artery, or I would have bled out by now."

"Way ahead of you." Miguel took out a sling bandage and a trauma pad from his pack. "Hold the pad here and push hard," he instructed John while he rolled the bandage into a four-foot length.

"You've done this before," said John.

"You have no idea. Okay, this next part is gonna hurt." Miguel wrapped the sling bandage around John's thigh, pulled it tight, and tied it off. John grunted and turned pale but didn't pass out. "Good for you. Now let's get going. Can you hop on one leg?"

John nodded.

Miguel got John to his feet and put John's arm over his shoulders. "Just like a three-legged race from when you were a kid, remember?"

They headed through the Ponderosa pines toward the mine entrance. Ten steps, twenty-five steps, and the sides of the path started to rise around them. They were so intent on just taking the next step that they didn't hear the helicopter hovering above them. Fifty-three steps and they spotted the entrance in the cliff side. Just a few more steps and they'd be there.

***

Baka slowly released his breath and squeezed off a round.
Good night.

***

Miguel crumpled to the ground and lay facedown in the dirt. John fell and rolled off the path. He clambered behind a boulder.

"Miguel!"

John saw the entry point just below Miguel's left shoulder blade. His expert eye tracked the path the round had taken through Miguel; the exit would have to be just to the left of center chest. Miguel was dead.

The chopper had moved off but looked like it would circle around. No doubt the other assholes were close behind.

Move it, Johnny boy.

222

He craned his neck around the rock and saw the entrance, not twenty-five yards away. Adrenaline got him to his feet; grit carried him the rest of the way.

***

"One down. Don't approach him. I lost the others," said Baka. "Don't go into that ravine. It's a kill box. We'll circle around up here. They must have left the path. I'll search for them and direct you in. They couldn't have gotten far."

28 The Last Leg

The waves were relentless. Aida spent the energy Max had given her fighting to keep her balance against their pounding force and to stay near her family. After that was gone, the waves punished her until she was a mere blade of grass tossed about by the whim of a tornado. The unnatural waves whipped the background swells and crests of the Wave World into a violent frenzy, and she lost sight of Greg and Nat. She was alone and powerless. A numbness took hold of her, and the only pearl she could see was his—Baka, the monster, the hunter, the killer, her murderer. Even through the waves, he drew ever closer, heading in the same direction as she. Their pearls drew even with each other like two horses running the last length of a race, neck and neck to the finish line. Their paths would touch soon.

As she felt the last of her life ebbing away, she thought it cruel of God to have her spend her last moments of life separated from those she loved most and in the company of this revolting beast. She immediately regretted this sentiment against the Almighty when she saw a death fold form and open in front of her.

Then she realized. *If I'm dead, he'll call off the chase, and Greg and Nat will be safe.*

She always had understood the power of personal sacrifice.

Nobody lives just for themselves.

This was what had driven her into medicine, what had validated her life as a mother and spouse. She found the greatest value in herself when she was helping others. It had been a life well lived, and now it would be a life well ended. If she could have smiled, she would have.

***

"They've started again," Johar announced into the communication loop, which now included the executive assistant director for science and technology, Theresa Waters, and her boss, the director of the FBI. After the first set, Waters, who headed the OTD, advised him of this unique threat. The director needed to see it for himself, so here he was.

The patterns were identical. Concentric circles of red dots expanded cross the continent from their origin in southwest Washington.

"This is incredible," the director let slip on his open mike. "Are we recording this?"

"Yes, sir, in triple redundancy," Johar replied, then cringed, wondering if someone else should have answered.

It didn't matter to the director who had answered. He had what he needed. "Tell Seattle to go now. I'll get this through the AG and ISC."

***

How long? How far? Aida wondered.

The binding tightness of longing and sorrow and some fear contested with the joyful warmth of loving memories and gratefulness for her life in her heart. Baka's pearl was just out of reach now.

Soon. It will be very soon. Lord, keep them safe.

Wild waves rocked her, and she witnessed two of them merge, immediately growing to double the size of the originals. Borne on the crest of this rogue wave, a jumbled cluster of pearls illuminated her view. She saw it would pass through her before she reached her end. Out of a desperate desire not to be alone, to be with other people one last time, Aida reached for them just as the rogue wave hit her.

225

Tumbled and tossed, she still stretched for the lights. They came to her, and she grasped for them. She saw that another event line followed closely behind them. It was like the one in the plane.

Fire.

She went, sparkling like a bottle rocket and, in utter disbelief, found herself standing on the bow deck of a large boat facing the two-story cabin area, the wind pushing on her back.

The roiling smoke that billowed from the rear of the vessel filtered the light from the rising sun, keeping it from blinding her. She heard screaming mixed with loud voices giving instructions to move to the lifeboats, but she knew that wouldn't work; the fire had cut them off from passengers.

Aida saw people inside the cabin, mostly adults, dressed in work clothes, as if they were heading for their shifts, and they saw her too.

"This way! Come this way!" she shouted, waving to them. They would all be safest in the front of the boat. A man locked eyes with her, nodded, and grabbed his family. They exited the cabin to move toward her.

***

"This is Roger Roget, KTLA morning news. There's breaking news right now off the coast of Long Beach, a fire on the *Catalina Catamaran* ferry. It's on its first run from Long Beach to Avalon, the five-thirty a.m. sailing. The boat's stopped in the water about halfway between Long Beach Harbor and Avalon. That's about eleven or twelve miles from the nearest land. Nearby vessels are coming to its aid. The Coast Guard station in Long Beach is responding. I understand we have live video from KTLA News One chopper. Here's Dawn Olvera with the latest."

"Thanks, Roger. As you can see, this is a very dangerous situation. The rear of the boat is completely engulfed in flames, cutting the passengers off from at least some of the lifeboats. There's a lot of confusion on the deck and in the main passenger areas."

The images of the burning boat and terrified passengers trying to find any safe place were immediately splashed on screens across the US, then picked up by the international media and beamed all over

226

the globe. No fewer than six broadcast-quality cameras were recording every square inch of the deck.

"The forward area near the bow of the boat is clear," Olvera continued, "and...and...I see a woman, waving to her fellow passengers, calling to them to come forward."

***

The first twelve minutes of the raid went by the book. No surprises, no resistance, just startled staff and patients. Kozlowski's long night, now turned early morning, bore fruit when they encountered architectural features that weren't in the building plans. An elevator had been locked off before the response team pushed in. They had to cut the power to certain sections of the building in order to override the building control systems to access it. That was another surprise. Massive amounts of power were feeding into the undocumented lower levels of what turned out to be a complex.

Everyone on the upper floors was detained; some were arrested. One in particular was pulled from the third-story executive office. He refused to talk, but staff identified him as Jerome Gilden.

It took the agents another thirty minutes to breach the considerable security of the lower levels. Once Kozlowski got inside, he didn't know what to think. Again, there was no armed resistance, just frightened nurses and technicians. They found Dr. Qian's limp body huddled below his computer station. As Qian had no visible wounds, Kozlowski assumed it was death by drug overdose. In a day or two, toxicology would confirm this. What the OTD's digital forensics experts found on Qian's workstation was evidence of his penultimate act. He had typed a single command line, launching a program. It read: *PURGE*.

Explanations for the two separate surgical suites, the pentagonal room, and the four smaller rooms came faster than Kozlowski expected. The occupants of the pentagonal room were separated and questioned. Some kept quiet; some didn't. And from those who were willing to cooperate, he learned of the now-deceased victims in the four sarcophagus-shaped containers. Within forty-eight hours, the entire intelligence community descended on The Project, and a day after that, the complex was classified top secret, special compartmentalized by the Department of Defense.

***

Aida heard the *thomp-thomp-thomp* of at least three news helicopters around the boat. People were leaving the cabin and coming to her. She climbed on top of a deck locker by the railing so she could be more easily seen and kept calling to the passengers. Some had their mobile devices out.

***

"Passengers are making their way onto the front deck of the boat now," Olvera reported. "Some have jumped over the side into the water, expecting to be rescued by other boats. The woman in white has climbed on top of a bench or something, still waving, still gesturing to everyone, calling them to the safest part of the boat. A whole flotilla of private fishing boats, sailboats, and all kinds of vessels are only a hundred yards away now."

***

Aida saw that passengers were turning to help other passengers, and some were starting to come near her. The wind had caught the side of the boat like a sail and turned it in the water so the smoke no longer blocked the rising sun. Although its brilliant glare overwhelmed her, she didn't turn away.

My last sunrise, she thought as the rubber band tugged on her mind.

Then, in front of everyone on national and international commercial and social media, Aida vanished.

29 *Oro y Azul*

Natalia and Greg caught John as his right leg gave out and he tumbled through the mine entrance. Miguel's field dressing, now saturated from John's exertion, remained firmly in place.

"Where's Miguel? What about my brother? Is he still out there?" Francisco demanded.

"Miguel died," John choked out through burning pain and fatigue. "The asshole in the helicopter shot him through the heart. I'm sorry—I couldn't pick him up."

Francisco steadied himself on the tunnel wall, then slowly sank to the floor. "We can't just leave him out there lying in the dirt. We've got to get him!"

"*En el nombre del Padre, y del Hijo, y del Espíritu Santo.*" Mollie quietly blessed herself and prayed for the soul of her sister's son. Her whispers were almost drowned out by the grinding sound of the helicopter echoing through the ravine and into the mine. "*Mijo,* if you go out there now, you'll get shot too."

"*Tía*...this is wrong." Francisco struggled to his feet and took a step toward the entrance.

Greg spoke up. "Please, Francisco. I know my wife wouldn't want *anyone* to die for her. I'm so sorry about your brother."

"My dad's right. She'd want us to try to find a way out of here," Nat pleaded as she worked to change John's bandage.

John got through to him. "Francisco, you two brought us here for cover, and we've reached the objective. We're safe for now, but we have to keep moving. Is there another way out of here?"

229

"I don't know anymore. Maybe, but we haven't been here in a long time. We'd have to look."

"Okay, so let's get looking," said Mollie. "If we can find our way out without being seen, we'll have a chance."

Resigned to the logic of it, Francisco picked up his flashlight and shined it down deeper into the silent blackness of Oro y Azul before setting off. Mollie and Greg followed close behind and shared a light between them. John stayed behind to tend to Aida, and Nat stayed behind to tend to John.

Nat could still see the bobbing flashlights on the walls of the tunnel when Francisco yelled, "Oh, shit! Get back, back, back, back!"

The muffled scuffling of their footfalls grew as the three of them trotted back up the tunnel, their lights flicking into John's and Nat's eyes.

"Point the lights down!" said John in hoarse whisper. "They'll be seen outside."

"We've got worse problems than that!" Francisco said. "There's a shitload of water-gel explosive and electrical blasting caps in some lockers down there. One shot into the tunnel, and we all go up!"

"What's beyond that?" John asked.

"It looks like the tunnel ceiling caved in. It's blocked. No way back, no way forward," answered Greg, who sounded more than a little panicked.

Outside, the helicopter made a slow pass, low enough to shake dirt loose from the ceiling.

"All right, everyone, settle down," John said. "I think I have an idea. Those electric blasting caps, how many yards of wire?"

"Two full spools. Maybe a hundred and fifty yards each," Francisco said.

"Okay, good," said John. "We're gonna use that water-gel to take out the chopper."

"How the hell are we gonna do that? Throw it at 'em?" Francisco scoffed.

"No, listen. We lay out the electric blasting caps and cable around an LZ and wire up the water-gel in the center. The cap wire is like an antenna; it picks up any random electrical discharge. That's why we stopped using it in the service—too many premature detonations. In

230

this dry air, those rotors are generating more than enough static electricity for the cap wire to pick up. You were in the service, over in the sandbox, right?"

Francisco nodded.

"Remember the halos the helicopters generated at night when they got down low? The sand and dust would pick up a static charge and light up."

"He's right," Greg chimed in. "In this dry air, the difference in potentials between the ground and the helicopter…" Seeing he'd lost them, he changed his wording. "The static charge that gets built up will be considerable. When the helicopter gets low enough, it would ground out, causing an electrical arc."

"What if it doesn't arc?" Francisco shot back.

"We can trigger it from here. The batteries will be enough, but…" John paused.

"I'll go," said Greg. "You were going to say we need to lure them down. There has to be bait. I'll run when they get close…to get clear of the blast." This last part was to Natalia.

"No, it should be me," John said. "There was a note in the ambulance written to me. It said you all would need me and thi—"

Natalia cut him off. "Don't be stupid. You can't run, and you're the only medical care my mom has. Dad, I love you, but you're too slow—you'd never get clear—and it has to be someone they want alive. They'd want to use me to get to Mom." She looked at Mollie and Francisco. "It has to be me." No one spoke. The only sound in the dry, dead air of the mine was the helicopter, fading in the distance.

***

Natalia felt cold and lightheaded as she gulped the arid dawn air in short, quick puffs. Like an electrical shock, numbness from her clenched muscles ran down her arms, cutting off the blood to her hands and fingers, chilling them even more. She felt the raw horsepower of the helicopter vibrating the ground as she crouched under the branches of a juniper. Although she heard its rumble nearby, she couldn't see it. Suddenly the harsh mechanical beating of its rotors blasted her out of her hiding place as the chopper popped

231

up from behind the cliff face it had been using for cover. Natalia darted between the trees and brush, trying her best not to be seen while knowing she would be. Bile rose in her throat, making her gag. She swallowed hard to get the taste out, but her mouth was dryer than the high desert she was running through.

For plan A, her father, Francisco, and Mollie had laid out the cap wire in a crisscross pattern and connected the tubes of water-gel explosive to it in a clear area about forty yards beyond the mine entrance and the safety of the ravine. It was a crude net, but they only had moments between passes of the helicopter to sprint across the clearing with the spool of cap wire, unrolling it behind them.

John's plan B had them run another pair of wires back to the entrance. One of which already was fixed to the positive terminal of a lantern flashlight battery. All it would take was a stroke from the other wire to trigger the detonation if plan A didn't work.

***

"There, it's the girl. That spooked her out!" Baka said. He opened his comms. "I've got eyes on the daughter. She's running back toward the ravine. Units one and three, what are your positions?"

"Unit one here. We're about half a click due north of you."

"Unit three. We're about the same to your southeast and down a steep incline."

Son of a bitch. I have to get her myself.

"Go in low, follow her, force her to the ground. I'll hop out and grab her," he told the pilot. "Units one and three, get your asses up to my current location. We're going in to grab the girl."

***

"Oh, God. Oh, God. Oh, God!" Natalia gasped as she sprinted toward the edge of the clearing. The deafening rotor wash tore savagely at her, knocking her down and blinding her. Something snapped in her right ankle. She squinted against the stinging sand and saw the clearing not ten feet away. The chopper passed just feet overhead and swung around. She leapt to her feet to dash across the maze of cap wire hidden in the New Mexico dust. Adrenaline kept

232

her from feeling most of the pain that shot up from her ankle, but at best she was moving at half speed as she crossed the center of the clearing.

***

"Stupid girl. She's in the open and injured. Set down," said Baka. This was too easy.

***

The copter swung in, the landing struts skimming the tops of the juniper as Natalia made it to the treeline on the other side of the clearing and ran to her father. He scooped one arm around her, and the two of them hobbled toward the ravine. "We saw you fall. C'mon," he said. "Move. Don't look back."

The helicopter flared out over the clearing, the blast from the rotors digging into the sand, spraying it up into the air where its own downdraft caught it again and thrust it down in blinding cloud. Feet from landing, Baka saw a pile of whitish tubes, like sausage casings, with wires running from them.

IED!

"Pull up! Pull up!" he screamed.

The copter lurched to one side as the pilot tried to comply, bringing the aluminum landing strut within inches of the ground. Relative to the ground, the copter had built up a large positive charge, and nature hates an imbalance. Electrons surged down the charge gradient from relatively positive to neutral ground, met an inches-wide gap between the two, then jumped the gap in a visible arc.

Without breaking stride, daughter and father went right off the lip of the ravine. The concussion from the explosion caught them in midair, slamming the wind from their lungs and blacking them out. They fell senseless to the ravine floor between the rock walls.

***

"Unit one, unit three, what the fuck was that!" unit two called out over the comms. The noise from the massive explosion rolled across the Chama Valley and assaulted the peace of the multihued cliffs and buttes of Georgia O'Keeffe country. Three hours had passed since the recovery team had chased the subjects into the hills, leaving the two members of unit two to watch over the monks. Matthew and the others sat stone-like in the temple, waiting.

"Ah, aerial cover is down. Repeat...aerial cover is down," unit one said in disbelief. "Unit two, we have one wounded, and Baka is gone. What are your orders?"

Unit two called, "Full abort. How long to get back here?"

The head of unit two and second-in-command walked out of the temple and away from the monks. Neither man was paying attention to the monks now, and thus they never saw the blows to the pressure points below their left ears that felled them.

"Unit two, we're at least sixty to ninety minutes out," replied unit one. "Unit two...unit two? Unit two, come back!"

***

Right after the explosion, Aida took a turn for the worse. Francisco had taken off at a run toward the Chama Valley Zen Center for help and transportation. Greg and Nat came around a few minutes later, but it would be days before the ringing in their ears stopped, so John had to yell for them to hear him.

"Aida's pulse is rapid, and her breaths are coming short and shallow," John told them. He didn't need to say any more. They all knew what this meant. Nat knelt on one side, Greg on the other. John sat by her head, readying himself to resuscitate her. All of them were pushed beyond the limits of their physical and emotional endurance. Grief ripped at their souls as it squeezed out tears from their desiccated eyes. Exhausted, agonized, crushed, they could only hold her, wait, and watch. Aida's chest rose and fell in rapid succession, then stopped.

Then she took one long, gulping breath.

***

234

The brightness of the sun grew, its light blotting out all else in Aida's view.

So this is death.

The light intensified, but something changed. She felt herself drift peacefully, weightless. Darkness crept in around the edges of the diminishing light. She felt hands in hers and smelled the musty richness of cool earth. Voices, talking too loudly over one another, called her.

"Mom?"

"Aida?"

Her eyes hurt; she looked to the side of a flashlight that someone was holding directly over her head and saw her daughter and her husband. The weight of the ordeal was written clearly on their tear-streaked faces but now was supplanted by the release of joy. They sobbed and held her.

"You two look terrible," Aida said, "but you're alive. We're all alive." They continued to hold one another in the silence of the mine entrance, not speaking, just being. Finally, Aida said, "I have to sleep."

"That's a good idea," John said, then turned to Greg and Nat. "I need to get her vitals."

Aida craned her neck up to see John's face. She gently stroked his cheek. "John…" She then closed her eyes and fell into a dreamless sleep.

30 The Supercell

The cool, dry Canadian air of the high-pressure dome that had been visiting University City over the past few days and bringing blessed relief to all was being evicted by a giant, angry, low-pressure system pushing its way up from the Gulf of Mexico. Its torrid heat and high humidity smothered the Great Plains, making the air gelatinous and unpleasant to breathe. As was typical for the time of year, thunderstorms formed along the frontal boundary between the two battling leviathans, though the outcome of this match was never in doubt. Lightning ripped across the clouds, and some cells dropped torrents of rain and hail before they spun up tornados. Twenty miles due south of University City, an updraft of ground-level heated air paired with a downdraft of cooler air from higher up and a strong wind shear to set a cyclonic twisting into motion.

The severe weather warnings were lost on Beverly Michelson as she entered building 87. A singular thought had occupied her all afternoon.

I can get over and come back.

Seeing the console and the settings that had sent Aida over cemented it in her mind. She understood what had gone right when the lab tech had tried to sabotage the QUESAM device, and more important, she understood what had gone wrong. Enough energy had surged through the QUESAM at just the right places to force Aida's cortical systems of attention out of the normal alpha wave rhythms into something else, and there it remained, stuck, like dislocated joint. What was needed was another surge, at the normal alpha wave frequency, and strength to reestablish the proper patterns. That was the part that Aida didn't receive.

But Michelson knew better. She understood the underlying neuroanatomical mechanisms and physiology of attention better than anyone else.

I've discovered something new. No one else in all humanity knows what I know.

The fact that she was the one to see and understand this concept and its application didn't really surprise her. She knew her brilliance was the driving force at The Project. Gilden had money and influence, true, and Qian had built the imaging system for the quantum world. But money was a commodity that could be obtained from any number of sources, and skills like Qian's could be purchased. These two people weren't unique, and she had no further use for them. As she imagined the possible uses of her knowledge and the power it would bring, a grin of unwholesome delight twisted her lips.

***

"I'm Dr. Beverly Michelson," she told the night security guard at building 87, then flashed a University Hospital ID. "I'm working with the NIH grant auditors in the Doxiphus lab. We were in there earlier today. The auditors flew out this afternoon, but they have some additional items they've asked me to follow up on. Would you open the lab for me, please?"

"Of course," the guard replied.

They didn't talk as he led her to the lab and unlocked the door. Michelson strode in like a lioness into the den of a rival she had just slain and flicked on the lights.

"Remember to pull the door closed behind you when you're done. It'll lock itself," the guard said as he turned to leave.

"Thanks again. I'll only be a few minutes, twenty tops." She smiled at him. "I'll check in with you on my way out."

He flushed at her attention and dropped his keys. He then grunted as he bent over his large belly to get them and was red-faced when he straightened up. "Uh, thank you…uh…Dr. Michelson. That would be great," he said, and hurried down the hall.

237

***

Ten miles south of University City, the updraft, deep inside the forming cell, was now rotating at a faster rate around a central axis and grew into a mesocyclone. Moving at fifty miles an hour, the storm would be on the outskirts of the city in minutes. The top of the cloud vaulted up above twenty thousand feet and skewed to the south as the base of the storm raced north, forming the classic anvil shape of a supercell. The bottom of the storm itself was round and hung down from the main cloud body like a sucker off an octopus arm. Viewed from the side, it looked like a wall, and hence was called a wall cloud. The main body of the storm, between the wall cloud at the base and the anvil on the top, was tightly compacted by the circulating winds and rotated ominously. Tentacles of lightning flashed from ground to cloud and cloud to ground. Taken as a whole, a supercell storm frequently left storm chasers with the impression of a titanic, malevolent man o' war jellyfish floating across the landscape in search of prey.

***

The chair reclined as soon as Michelson settled in, and in the absolute silence of the inner room, she was uncomfortably aware of her rapid breathing and moist palms. In a few moments, she would glimpse the unveiled essence of reality.

There won't be any sensation from the initial stimulation impulse, she reminded herself. The strength of the currents she was working with would barely be felt as a tingle on her scalp. It was the frequency, duration, and location of the target pulse that were significant. She reviewed the run parameters in her head.

Initial twenty-millisecond pulse, then a countdown timer of three minutes, then the correcting pulse for three hundred fifty milliseconds, and I'm back.

***

In the green air outside of building 87, tornado sirens had been sounding for three minutes, warning everyone in the path of the

238

approaching supercell to take cover. The supercell dropped baseball-size hail and also had produced a classic hook echo on radar, indicating funnel clouds.

***

There was a hissing from above and behind Michelson as the open end of the tube extended itself into place. The air pillows inflated, stabilizing her head, while her feet twitched in uncontrolled excitement. When she heard the whine of the charging capacitors, she reflexively clenched her eyes shut. Intense brightness, like thousands of flashes going off simultaneously, blinded her. In a few moments, her vision cleared.

She gasped. There was no way she could have prepared herself for what she saw: a glowing fabric, woven from threads of light by small shiny points set in the dark space time of the universe. Qian's representation, for all its technical wonder, was no better than a blind monkey fingering in the sand trying to reproduce the ceiling of the Sistine Chapel.

"Hello, hello. Can you hear me?" she said as she looked for the observers from The Project.

***

A quarter mile from building 87, lightning struck the secondary power substation that serviced the core of the campus, including building 87. The surge blew out lights and transformers throughout the heart of the campus. The QUESAM device also was on the receiving end of the surge. It funneled through the tube, into Beverly Michelson, and then to the chair as it made its way to the grounded platform. Her body convulsed once in a horrible contraction, then fell limp.

An hour later, when security was sweeping the blacked-out building, they found her sitting in the stim room chair, mouth open, drool running down onto her chin and her excrement dripping onto the floor. She was alive but unresponsive.

***

239

Matthew watched the event line approach Michelson and didn't interfere. He knew her name, who she was, and what she had done. She was *akusala*. Her awakening to the Wave World was unlike Aida's, however. When she flipped, she became immediately aware. Her pearl lacked the luminescence of Aida's, and she vibrated out of time with the background rhythms of creation. The light of her consciousness roamed wildly, and she called out, seeking someone. Her consciousness was trying to orient itself when the event wave washed through her.

He watched and sensed an immediate change in her. The dancing light of her focus dimmed and fell inanimate, gazing awkwardly out at an angle to her previous path. Her pearl moved forward, no longer turning, bereft of decision threads. She called out no more.

***

In the abyss of her psyche, Michelson was aware of what she saw on some level. The miracle of the Wave World passed unappreciated before the remaining tenuous spark of her consciousness as she lay inert in both worlds.

31 Coming Back

Theresa Waters and Dan Kozlowski sat in her office at the OTD, watching a replay of the Los Angeles report on the fire on the *Catalina Catamaran* and the extraordinary events that had taken place that day.

"This is Roger Roget, KTLA News, with a special report. Speculation about the identity and fate of 'The Angel of Avalon,' as the appearing-disappearing woman is now known, is running rampant around the world. No one, however, has positively identified her. Theories range from her falling overboard and being lost, to her being digitally edited in as a ratings grab. Others claim she was an angel sent to help those aboard. Digital image analysts, special effects wizards, and CGI experts are offering up their own theories as to what happened, but none have provided a definitive explanation.

Though no more than one hundred ten people were on the deck that morning, more than seventy-five hundred people have claimed they were present on the thirty-by-twenty bow deck of the boat. And now they are trying to sell their stories of the event. Of those survivors who were verified as being on the deck that morning, probably the most genuine and reliable account comes from Dave Chatsworth, who was with his family when he first saw the woman through the cabin window."

The news program cut to an interview with Mr. Chatsworth.

"There was no way to keep track of everything that was going on, what with the smoke, the alarms, people shouting instructions, and others screaming and running all over the place. She was probably another passenger. I mean, why not? It makes the most sense. I don't know where she went; maybe she wants to stay anonymous. But she helped save a lot of people, I can tell you that."

The screen cut back to Roger Roget.

"What cannot be refuted is the effect the event has had on the world. The hope that has come from it has rooted itself in the minds and hearts of almost everyone who has seen it. It isn't just the hope that they derive from seeing people help each other but also the hope instilled by the possibility of a chance that what they saw was real. It is a bit of evidence for people to consider in those quiet, introspective moments of utter honesty when they face the question that everyone faces at some point in their lives: 'Is this all that there is?'

And from the viewpoint of this reporter, such thoughtful consideration and the altruistic actions that rise from that consideration can only benefit the human condition.

I'm Roger Roget. Good day and best wishes."

Waters stopped the replay.

"So what do we have?" Kozlowski asked, knowing that the head of the OTD hadn't flown him in to watch a video that was available everywhere.

"I need your help," she said. "You'll have to take a detour to New Mexico on your way back to Seattle. You can read the files on the way."

***

Four days after Aida had woken up in the entrance of the Oro y Azul mine, there was a knock on the door of her room at University of New Mexico hospital in Albuquerque. The visitor was a bland-featured woman with dark hair and quick, intelligent eyes. She was dressed in a conservative dark business suit and carried a file folder. A man was with her. He was prematurely bald, sported a thick brown Van Dyke beard, and had an athletic build.

"Excuse me," the woman said. "Are you Aida and Gregorio Doxiphus?"

"Yes," Greg answered.

"Please forgive my intrusion. I'm Theresa Waters with the FBI." She showed her federal ID, put it away, then shook both their hands,

242

grinning as she did so. "You can call me Terry. This is Special Agent Dan Kozlowski. He runs the Seattle field office." Kozlowski proffered his ID as well.

"We've already told the police and other FBI agents everything that happened," Greg started, a little more defensively than he'd intended.

"Yes, I know, and we thank you for your complete cooperation." Another smile. "Would you mind if we closed the door?" Waters asked.

"Actually, yes," Greg said. "We would mind very much. You need to lea—"

Waters held her hands up. "Of course. I'm sorry. That was insensitive of me, given everything you've been through." Her apology seemed genuine.

Aida saw that and told Greg, "It's okay. Would you like to sit down, Terry?"

"Thank you, but we won't be staying that long. I'm not here to talk to you about the events in your lab or what happened here in New Mexico," she said, approaching Aida and opening the folder, which had some photos in it. She laid the first one on the rolling table for both of them to see. They were clear and crisp, not like the blurred images they had seen on TV. "I assume you've seen the incredible story of the woman who appeared on the ferry boat off Long Beach and then mysteriously disappeared after she helped rescue the passengers."

Greg replied noncommittally, "Sure. It's all over the news. Do you know who she is?"

"Well, no one got a good shot of her face," Waters went on, "but curiously enough, there are reports of a woman, identically dressed, who simply appeared in a jungle in Africa right next to plane that had crash-landed. She helped a dozen or so children and one mother escape the burning wreck before it exploded, and then she disappeared. That happened last week." She took out another picture; this one was blurry. "Then, about three days later, she appeared again, at the site of the recent tsunami in Southeast Asia. Right on the beach. A security camera recorded her running and waving her arms. It looked like she was trying to warn people. And here she is

on the *Catalina Catamaran* less than six hours later in California."
She finished arranging the photos side by side.

"You have family in Greece that you travel to see," she continued.
"You know all interactions at customs checkpoints are recorded on
video, yes?"

Greg and Aida studied the pictures and remained silent.

"As I said, there are no clear views of the woman's face, but we
have tools that can identify people by their stance, how they move,
their build, and so on. These tools confirm that it's the exact same
woman in all the pictures. You have to agree that there's more than a
passing resemblance between all the images of her."

"What's your point, Agent Waters?" Aida said with a chill in her
voice.

Unfazed, Waters replied, "It's Assistant Director, actually. I'm
head of the Operations Technology Division, and now that we
understand each other, I hope we can have an open and honest
conversation."

Waters waited a moment for a response from the couple. Greg
was standing now, and he and Aida were clasping hands. They didn't
say anything. Waters never had excelled at gaining the trust of
people she interviewed when she was in the field. She knew a gentler
tack was needed.

"I'm not here to cause you trouble. We're here on behalf of
several government agencies to ask for your help." She picked up the
photos and placed them back in the folder, then took a step back.
"Dan, would you continue, please?"

Kozlowski rolled a stool up to the side of the bed and sat down.
This placed him below the eye level of both Greg and Aida. He kept
his hands folded in his lap and made eye contact with them.

In a calm, low voice, he said, "Four days ago, based on an
anonymous tip from a location here in New Mexico, I led a raid on a
facility in Washington state that was home to a public service
organization called The Project. On the surface, they were providing
medical and social services to the homeless, mostly veterans from
the Puget Sound area. During the raid, though, we found some
exceptionally disturbing things that we don't understand." Kozlowski
produced his own photos. "It appears that The Project, which was
run by a man named Jerome Gilden, in association with Dr. Beverly

Michelson—we know you both know her, by the way…anyway, The Project was actually harvesting homeless people and, after performing a neurosurgical procedure on them, using them in a way we don't understand."

Kozlowski had laid out photos of Gilden and Michelson, the surgical suites, the production floor, and the head of a partially decomposed body with wires and tubes running from it. The head and what remained of the body lay inside a sarcophagus-shaped container. Greg looked away, and Aida covered her mouth with her hand.

"Oh, God," she said as she looked at the last photo. Imprinted in small letters on the interior of the sarcophagus was "Observer 119, R. Stevens."

"It's disturbing, I know," Kozlowski said. "Gilden is now in federal custody."

"And Dr. Michelson?" Aida asked.

"She was found in your lab, Dr. Doxiphus, in the stim room. It looked like she was attempting to use your kweesam de—"

"cue-sam. It's pronounced cue-sam."

"QUESAM device. She's in a coma at University Hospital. Dr. LaVista's opinion is that she's in a permanent vegetative state, though it's too soon for a formal diagnosis."

Aida blanched in obvious surprise.

"Back to our request…" Kozlowski chose his next words with precision. "We'd like your help, after you're discharged, in analyzing what we found at The Project. You'd be consultants, and we'd pay you for your services."

Greg equivocated, "This is hardly the time. My wife needs to recuperate, and we need to get back to University City and the lab."

Kozlowski tapped the corner of the folder on the nightstand. "I'm sorry to be the one to tell you, but the NIH has pulled all funding for your research after your and Dr. Michelson's accidents, and I had to seize all your materials, including the QUESAM device, as part of our investigation into what happened at The Project." His delivery was gentle but firm, and the message was clear.

Aida touched the photo of Ray Stevens and drew it closer to her. "I expect to be discharged in a few days," she said. "We'll need two weeks to wrap up some personal business in University City and here

245

in New Mexico." Her gaze bore into Waters. "We have two funerals to attend. How can we contact you, Dan?"

Kozlowski reached into his jacket, took out a card, and handed it to her. "Here's my work, personal, and home numbers. Don't worry if my wife or one of my kids answers. Just let them know who you are." He gave a sympathetic smile. "Take your time. Let us know when you're ready."

***

Four Black Hawk helicopters flew low in formation below the heavy cloud deck. With their running lights off and the sound suppression systems muffling the *wump-wump-wump* of the rotor blades, they were engulfed in the darkness as they tried to be holes in the night sky. The pilots relied on night vision gear to avoid midair collision. In addition to a minimal crew, each helicopter carried three passengers. Two were Federal Bureau of Prisons guards. The third was a hooded man in leg irons, belly chains, and handcuffs. Unknown to all involved, the prisoners in three of the helicopters were actually federal employees who had been selected for their resemblance to the true beneficiary of this heavily armed transport. The fourth prisoner had been fitted with a sound-canceling headset and blinders under his hood.

One by one, the four transports landed on a desolate, flat valley floor in Florence, Colorado, and discharged their passengers. Each set of three was taken into the administrative maximum facility, called Supermax.

***

After shuffling along for an interminable amount of time, Jerome Gilden felt the hands on his arms tighten, signaling him to stop. As he stood still, he felt the hood being pulled off. The earpieces and blinders were removed, and he squinted at the fluorescent lighting of the stark seven-by-twelve-foot concrete cell. He had no idea where he was, and the US government had done everything in its considerable ability to ensure that no one else did either.

246

In the coming months, he would have only one human contact, a voice he would come to know as Mr. Thomas, a charming fellow who asked him questions through one-way glass about The Project and what they were trying to do. He was particularly interested in trying to understand the connection between The Project and the waves of violence that had rippled around the world. For the most part, Gilden kept his silence. But even he knew he wouldn't be able to hold out indefinitely.

***

Miguel's funeral was first. Throughout the wake, rosary, receptions, funeral Mass, and internment, Aida found herself surrounded by familiar strangers: Mollie and Francisco, the monks, and Matthew. Although she had seen them all before in the Wave World and even talked to some of them, the first physical meetings with everyone except Matthew and John were strained and uncomfortable.

She felt as if she were a voyeur, and in a way, she had been. She had watched them without their knowledge or consent. She had seen them going about their lives, sometimes under horrendous circumstances. She had felt their emotions. While she found that level of intimacy grounding and reassuring when she was trapped in the Wave World, now that she was back in the Particle World, she felt ashamed of the experience and her reaction to it. As a physician, no matter how physically close an encounter with a patient was or the degree of sympathy she felt, there was always the barrier of the clinical practitioner between her sense of self and that of the patient. Now, the physician in Aida felt she had violated people's privacy by peeking in uninvited.

Matthew understood this and pulled her aside at the funeral home before the rosary started. "Aida, you've seen the world in a way that almost no one else ever has or will again and that even fewer could ever understand. You certainly weren't prepared for it. Don't judge yourself or what you did while you were away. You're being unfair to yourself. You did such wonderful, unselfish things. Don't try to explain it to anyone unless you have some shared frame of reference. That'll only bewilder them and frustrate you." He embraced her

247

warmly. "I know you and your family are coming up to the center for Max's cremation, but after that I want you to spend some time with us when everything gets settled."

During the funeral Mass, Greg, Aida, Natalia, and John meant to keep a respectful distance and sat in the back of the church. But Mollie wouldn't have any of that and insisted that the four of them join the family in the front pews.

"We've been through all kinds of trouble together. You all belong with us now."

Aida gave Greg a look to silently ask, *Should we?*

Smiling, Greg nodded and mouthed, *It's okay. Go with it.*

He knew Mollie was in charge, and that was that.

Aida sat between Mollie and Greg for the Mass. Mollie took her hand during the Gospel. It was Romans 14, and as the priest intoned, "For none of us lives for ourselves alone, and none of us dies for ourselves alone" over the flag-draped coffin, Aida understood and wept quiet tears.

***

Before Max's funeral rite, Matthew had asked Aida to join him in the courtyard privately. "It's only natural to feel guilty. But keep in mind that his staying with you was his choice. It was what he needed to do."

Aida nodded weakly. Intellectually she could acknowledge this, but emotionally accepting it was a long time off.

"I'm happy for him. Perhaps he has broken free of the samsara," Matthew said.

"And if not?" she asked.

"Then he'll reincarnate and bring better things into the world." Matthew embraced Aida, then said, "Greater love hath no man than this, that a man lay down his life for his friends."

She sniffled and dabbed her eyes. "You're quoting the Bible?"

Matthew smiled. "Truth is transcendent."

***

The rite had started in the temple, where a large framed photo of Max was displayed on the altar along with a statue of the Buddha. The photo and statue were decorated with wreaths of flowers, and baskets of fresh fruit lay before them. The monks placed Max's casket in the center of the temple room, almost exactly in the same spot where Aida had lain. After initial prayers were recited in the temple, they carried that casket out to the parking area, where there was little risk of the heat scorching the tree branches overhead or the fire spreading. They placed the casket on the waiting pyre.

No one cried; Matthew had explained to them that Buddhist funerals were intentionally peaceful, calm affairs. It was believed this helped the soul of the deceased to move on. Attendees were encouraged to perform charitable acts in the coming days and to pray that the merit for those acts be passed on to the deceased. Lastly—and this seemed an unavoidable consequence of any funeral to Aida—attendees were to contemplate the impermanence of life and their own mortality.

They died because of me.

That was all she could think as the flames of Max's funeral pyre licked the edges of the pine casket and the shrine. The monks encircled the flaming platform and chanted. Their robes had a golden fluid richness to them in the setting sunlight.

If I had flipped back when I'd had the chance, Max probably would be alive right now, Aida thought. *My being on the beach certainly didn't help many people. I can't save everyone.*

She knew she was whipping herself and regretted it. Max would have told her to forgive herself, and she owed it to him to try. Grudgingly she took the thought a step further.

But if I had flipped back when we were all here in the temple, who knows what would have happened to the people on the boat.

The weight that pressed down on her mind shifted, and while it was still there, perhaps it wasn't impinging on her quite so much.

In the twilight after sunset, the main ceremony ended, and participants moved back into the converted adobe hacienda. A few monks stayed with the smoldering pyre and would attend to the fading embers throughout the night. In the courtyard, Mollie had put together a small reception with food and drink. Greg and Aida served themselves small plates and found a bench. Greg wasn't interested in his food and instead drank in the night sky.

"I'm sorry we never spent time in New Mexico before this," he said. "There's something special about this place—an approachable grandeur. It's hard to describe...well, at least for me, anyway. I'm sure a poet would do a better job."

Aida smirked. Greg was right.

"Georgia O'Keeffe said, 'If you ever go to New Mexico, it will itch you for the rest of your life.'" She took his hand and leaned her head on his shoulder.

"I feel the same," he replied, and kissed the top of her head. Though the sentiment was unspoken, they both realized this was the first moment when they'd been alone and in peace for weeks. No hospital rooms, no police or FBI. There was a blessing in the stillness, and they welcomed it. After a time, Greg said, "I'm gonna get some more water. You should have some too. It's arid here." He undoubtedly would be doting on her for months. She decided it probably would take that long before she would want him to stop.

Aida sat alone on the bench, the light from the waning moon behind her. Higher up, over the walls of the courtyard, the hills and mesas cast muted shadows across the landscape. An ember, glowing yellow-orange, drifted overhead, caught on a breeze. In her left ear, as if he were just inches away, she distinctly heard Max say, "I'll see you again."

32 Healing

A soft snow fell on the peaks and mesas of northern New Mexico. Timid, tender flakes clung to the evergreens and, with their purest white, dressed them for the holiday season. Aida spied the still-falling snowflakes through the kitchen window and smiled on this Friday morning. She poured herself a cup of coffee and immersed herself in the experience of it. It was the simple, everyday things she appreciated the most now, after her "trip." That's what they all had decided to call it. The innocuous name made it easier to talk about, and talking about their shared trauma seemed to help the most. Little by little, over the eighteen months after her trip, a sense of normalcy was returning to their lives.

She sat down at the kitchen table, the warmth of the mug making her fingers tingle. There was time enough before Natalia and John's arrival this afternoon for her to have a leisurely morning. Tomorrow was the twenty-fourth, and they were throwing their annual Christmas open house, so their home would be almost manic with preparations in a few hours. She and Greg were expecting a houseful, though some would be missing.

Max and Miguel...you said we'd meet again, Max.

After Max's funeral, the four of them had gone back to University City to get Natalia settled back into school to finish the semester. Aida and Greg had suggested Nat take the rest of the semester off, but she thought getting on with life would help ground her and from there she could better work through everything that had happened. Nat did leave the dorm and move back home, though. Being back in

251

the house was like being wrapped in a warm blanket for all of them. Too soon, though, they had to contact Agent Kozlowski. At least Nat had been able to watch the house in their absence.

Washington state…The Project.

The thought of what they'd found still sickened Aida. Only the fact that she and Greg had a direct hand in shutting it down eased her conscience—that and their agreement on the flight to Seattle not to be as forthcoming with the government as they could be. She remembered whispering into Greg's ear as the plane accelerated down the runway and the engines filled the cabin with their roar. "We have to steer them away from the Wave World."

He nodded and leaned into her ear to reply, "We can keep them focused on the neurophysiology of Michelson's work and ours. They don't know about the quantum mechanical implications of the altered perceptions."

Revealing those implications was what they had to guard against. The ability to transparently see causes before they coalesced into significant events and thereby be better able to predict those events couldn't be entrusted to any government or corporation. Or anyone, really. The first part was easy enough; their research had been in the field of brain-function mapping with concomitant therapeutic applications, and they could play off Michelson's work as a rogue investigation into the nature of human consciousness.

Not revealing the second part was the trick. They both knew they'd be under observation themselves, particularly Aida. Theresa Waters had made it clear that she knew it was Aida who had appeared to be in different places nearly simultaneously and, by extension, that there was more to all this. Plus, the Feds had Gilden in custody and undoubtedly were questioning him. The FBI and the other agencies that Waters and Kozlowski were fronting for were extremely interested in what Aida had experienced while she had been unconscious and in why The Project had been so determined, to the point of committing multiple murders and international terrorism, to get their hands on her. The government was watching Matthew and the monks of the Chama Valley Zen Center as well, though they hadn't taken any intrusive actions there yet.

Aida and Greg had to sign stacks of federal secrecy forms, swearing not to reveal or discuss their work at The Project to anyone, under penalty of federal prosecution, and to fully cooperate with the ongoing federal investigation. This got them both a top-secret, special-compartmentalized clearance, and they set to work.

Kozlowski tried to split them up to work on analyzing different technical areas: Aida the biomedical, Greg the imaging system. They saw this as an obvious ploy that would result in their both being surreptitiously examined by the assigned team members over the coming weeks. They instead proposed, then insisted, that they work together, analyzing a single project area at a time.

"We'll make faster progress if we work together. Our research, after all, has always been a joint effort," they reasoned with Kozlowski. After a day of contentious discussions, Kozlowski and the project overseers to whom he reported relented. Four and a half months later, after they had disassembled, identified, cataloged, and analyzed every bit of equipment, data, and computer code that hadn't been destroyed, they were released from their capacity as consultants and allowed to return home. Their final report was accurate, detailed, insightful, and entirely truthful in every aspect that could be empirically quantified. They expected to be put through lie detector tests and had prepared for that eventuality.

From the records, data, and analysis, Aida remembered that the final report had shaped up like this.

The Project was attempting to understand human consciousness. Under the direction of Dr. Beverly Michelson, it had identified individuals who were gifted at using their natural ability of covert attention—that is, they were good at paying attention to things they weren't consciously focusing on—and performed highly illegal, immoral, and unethical procedures on them. This line of query was logical, as it is well known that focus and consciousness are intimately related at a neurophysiological level. The report didn't venture into what had motivated The Project into taking these horrific actions, as, one, it would have been pure speculation and therefore unprovable, and two, it was unnecessary. Here the report was blunt. Gilden was in custody, so the Feds should get their information from him.

The report continued:

Once the victims had been subjected to the experimental and ultimately fatal procedures, The Project was then probably attempting to visualize their consciousnesses via a live feed. The report could arrive at no definitive conclusions in this regard due to the complete destruction of the programs, storage hardware, and data.

The report did speculate on the course of events, though. It said:

"Given the dozens and dozens of victims The Project killed, it is highly likely that their efforts didn't meet with the intended success. The Project might have started with a marginally intrusive surgical procedure they hoped to pass off as some type of therapeutic brain surgery. But when they didn't get the desired results and the victim subsequently died, they chose to pursue ever more abhorrent and drastic paths.

"End of report."

Their work was lauded, and the report impressed the project leads, though they could never publish it. During their time at The Project, Aida and Greg and the university had mutually agreed to part ways. Not at all coincidentally, they were both offered top research positions at Los Alamos National Laboratories. Moving to New Mexico made sense. Aida needed to be near Matthew so she could practice focused meditation, and the onus of what had happened in their lab made staying in the tight-knit academic community in University City untenable. Greg accepted his position, but Aida declined hers and instead became a consulting neurologist at various hospitals and clinics across northern New Mexico.

And so here we are…

The doorbell rang. She hadn't been expecting anyone for a few hours. Greg would be home at noon, and Nat and John weren't due to land in Albuquerque until a little after two. She looked out the front window and saw Matthew waiting on the stoop, stomping his feet and rubbing his hands together for warmth. She welcomed him in.

"Matthew, come in before you freeze."

"I hope it's okay that I came a little early," he said. "I wanted to beat Mollie here. She's been cooking for days. She'll be bringing a truckload of food along soon."

"Of course it's okay. Can I get you anything? The coffee is still hot," she offered as she took his coat and he doffed his boots in the entryway.

"Coffee would be wonderful. Thank you," he said, following Aida to the kitchen. "How is your practice going?"

She knew he wasn't referring to her budding medical activities. "Very well, I think. I'm able to stay attached to the moment without purposely occupying myself with some activity. I haven't had any near flips since..." She thought about that as she poured him a mug of coffee. "Early spring, around Easter."

The near flips had been unsettling. They started when things in her life had calmed down and Aida's mind wasn't so caught up in dealing with the trauma of her trip, The Project, or their relocation from University City to New Mexico. They happened when she was falling asleep and sensory information associated freely with unorganized thoughts, putting the mind in the middle of a scattered, chaotic kaleidoscope of reality. She would have a moment or two of feeling as though reality were slipping away, and sometimes she'd catch a glimpse of the darkness and the lights. Then she'd awake fully, startled and breathing heavily. Matthew had been watching her during one of these episodes and nudged her focus back to the Particle World.

"That's good. Keep at it. The only way to strengthen a mental habit is to practice," he said, and took a sip from his mug. His bright eyes rested on her, observing her in excruciating detail. She hated when he did that; it undermined her confidence in her own ability to judge her state of being. He was looking for something.

"I'm fine, Matthew. Why are you still eyeballing me? What is it?"

He put down the mug and sat back in his chair. "It's Beverly Michelson. I didn't want to bring this up now, right before the holidays and your party. But I had to see you for myself."

"Tell me," she said, the morning's leisure evaporating from her voice. "Is she awake?" Aida, who had been leaning against the counter, now stood rigid.

"No, she's still in the Wave World, but she's becoming more active. Her consciousness is gathering itself, reassembling. She's unbalanced, though. Her psyche never integrated the reality of her experience. I'd say at best she's only partially conscious of herself and her surroundings."

"That sounds pitiable but not threatening." Aida was still working on feeling compassion for the woman.

255

Matthew continued. "Even in her current state—which I think must be something like a delirium, as you've taught me—her mind is reaching out to grab on to something, anything, to anchor itself to. She holds you responsible for many of the problems that are of her own making, so it's natural that you'd be a target. I just wanted to make sure she wasn't seeking to latch on to you."

Aida shrugged. "I haven't noticed anything unusual."

"That's good. We haven't seen her try to focus on you, but we can't be as vigilant as we used to be."

"Then let's let it be," she said, and put her mug in the sink. "Besides, I just saw Mollie pull up. Wow, you weren't kidding. The whole back of her truck is filled with coolers and boxes."

***

Later that night, Aida, Greg, Nat, and John were in the Santa Fe Plaza, where people had been celebrating Christmas for more than four hundred years. It was a frigid night; snow crunched under their feet, and their breath condensed in moist clouds as they moved with the crowd following the Las Posadas procession around the square. Both Mollie and Matthew had told them not to miss this celebration.

Las Posadas is a re-creation of the journey the pregnant Mary and her husband, Joseph, took through Bethlehem looking for a house in which Mary could give birth to Jesus. The troupe of actors went from door to door, singing in Spanish and asking for shelter. Above, on the rooftops and balconies, devils dressed in red with horns on their heads and pitchforks in their hands sang out, setting the hearts of the homeowners against the holy family.

The crowd booed and hissed against the devils as they sang their part, and then the group proceeded to the next house. After a dozen or so, the crowd would arrive at the church or another large area where they would be welcomed, and all would come inside to warm up and eat and drink.

Arm in arm, Nat and John strolled ahead of Greg and Aida. The two of them had been a couple pretty much since their return to University City. This was their second Christmas together, and they were unmistakably happy. Uncharacteristically, John had been a little twitchy since they'd arrived that afternoon.

256

Natalia turned around to speak to her parents. "Hey, Dad. I'm going to get some hot chocolate. Do you guys want some?"

"That would be wonderful," said Greg. Nat flashed a wide grin at her mother and walked off, taking her time. Greg whispered to his wife, "She's not being too obvious, is she?" which earned him a poke in the ribs. Aida took John's arm and maneuvered him between her and her husband, and the three of them continued down the street. Aida saw that John was sweating under his wool cap.

"Greg, Aida," he began, then caught his toe on the edge of an upraised brick in the sidewalk and stumbled. "I...uh...well...I love your daughter very much and you two as well. I know I'm only a medic, but your daughter has convinced me to go back to school. I'm working on a bachelor's part-time, and I want to go into the physician's assistant program when I finish. But I have to keep working, and—"

"John," Aida interrupted, "is there something you want to say?"

John stopped and took a deep breath. *Underwater demolition was easier than this*, he thought.

"I want your permission to propose to Nat."

"We take this very seriously," Greg said. "This is a lifetime commitment for both of you."

"I know," John responded. "That's not the part that worries me. Asking you two is the hard part. She's my world. I don't ever want to be without her."

"Greg, be nice," said Aida. "John, honestly, we were starting to wonder what was taking you so long. Of course you have our permission and wholehearted blessing." She embraced him and kissed his cheek.

Greg beamed at his future son-in-law, shook his hand, and clapped him on the shoulder. "Welcome to the family, son. Does Nat know you're going to propose?"

"We've been talking about it for a while, but no, she doesn't know anything about this. I want it to be a surprise tomorrow night," said John.

Later, Aida would tell Greg how sweet she thought it was that John believed Natalia was completely in the dark about his intentions this Christmas.

"She just finished her last semester of undergrad work," Greg said, "and then she's moving straight on into her graduate work. And you're in school too." He looked at his wife, who nodded. "We only ask that you wait to have the wedding until after she finishes her master's." Nat was in a five-year bachelor's/master's program in neuroscience that she would be finishing in a little more than a year.

"That's about when I'll be finishing my undergrad. We were thinking of that time frame too."

Nat emerged from the crowd holding a drink carrier with four steaming cups. "Here we go…everything okay?"

"Yeah, we're good," said John, and they moved to catch up with the procession. "So when do they get someone to let them in?"

***

The day of the Christmas open house was clear and crisp. All the monks came, along with many members of Mollie and Francisco's family. Aida had invited some of her coworkers, and Greg had asked his team members to come as well. The advantage of an open house was that the guests could come and go as best fit their schedule. The food, an odd mixture of traditional New Mexican and Greek fare, complemented each other well. The sweetness of baklava or Christopsomo after tamales with coffee was a new experience for all. At the end of the day, with the piñon fire burning in the kiva fireplace and the Christmas tree lit up, John pulled Nat out in front of everyone, got down on one knee, and presented her with a small box.

"Natalia, will you marry me?"

She pulled him up off the floor, gently took his head in her hands, kissed him, and said, "Of course."

Both Greg and Aida teared up as applause, shouts of congratulations, and several excellent *gritos* filled the house. Their lives were indeed whole and healthy again.

***

Three hundred miles to the north, a man was screaming in the night.

"Get away from me. Stay away from me. *No!*"

The guards at the federal Supermax in Florence, Colorado, had seen this all before. In fact, it was pretty much expected. Lock up a person in isolation for twenty-three hours a day for months that stretched into years and they broke down. This one had had it worse, though. His only human contact, if you could call it that, was with a voice he heard while sitting alone in a room staring at a one-way mirror. What the man saw in the reflection didn't remotely resemble the face he had known eighteen months ago. The time had been hard on Jerome Gilden, aging him prematurely. The bitter, rapid decay he had fought against with his considerable will now ate away at him, both inside and out.

This torment, this unwelcome visitor in the night, though, was something new. It usually came as he was trying to fall asleep, which was his only true escape from this place. When it came, he felt as if something was clutching at his mind, trying to dig itself into him. He would lie there, fully aware, watching the room spin around him, and sink further into his terror. It would have provided him scant comfort to know the cause of his anguish was that someone was thinking about him or that a nameless, faceless monk had been wrong on one crucial point. Aida Doxiphus wasn't the last person who had been on Beverly Michelson's mind.

References

Bradford, David. "Brain and Psyche in Early Christian Asceticism," *Psychological Reports*. 109, 2, 461–520.

Breedlove, S. Marc, Neil V. Watson, and Mark R. Rosenzweig. *Biological Psychology: An Introduction to Behavioral, Cognitive, and Clinical Neuroscience*, 6th ed. Sunderland: Sinauer Associates, 2005.

Brownfield, Charles A. *Isolation Effects of Restricted Sensory and Social Environments on Human Beings*, 3rd ed. United States of America: Random House, 2010.

Calder, Nigel. *Einstein's Universe*. New York: Greenwich House, 1979.

Close, Fred. *The Infinity Puzzle Quantum Field Theory and the Hunt for an Orderly Universe*. New York: Basic Books, 2011.

Cruz, Joan Carroll. *The Incorruptibles*. Rockford: Tan Books and Publishers, 1977.

Chib, VS., et al. "Noninvasive Remote Activation of the Ventral Midbrain by Transcranial Direct Current Stimulation of the Prefrontal Cortex," *Translational Psychiatry*. 2013, 3 e268, https://doi:10.1038/tp.2013.44.

Gallagher, Winifred. *Rapt Attention and the Focused Life*. New York: Penguin Group, 2009.

Gribbin, John, *In Search of Schrodinger's Cat: Quantum Physics and Reality*. New York: Bantam Books, 1984.

Kumar, Manjit, *Quantum Einstein, Bohr and the Great Debate about the Nature of Reality*. London: Icon Books, Ltd, 2014.

Lama, His Holiness the Dalai. *The Universe in a Single Atom: The Convergence of Science and Spirituality*. New York: Broadway Books, 2005.

————. *How to Practice the Way to a Meaningful Life*. Translated and edited by Jeffrey Hopkins, Ph.D. New York: Atria Books, 2002.

Landlaw, Johnathan, Stephan Bodian, and Gudrun Buhnemann. *Buddhism for Dummies*, 2nd ed. Hoboken: Wiley Publishing Inc., 2011.

Lanza, Robert and Bob Berman. *Biocentrism*. Dallas: BenBella Books, Inc., 2009.

Monti, Martin M., et al. "Willful Modulation of Brain Activity in Disorders of Consciousness," *The New England Journal of Medicine*. 362, 7, 579–589.

Owen, Adrian M. "Is Anybody in There," *Scientific American*, May 2014.

Pollak, Andrew N. MD FAAOS, ed. *Emergency Care and Transportation of the Sick and Injured*. Sudbury: Jones and Bartlett Publishers, 2005.

Ricard, Matthieu., et al. "Mind of the Meditator," *Scientific American*, November 2014.

Rosenblum, Bruce and Fred Kuttner. *Quantum Enigma Physics Encounters Consciousness*, 2nd ed. New York: Oxford University Press, 2011.

Rowan, A. James and Eugene Tolunsky. *Primer of EEG With a Mini-Atlas*. Philadelphia: Butterworth Heinemann, 2003.

Tloczynski, J., et al. "Perception of Visual Illusions by Novice and Longer-Term Meditators," *Perceptual Motor Skills*. 2000, 91,1021–1026.

Tortora, Gerard J. and Nicholas P. Anagnostakos. *Principles of Anatomy and Physiology*, 4th ed. New York: Harper & Row, 1984.

Wolf, Fred Alan. *Taking the Quantum Leap: The New Physics for Non-Scientists*. New York: Harper & Row, 1989.

About the Author

I live with my family near Seattle, Washington. I have a background in psychobiology, neuroscience, and law. Currently, I'm a technical writer in my day job and I have hobby-level interest in quantum theory, astronomy, HAM radio, and am a member of the Pacific Northwest Writers Association (PNWA).

I hope you enjoyed *Flip*! I'd really appreciate it if you left a review wherever you review books.

I invite you to visit my Facebook page (http://bit.ly/cjfoxauthor) and join my email list (http://bit.ly/flipmailinglist). I keep you in the loop on the continuing development of the Wave World storyline.